"What are you afraid of, Justin?"

That snapped his spine straight. "Nothing."

"Then prove it. I dare you to spend the next ten weeks here, at the clinic."

"Dare?" Was she joking? This wasn't kid stuff... To him, it was life-and-death. And the way Brielle got under his skin, opened him up, was downright dangerous. If he accepted, he'd need to keep his distance. "I'm not going to any group talks."

She pondered that a moment then sighed. "Fine. Go only if you want to, which I'm betting will be plenty."

"You're pretty sure of yourself."

"I am."

He found himself smiling. When was the last time he'd smiled for no reason? He liked Brielle's gumption.

"So," she pressed, looking so flushed and vibrant he wagered touching her would be like grabbing hold of an electric fence. He could feel the spark from where he sat. "Do we have a deal?"

He shoved back his chair and held out his hand. "Dare accepted."

Dear Reader,

Welcome back! I've been eager to share the next story in my Rocky Mountain Cowboys series with you. The Cade and Loveland ranching families, neighbors who've been feuding for over a hundred years, are full of such interesting and complicated characters. They each face, and overcome, personal challenges in unique and inspiring ways.

Since losing his twin, brooding daredevil rancher Justin Cade's not so much searching for meaning in life as he's challenging it, cheating death by taking extreme risks. But when life puts him on a collision course with a beautiful woman he initially mistakes for an angel, he sees he has a reason to live after all.

Former army chaplain and PTSD sufferer Brielle Thompson's plans to start over are threatened when the rehabilitation clinic she supervises may close. She's determined to save the facility, its patients and the tormented rancher she crosses paths with one fateful night. As she and Justin join forces to save the clinic, she discovers there's more to him than a danger-seeking, Harley-riding cowboy. Despite his gruff exterior, he has a big heart—one that might heal her own if she dares open it to Justin and love.

Happy reading!

Karen Rock

HEARTWARMING

Bad Boy Rancher

———

Karen Rock

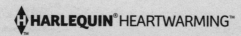

Recycling programs
for this product may
not exist in your area.

ISBN-13: 978-1-335-63359-0

Bad Boy Rancher

Copyright © 2018 by Karen Rock

Printed in U.S.A.

Award-winning author **Karen Rock** is both sweet and spicy—at least when it comes to her writing! The author of both YA and adult contemporary books writes sexy suspense novels and small-town romances for Harlequin and Kensington Publishing. A strong believer in Happily-Ever-After, Karen loves creating unforgettable stories that leave her readers with a smile. When she's not writing, Karen is an avid reader who also loves cooking her grandmother's Italian recipes, baking and having the Adirondack Park wilderness as her backyard, where she lives with her husband, daughter, dog and cat, who keep her life interesting and complete. Learn more about her at karenrock.com or follow her on Twitter, @karenrock5.

Books by Karen Rock

Harlequin Heartwarming

Falling for a Rancher
Christmas at Cade Ranch
A Cowboy to Keep
Under an Adirondack Sky
His Kind of Cowgirl
Winter Wedding Bells
"The Kiss"
Raising the Stakes
A League of Her Own
Someone Like You
His Hometown Girl
Wish Me Tomorrow

To my sister Cathy, my "Irish Twin." Being your sister has been such a defining part of my life and my identity. I wouldn't be the person I am, the writer I've become, without you and the unbreakable bond we share.

All my love... Always.

CHAPTER ONE

"HAPPY BIRTHDAY, JESSE." Justin Cade raised a beer to his reflection then gulped half of the microbrew. He scrunched his face at the citrus tang, forcing down the rest.

"Bah!" He scraped his tongue with his teeth. "How'd you drink this fancy stuff? Fruit and beer? Might as well be a wine cooler." He crumpled the can in his palm and chucked it at his bathroom's wastebasket. "Here's to us turning twenty-six. Or me, anyway."

He frowned at his identical twin's face, shrouded by Justin's dark beard and mustache. A purple bruise from a barn brawl circled his left eye. Black stitches closed a jagged gash on his cheek caused by this week's dirtbike crash. Despite the camouflage, Jesse still peeped through. "You should be here, dude."

Yellow-green eyes, surrounded by a ring of brown, blazed back at Justin. He bared his teeth, stomped from the cubicle-size space then flung himself into the single foldout chair in his cabin's combination kitchen-living-dining area. It faced an antenna-topped TV perched on empty feed crates from his family's cattle ranch. A crammed gun cabinet, a wobbly card table and a sagging couch comprised the rest of his furnishings.

Mismatched sheets obscured the front windows and the dark night behind them. An ancient coffeemaker moaned as it dribbled thick, black brew into a glass pot. The bitter smell mixed with the woodstove's aromatic hickory logs, a melancholy scent that reminded him of times spent chopping stacks with his brother, each refusing to quit until their pile topped the other's in height.

A one-eyed kitten he'd fished from a storm ditch leaped onto his lap and purred louder than a combine engine. Since he planned on dropping her by the barn, he hadn't named the scraggly black-and-white thing. No sense keeping her. He barely cared for himself, let alone a kitten that weighed less than a tissue.

His work-rough fingers stroked the quivering fur ball, rising as her back arched and her miniature tail flicked in contentment. "Don't get used to this," he grumbled, scratching behind her ears. She rubbed her whiskered face against his hand and purred louder.

He flicked on the TV, peeled off the chair then sauntered to the kitchen counter. Furball wove in and out of his legs. The peppy Monday-night football announcers grated on his ears. He grabbed his ringed mug from the sink and filled it with coffee. Time to clear his head. After herding cattle this morning, he'd dropped back into bed, fallen into an uneasy sleep, then woke even more exhausted. Too bad he hadn't slept right through.

He eyed the loaded rifle over his front door.

Sometimes he wanted to stop the world and hop off it for a while. That idea was particularly appealing today.

Steam curled from the coffee's dark surface as he raised it to his mouth. At the last minute, his stomach churned and he chucked it, mug and all, into the sink. A satisfying crash exploded. He grabbed a six-pack and a carton of milk from the fridge, freshened Furball's bowl, then dropped onto the couch and popped the top off a Miller.

The hell with sober. He wasn't going anywhere. Least of all to Mount Everest, Kilimanjaro or any of the seven summits he and his twin had vowed they'd scale before turning thirty. Before Jesse's opiate addiction. Before he wound up murdered over it.

Justin took a long drink then flopped on his back. His boots dangled over the couch's arm. A purring Furball sprang onto his stomach and needled her claws through his worn T-shirt, pricking the skin beneath. Drawing blood, he'd bet.

Not that he cared about injury.

He welcomed it.

Jesse's passing had muted all feeling except pain. Pain reminded Justin that he still lived. It also reminded him that *he* should be six feet under—not Jesse. The woodstove's flickering light gleamed on his shotgun's barrel.

Jesse was the better twin. He'd dreamed while Justin made trouble. The fact that death took Jesse, who'd never hurt anyone besides himself, and left a reckless, sullen cuss like Justin behind proved the universe had no plan—or if it did, it sucked.

The kitten's delicate pink tongue appeared in a wide yawn. She closed her eyes as Justin scratched beneath her chin. His gaze traveled to Jesse's globe, covered with color-coded pushpins. Green represented places they'd been, yellow for places they'd hoped to see and red places they'd intended on scaling. Conquering. Their chance to view the world from above, riding it astride while it spun.

Then Jesse's addiction had snatched it all away.

Justin's trigger finger curled.

Furball inched up his stomach and huddled

against his thudding heart. He rested his chin atop her silky head. Growing up in Carbondale, Colorado, a small town smack-dab in the center of the Rocky Mountains, a place where cattle outnumbered humans ten to one, he and Jesse planned elaborate adventures while riding the old, familiar range. It'd never occurred to him that his twin would escape this place with a needle instead. Before drugs, they'd done everything together. The dynamic duo, their grandpa used to call them. Inseparable, their grandma had added. She never got their names straight—not that he or Jesse cared. They'd been a team. A unit. Two halves of a whole.

Now Justin escaped his own way, chasing thrills, the riskier the better, adrenaline his drug of choice. What did he have to lose? His life? It hadn't amounted to much anyway. His older brothers, Jack, James and Jared, had found love and started families. His younger sister, Jewel, devoted her life to improving the ranch, and his ma had recently gotten a new lease on life with her grandchildren and a beau.

Him? His constant foul mood made him unfit company. His family would be better off without him skulking around, unable to move past Jesse's death after three and a half years. His grief didn't have an expiration date. Acting normal, happy, around others stressed him out. Living took effort, and sometimes, like today, he didn't have the energy for it.

The shotgun drew his eye again.

Sooner or later, he'd even up the score and join Jesse. He'd reneged on his promise to his dying father to look after his twin. And his death would satisfy Carbondale's rumor mill. Jewel reported that neighbors whispered about him behind raised hands as he roared down Main Street on his souped-up chopper.

"That daredevil will follow his brother to the grave and break his poor mama's heart."

"The boy's like to lose his neck."

"Got a death wish, that one."

A wish? No. His extreme antics were a challenge. He dared death to come for him—like it had Jesse. And he experienced a grim satisfaction every time he cheated it. When he went, it'd be on his terms.

He stroked his eyes over the shotgun then leveraged himself upright.

A knock sounded. "Uncle Justin?"

Justin shoved the six-pack behind a couch cushion and stood.

"Here."

Why had his six-year-old nephew sought him out on a school night? He flung open the door. "Hey, kiddo."

His gaze roamed over Jesse's son's face. Almost two years ago, Javi and his mother, Sofia, had arrived at the ranch, upending the strict order his older brother James had imposed following Jesse's death, and stealing James's heart. They'd married ten months ago and now expected their first child soon, a cousin for Jack and Dani's six-month-old boy.

"Grandma says dinner's ready, and you should come up."

Justin scratched the back of his head. Furball batted at the rodeo buckle encircling his boot—the buckle had belonged to Jesse. Why the invitation? Ma knew he didn't leave his cabin much, especially on *this* day.

"Tell her I'm sleeping."

Javi's dark hair swished across his forehead as he cocked his face and perused Justin. Except for Javi's left-side dimple, he took after his mother in every way. "You don't look asleep."

"Maybe this is a dream."

"Then how come I'm awake?"

"Who says you are?" Justin put Javi in a headlock and they roughhoused, Javi's laughter foreign in the bleak space of the cabin.

"Okay. Uncle! Uncle!" Justin cried after letting Javi twist his arm behind his back and crashing to his knees. "You win. Now go on home. I'm not the best company tonight."

The shotgun glistened, beckoning.

Javi eyed him. "You do look kind of scary."

Justin shoved a hand through his hair, making it stand on end. "Good."

Javi tugged Justin's beard. "Like a bear. Except I'm not afraid of you."

"Shoot." Justin shrugged and stood. "Must be losing my touch."

"Now will you come with me?" Javi wagged a finger at him. "Plus, you don't have a choice."

"Why's that?"

"Pa's orders."

Justin's lips vibrated with the force of his sigh. Marrying Sofia had tempered some of James's controlling ways, but not all—not enough.

"He says he'll drag you back himself if he has to…though I told him I could do it. See?" Javi pushed up his sweatshirt sleeve and flexed his biceps. The flat muscle twitched.

Despite his dark mood, Justin smiled. "Not bad. You've been eating your spinach?"

Javi scooped up Furball and turned in a circle, the wide-eyed kitty dangling at the end of his fingertips. "Yep. And I'm almost seven now. Mama says I'm getting big."

Justin rescued the bristling puffball and dropped her gently back on the couch. "Guess I'd better go quietly."

"If you know what's good for you. Hey! Can I tie up your hands, and you can be my prisoner?"

Justin shook his head at the imaginative boy.

"I'll come." *Not willingly*, he added silently, donning his Stetson and leather jacket. Justin dropped his keys in his pocket and followed Javi up the path that led to his family's homestead.

Built in the late 1800s by his silver prospector ancestor, the rough-hewn cedar structure sprawled at Mount Sopris's base. The two-story house's windows were dark. Strange considering the hour and his mother's dinner invitation. Had they lost power?

Starlight revealed the log pillars propping up a steep portico and the peaked gables breaking up the roofline. A swing rattled on its chains in the recesses of a wraparound porch. The empty corrals that led to newly harvested hay fields lay empty, the horses stabled, the longhorns grazing in one of the twelve pastures used on their ten-thousand-acre organic beef ranch.

Once the sight of his home, glimpsed after a long day in the saddle, had filled him with relief. Now dread settled heavy in his gut. He'd moved to one of the cabins after Jesse's death to escape the memories and be alone.

His heavy boots tromped up the stairs.

When he pulled open the door, lights blazed, temporarily blinding him.

"Surprise!" his family shouted.

Javi ran around him chanting, "Happy birthday! Happy birthday!"

Justin backed up a step. "No."

His mother, Joy, strode through the doorway. She shoved silver strands behind her ear and peered at him anxiously from behind frameless glasses. "It's been a long time since we…we wanted to do something nice, honey… Wanted to celebrate…"

His boots dropped down one tread. "No." He would not, couldn't celebrate his life. Not when his twin brother lay six feet under, buried along with Justin's broken promises, the ones they'd whispered to each other in the womb: fidelity, unity, brotherhood.

They'd always had each other's backs, until heroin left Jesse addicted and Justin betrayed and furious.

"We baked a cake," cajoled his pregnant sister-in-law, Sofia. A white kerchief kept her long dark hair tied back and contrasted with her tawny skin. A blue shirt stretched across her rounded belly.

Jared guided his legally blind fiancée, Amberley, through the door to join the group. His pressed shirt and crisp jeans made Justin squirm beneath his grubby Wranglers, frayed T-shirt and worn leather jacket.

"It's your favorite! Chocolate!" Javi scaled one of the pillars then dropped at James's frown.

A cool wind howled down from the mountaintops, rustling the leaves of the aspens dotting the property. Temperatures dropped fast at night during Rocky Mountain autumns; Justin zipped his coat against its bite and lowered himself another step.

"That was Jesse's favorite." His heart slugged hard, a battering ram in his chest. He couldn't face their smiles, their cheer.

"We did one layer of chocolate and one of strawberry, the way we used to." A pleading note entered his mother's voice. "Please, Justin, come in. It's time that you, that we—"

"Y'all enjoy it. I've got somewhere to go." He spun, sprinted to his hog and jumped on its low-slung seat.

"Where?" James shouted.

"Can I come?" His sister, Jewel, hustled after him. Her freckles burned dark on her white face, and the moonlight trickled down the length of her side ponytail.

He shook his head, donned his helmet, revved the engine and mouthed "sorry" before letting out the throttle and ripping into the black night.

His family meant well. They just didn't understand him or his unending grief. Jack, a bounty hunter turned Denver deputy sheriff, had moved on after he'd caught Jesse's killers. James had healed once he'd opened his heart to Sofia and Javi. Jared kept busy managing his fiancée's barrel-racing career. Even his mother has gotten on with life since the grandbabies came along and she began dating Boyd Loveland, of all people—their neighbor and patriarch of the family they've been feuding with for generations.

But him? He'd never let Jesse go. Who was he without his other half?

Not anyone.

Not anyone good.

Jesse made up the best parts of them.

Justin gazed at the full moon as he wailed around a hairpin turn. Heat waved up from the engine, and he breathed in the sharp smell of exhaust mingling with the pines lining this remote stretch of road. Sharp precipices dropped on either side of the two-lane rural route. At this hour, it should be deserted. He opened the throttle, and the speedometer ticked up until the needle vibrated on the hundred-mile-an-hour mark.

His body hummed, electric, alive, for the first time today. He gazed back at the road and glimpsed a moving van edging into the intersection. His pulse slammed in his veins. Too late to stop. He could either topple sideways onto the narrow shoulder and down the embankment or race to cross in front of the van.

He might make it, he thought, eyeing the lumbering vehicle.

Or he might not.

When it came down to it, what was the difference?

He'd joined the world today; this might be the right time to leave it, too… He pried his fingers from the handlebars and tipped back his head as the motorcycle rocketed downhill.

He'd roll the dice.

Let the chips fall where they may.

Thirty minutes earlier

"IN ONE-THIRD of a mile, turn left on Willow Brook Drive," Brielle Thompson's GPS droned.

"What? Where?" The moving van lurched as she shifted on the steep incline. The gears ground, then caught.

She peered at the lit screen then out at the dark, rugged terrain. Overhead, a full moon shone in a starry sky, illuminating Colorado's mountaintops. Her headlights picked up fir trees, thick brush, a narrow, pebble-filled shoulder. No willow trees. And no brook.

No turnoff ahead, either.

She groaned and wished herself back on any of the army bases where she'd spent her childhood, places where streets were ordered and her structured life made sense.

The two sets of dog tags dangling from her rearview mirror caught her eye. Her heartbeat stumbled. There was one base she never wanted to return to. Kandahar. It haunted her still. Somewhere amid the dust, heat and blood of Afghanistan, the pillar of strength she'd always relied on to hold her up had crumbled.

Would she finally regain it here in Carbondale?

"We're part of a long history of suffering," she'd heard her commanding officer say sympathetically before handing over her honorable discharge papers six months ago. He'd severed her from the only life she'd known—the military—and abruptly ended her tour of duty as an army chaplain, her bout with depression forcing her to abandon her comrades when they needed her most. "Thank you for your service."

The silent *dismissed* still rang in her ear.

Her fingers dug in a bag of soft sour candies and tossed them in her mouth. She sucked in her stinging cheeks and chewed through the pain. Lime. Lemon. Watermelon. Apple. Cherry. Orange. She ticked off each explosive flavor until they overrode her memories, shoving them down deep where they wouldn't get her into trouble again.

"Coming up on Willow Brook Drive," intoned the GPS.

She rolled down her window and the crisp, pine-scented air tore a strand from her bun and fluttered it across her mouth. A thicket of brush, scrub trees and conifers rose on one side. Opposite, the pines thinned and flashes of the starlit sky appeared through the spaces, revealing a drop-off. Not a stream or a willow.

This GPS made less sense than her civilian life. Her military world hadn't prepared her for life without a uniform. She was struggling to fit in. The bombardment of choices in fancy coffee shops left her bewildered and stammering. Workdays at her first regular job, as a psychologist at a mental health clinic in Chicago, ended when the clock struck five, objectives unmet. And it had filled her with restless anxiety.

As for her former coworkers, they'd kept to themselves, working independently. It was a different mind-set than the military, where you worked as a unit, brothers in arms, and had each other's backs.

She'd discovered that the real world was a lonely place.

Not that she'd let herself get close to anyone again. Not after… Her eyes swung off the road and landed on the dog tags. Not in a professional capacity. Not ever again. It could trigger a PTSD episode, one she might not survive this time.

Her new position as the head of Fresh Start, a mental health and drug rehabilitation facility in the remote Colorado Rocky Mountains, was her second chance at regaining her footing.

And she'd better not mess it up.

If she ever found the place.

"Recalculating," the GPS droned, sounding put out.

Brielle's head whipped left. What? She'd missed the turn? She groaned. Even a cheap gadget could navigate the real world better than she could.

The rural route stretched beyond her headlights, not showing a decent place for her big van to turn around. A sigh hissed through her clenched teeth. The facility's owner had texted her a half hour ago when she'd missed their meeting time.

Her. A no-show?

She lived by a schedule and was never late. As her army colonel father had bragged (when he used to be proud of her), Brielle was born on her due date, during the Army-Navy game's halftime, the timing so precise he hadn't missed a minute of the action.

So much for dependability.

She needed to message her new boss back, but she didn't trust the road's flimsy shoulders enough to pull over. Should she take a chance and text while driving? Was that legal in Colorado?

Given she barely knew how to drive a stick shift, or her whereabouts, exactly, she didn't need to add to her distractions. But if she didn't hurry, she'd lose another job, her fresh start over before it began. And then where would she go?

Not to her parents. After her breakdown, while she'd sorted out next steps, her mother had hovered and recited PTSD jargon she'd learned in online support groups. While her father ordered her to pull herself up by her bootstraps and loomed in her bedroom's doorway each night, shaking his head when she'd spent another day under the covers.

"Turn left on Laurel Moon Road," snapped the GPS.

Was it her or did the GPS lady sound snippy?

If so, she wasn't the only one losing her patience.

Brielle's beams picked up an unpaved road just ahead, no laurels or a street sign in sight.

Take it?

At the last moment, she veered left, the van protesting as she downshifted on the narrow road. Here, the dark pressed closer still, dredging up old, remembered horrors of what lurked just out of sight. Her breaths shortened. Quickened. She flicked on her high beams and wiped her damp palms on her dress slacks. A split-rail fence ran along either side of the road—if you could call it that, though path seemed more fitting. Hopefully no one approached from the other direction.

"Turn right," the GPS directed.

"Where?" Cattle with long, deadly-looking horns lifted their heads as she neared. She couldn't turn into a pasture. In fact, she couldn't turn at all. Abruptly the road ended at a locked gate.

"Awesome. Now what?"

"Recalculating," the GPS bit out savagely.

"Enough." Brielle flipped off her navigator, applied the brakes then popped the truck into Park. Her burning forehead dropped to the steering wheel.

It'd been a dark night like this when a soldier stopped by to see her before heading out on patrol.

"I don't believe in this war anymore," Jefferson had told her. "Everybody's angry. Crazy. Trying to kill you. Blowing each other up." He'd paused, and his eyes burned into hers. "It makes no sense—who gets killed and who stays alive. Sometimes you mess up, and it's okay. Sometimes you do what you're supposed to and people get hurt."

"You can't control everything that happens," she'd said. "You're only in charge of your own actions."

"No." He'd dropped his eyes and shook his head. "I can't even do that all the time." His face turned hard. "Once I thought you could help me. But you're a chaplain. Your hands are clean. You don't know what it's like to do what we do."

She'd tensed up as if he'd struck her. True. She didn't know what it felt like to take someone's life, or any of the horrors these courageous soldiers endured, but she'd been trained to understand. To empathize. To listen. To minister. Still, no books, classes or seminars prepared you for the harsh reality she'd discovered during her first deployment.

"No one's hands are clean except God's,"

she'd said slowly, as if convincing herself of her faith, her purpose, her mission. How did you spiritually minister to men who were still being assaulted? she'd wondered. "All we can do is pray He gives us the strength to do what we have to."

A fleeting smile twisted Jefferson's lips. She wasn't sure she believed her own words, or any words at all. What did words matter in Kandahar, where death struck indiscriminately? Its nonstop toll was a drip, drip, drip on the heart of every service member, boring a hole straight through for some, hardening it for others.

"Look at my hands." He'd shoved them at her, callused palms facing the ceiling, then he flipped them over and stretched out his fingers. "I look calm, right?"

"Are you?" Should she call his superior? File a report to request he skip today's patrol? Not that her requests were honored except in the most extreme cases...

"I never sleep anymore," he'd said. "But check out my hands—look at me. Look at my hands. It's like I'm calm."

But she hadn't really looked, not closely, not like she'd had to do later the next morning, when he and the rest of his platoon returned to the base in pieces. She'd been asked to help identify some of the questionable remains.

Her skin shook over her bones as each blood-soaked horror cascaded in her mind's eye. She'd seen too many brave troops lose their lives in defense of their country. And what'd she do? She'd succumbed to dark emotions and turned her back on her comrades when they'd needed her most, the deadly result one she'd never forgive herself for causing.

Never again.

She screwed her lids shut, snatched up another handful of sour candies and chewed so hard she bit her tongue. Warm, metallic-tasting fluid mingled with the synthetic fruit flavors.

"Don't think about it," she whispered to herself, knowing the dangers of reliving her experiences, the drowning depression that'd occur if she let herself sink back into them.

"Complete your mission," she ordered herself, then shifted into Reverse and headed backward from the dead end, her eyes trained on the rearview mirror, her mind compartmentalizing the way she'd been trained.

It only took one slipup.

The dog tags swung like a meat cleaver, ready to saw her in half.

Pain didn't exist unless she let it, her father always told her.

If a tree falls in the woods and no one witnesses it, does it make a sound?

If soldiers die in the field and no one survives to tell about it, did they make a sound?

She flipped on the radio as she jolted back onto the main road, drowning out her friends' screams. She heard them, often, when she wasn't careful to keep her mind empty or forgot to take her Prazosin before bed.

Those mornings she woke exhausted, restless and anxious, haunted by nightmares. Hopefully out here in Carbondale, in the middle of nowhere, she'd lose her past, her old self, and become someone new. Someone who no longer carried the gut-wrenching responsibilities of her former job—the memorial services for soldiers, friends killed in action, the therapy sessions after contact with the enemy, the perilous excursions outside the wire to minister to remote posts while under enemy fire.

Carbondale seemed peaceful.

Would it silence her demons and let her lead a normal civilian life at last? Or was she doomed to never fit in—to haunt the edges of the real world, straddling the line between it and war, unable to leave her past to fully join the present? She'd arrived at her Kandahar assignment starry-eyed with a head full of jargon and a heart certain of its ability to save everyone. Twelve months later, she'd left with nothing, not even herself.

Her cell phone buzzed on the seat beside her. She risked a glance down at the number, recognized it as her new employer's, then reached for it, slowing as she approached an intersection.

Her fingers closed on the metallic rectangle just as the dark shape of a biker raced into view, barreling straight at her.

Her pulse slammed in her veins.

Was he crazy?

She entered the intersection and had the right of way. Her heart jumped to the back of her throat, clogging it, stopping her breath.

Had he just lifted his hands from the bars?

Did he want to die?

No!

She slammed on the brakes. Too late!

An explosion of metal colliding with metal boomed and then she heard the sickening thump of something softer, human, hitting her truck with maximum impact. She recognized the sound easily.

For a moment, she smelled Kandahar's burned refuse, tasted the salty grit of its air, the blood, heard the screams, the groans, and she froze, hands over her ears, her curved body rocking.

Was she alive or dead?

There'd been times when she hadn't known.

She felt her legs, her arms, her face. No injuries. But how? An IED should have torn the Humvee and her apart.

Only…

She struggled to remember.

This was a van, not a Humvee.

And it wasn't a bomb, but a biker.

She straightened, scrambled out of the truck and raced to the passenger side. Her heart beat overtime, and her eyes stung.

A body lay crumpled on the ground, a man. Tall and lanky with a bruised, scraped face and a mop of dark hair. Beside him lay the twisted mass of his bike. His cracked helmet rolled a few feet away. She dropped to her knees and felt for a pulse just below his bearded jaw. A couple heartbeats later, it pressed back against her fingertips. Steady. She ripped off her jacket and covered him to stave off shock.

The stranger's thick lashes fluttered. Yellow-green eyes gleamed at her.

"Am I dead?"

A relieved breath whooshed out of her. "No."

He closed his eyes again.

"Crap."

CHAPTER TWO

BRIELLE'S LOW HEELS clacked on the court-house's marble-tiled floor as she strode down the hall ahead of the motorcycle driver's DUI hearing. In her pressed navy suit, her hair scraped into a tight, painful bun, she hoped her respectable, steady image belied her jittering nerves.

Where was room 8A? The hearing started in fifteen minutes and she wanted to arrive early. When the district attorney had contacted her with the date and time, she'd promised to attend. It was her civic duty after all…but deep down she sensed her eagerness stemmed from the rugged man whose tormented face had haunted her these past two weeks. His expression had reminded her of soldiers returning from battle—bleak and raw.

He could have been killed, yet he'd appeared calm and strangely disappointed when he realized he'd lived. He'd only managed to break a rib, tear a two-inch gash in his face and suffer a concussion, but that'd been nothing to him.

Did he have a death wish?

Why had he taken his hands off his handlebars?

Often, soldiers about to leave on patrol had stopped by her office on the pretext of asking for candy. They'd really sought reassurance, hope and faith that they'd return the way they left: alive. Whole. Physically and, with any luck, mentally. They valued their lives and saw each day they breathed as a reprieve until their next tour, and the one after that, the countdown to their deployment's end feeling like borrowed time. Yet the biker seemed cavalier about this precious gift.

Safety. Many didn't appreciate it until they'd lost it. Once gone, that faith never fully returned. You couldn't unknow things…couldn't unsee them…couldn't unlive them.

Brielle sidestepped a chattering attorney and client and strolled closer to the window. Outside, fall seemed to be gradually overtaking summer. Yellow now mixed with green aspen leaves. One cluster of red covered the side of an ancient maple. A child and parent stopped beside a spruce, snipped off some needles and dropped them into a baggie.

A student project, she surmised, recalling a happy memory from her elementary school days for a change.

Was her own darkness causing her to read too much into the biker? A traumatic past twisted the present, distorting the new to match the old. She needed a fresh start, something she'd never get if she kept picking the scab over her wound.

Sleep had eluded her since the crash, and she thought of the accident often. When she'd followed the ambulance to the hospital, she'd learned his name was Justin Cade, the youngest son of a ranching family and the town hellion, per an oversharing nurse who staffed an empty waiting room. The bored woman went on to divulge Justin had had a drug-addict twin brother, Jesse, who'd been shot dead by drug dealers on a back road right here in Carbondale. The community's only murder in over two decades.

When the nurse said "drug addict," she'd dropped her voice and whispered it, as if she'd uttered a filthy word. She'd pursed her mouth then said characters like that had no place in a sweet, sleepy town like Carbondale.

When she'd asked what brought Brielle to Carbondale and learned she would be running the new rehab and mental health treatment facility, the chatty nurse clammed up and busied herself sharpening pencils. Looked like Brielle might be one of those undesirables the nurse mistrusted.

Brielle paused at a water fountain and bent over to press the tab. She drank the icy stream, recalling the nurse's dismissal. While she hadn't expected the town to roll out the red carpet, it surprised her how few had dropped by the new facility. She'd written a letter to the local newspaper's editor inviting Carbondale residents to tour the facility and ask questions about the provided services before the first patients arrived next week.

She straightened, wiped her mouth, then continued down the hall. Other than a couple rubberneckers who'd looked plenty and said little, the townsfolk steered clear of Fresh Start. Worse, a couple of nasty letters to the newspaper's editor blasted the facility, calling it a threat to the community because it would attract the "wrong elements" and drop real estate values.

She blew out a frustrated breath. She needed Carbondale's support to succeed. While she'd stayed busy, reading through case files for incoming patients, hiring staff and inventorying supplies, her mind kept drifting back to how she could improve community relations…and to a rough-and-tumble cowboy who'd looked like he'd walked right out of a biker fantasy…

Speaking of which.

She pulled up short at the sight of the tall,

lean, bearded man tightening his tie knot. His light hazel eyes bored into hers then narrowed in recognition.

"You," he said, the single word sounding like an accusation. His hands fell to his sides, and he stalked toward her, smooth and graceful, a predatory animal. There was no other way to describe how he zeroed in on her. Like a wolf with hackles raised, Justin Cade seemed to flex every muscle in his possession.

Brielle swallowed hard and stuck her hand out. "Brielle Thompson." After a moment of hesitation, he clasped it with his callused palm. Warmth exploded up her arm at the brief contact. "I'm sorry about the accident."

He crossed his arms and his biceps bulged beneath the tailored suit material, curving it. "Wasn't your fault."

"I braked, but it all happened so fast."

"There wasn't anything you could have done."

She tilted her head so her eyes caught his. "What do you mean?"

He shrugged and his gaze flitted outdoors, landing on the parent and child she'd spotted earlier.

"Are you doing okay?"

"Suppose," he said without looking at her,

which gave her plenty of license to indulge her curiosity and study him.

Beneath his bearded scruff, he had a perfectly proportioned face: a strong jaw, high cheekbones and a straight, narrow nose. Normally she didn't like the mountain man look, especially after a lifetime spent around clean-shaven, tightly shorn military men. Yet something about his wild, untamed looks appealed to her. Challenged and drew her in.

"I tried visiting you in the hospital, but they wouldn't let me back."

"You're not family." He inserted a toothpick in his mouth. "Or a friend." His eyes slashed across her face then back to the outdoor scene.

Heat crept up her neck and into her cheeks. "True."

It wasn't like she wanted to be his friend. Getting close to Justin Cade, she sensed, would be as futile as trying to throw a hug on a cactus.

"I heard you broke your ribs. A concussion, too," she persisted.

His piercing eyes swung back to her, and the impact of his ferocious gaze was like a hand on her chest, shoving her.

"It's a fracture." He yanked at a green tie that brought out the yellow flecks in his eyes.

In fact, looking closer, she realized his eyes were lighter than she thought.

"That's a relief."

A line appeared between his thick brows. "You think I'm relieved about this?" he mumbled around the toothpick.

"How about grateful?" she snapped, losing her patience with the mulish man.

"Nope. Not that, either." His broad shoulders rose then dropped in a careless shrug.

Didn't anything matter to this guy? His face was a slipping mask, and beneath it Brielle saw pain. "I've seen a lot of good men and women who cherished life lose it too soon. You're lucky."

He scrutinized her for a moment then laughed, a bitter, hollow sound. "Lucky? Good one." He tipped his hat, pulled open a door labeled 8A, and disappeared inside.

Her eyes wandered over the entrance's fake wood grain.

Justin Cade might have deliberately taken his hands from the handlebars after all. Maybe he'd wanted to die two weeks ago, and she'd prevented it. Or it'd been some twisted version of Russian roulette with his life.

Did he court death?

She smoothed her hand over her hair, yanked down her suit jacket and wrenched open the door. After the trial, she'd steer clear of Justin Cade.

He didn't want to be saved, and those cases haunted her most.

"WOULD THE DEFENDANT please rise?"

Justin shoved back his chair and rose from the courtroom table slowly, ignoring the pain lancing through his side from his fractured rib. His heart drummed, and beads of perspiration broke out across his forehead. An overhead fan whirred in the expectant hush, and the room's wood-paneled walls seemed to close around him.

Out of the corner of his eye, he glimpsed the woman who'd driven the van he'd hit two weeks ago. Brielle Thompson, a former army chaplain from Chicago, he'd learned. She'd been hired to run Carbondale's new rehabilitation and mental health center, Fresh Start, and had been headed there when they'd collided.

Now she sat beside the county DA, ramrod straight, her strong jaw lifted, her face impassive. Varying shades of blond hair, from platinum to honey to a dark gold, smoothed over her head and twisted in a knot at the base of her neck. Although she hadn't glanced his way since the hearing began, he recalled her light green eyes in the hall and the way they'd seemed to look not just at him, but through him.

He didn't remember much about that night, except the image of her stricken face peering down at him. He'd even dreamed of it, a reprieve from his usual loop of Jesse calling for him, insisting this time he'd changed, and Justin angrily refusing to believe until it was too late...

"How does the defendant plead?" asked County Judge Charlotte James.

Her daughter, Amberley, who dated his brother Jared, had warned Justin not to expect leniency on his DUI charge. Judge James had lost her sister in a drunk driving accident and imposed the maximum sentence when hearing these cases. She leaned forward, her forearms extended atop the tall bench, a gavel beside her right hand. Her black robe billowed around her tall, thin frame and the narrow oval of her face creased in disapproval. Gray threaded through her shoulder-length brown hair.

Justin cast a quick glance back at his family. James glowered while Jared mouthed "good luck." Jewel chewed on a nail while his mother's eyes glistened. Her lips pushed together so hard the color leached out of them. Regret settled sour in Justin's gut. He'd caused his family pain.

Again.

Jail would get him out of their hair for a while. Behind bars, he'd also escape their pitying, anxious looks…their useless attempts to pull him from his grief. He squared his shoulders beneath Jared's borrowed suit jacket. "Guilty, Your Honor."

An annoyed huff escaped his family's attorney, Chuck Sloan. A portly man with a thick mane of white hair and a perfect set of teeth, he resembled a well-fed cat used to pampering, not scrapping. He'd insisted they plead not guilty to provide better leverage in a plea bargain, but Justin refused. He'd chugged the beer before hopping on the bike. No one had put a gun to his head— a preferable choice, in hindsight, to driving under the influence.

His mind drifted as Judge James called for the accident report, witness statements and the toxicology reports.

He could have hurt someone, an unforgivable, selfish act. Granted, he'd believed the remote road would be empty and his motorcycle little threat to a moving van, but he couldn't excuse his reckless disregard for another's life. Brielle Thompson, by all accounts, was an exemplary person, a woman of the church, practically a saint compared to a sinner like him.

Yet despite her brisk bearing and guarded

expression today, he recalled the dark anguish in her eyes after the accident and her sudden fury just moments ago in the hall. She'd looked haunted, desperate, desolate—an expression he recognized. It often peered back at him in the mirror.

Was this godly woman possessed by demons, too?

After listening to the officer on scene's testimony, as well as a brief statement from Brielle, Judge James steepled her fingers, her elbows planted atop her desk, deep in thought. The room descended into a tomb-like silence. A mother, failing to soothe her fussing baby, hustled up the central row of seats and out through the door.

"With a blood alcohol level of point oh nine—" Judge James waved the toxicology report a few minutes later "—your license is suspended for nine months."

"Yes, ma'am." Justin laced his fingers in front of him and rocked back on the heels of his boots, nodding. More than fair. Besides, he didn't need a license to race dirt bikes or go mudding off-road. As for driving, he'd catch a ride with one of his siblings if he needed to go somewhere. Other than the pool hall and a weekly poker night, he rarely left the ranch anyway.

Since Jesse's death, he found it hard to leave the place. Everywhere he looked, he saw Jesse. Walking away felt like he was abandoning his twin all over again. Besides, the wanderlust that'd once seized him had died alongside his twin. It'd be disloyal to explore the world without him. If Jesse couldn't leave Carbondale, neither would Justin, no matter how many sunsets he watched…wondering what lay beyond the horizon.

"As for sentencing," Judge James continued, "I'm prepared to offer two options for consideration before next week's sentencing hearing. Six months in the county jail or…"

His mother's gasp halted the judge's words. Her eyes brushed past Justin to his parent and softened momentarily. Was she dialing into his ma's worries? Did she fear Justin would travel the same dark road as his brother, sure he'd break her heart? Joy had already lost one son, and now she was losing another…

Justin's body ran hot and cold. Jail. Hearing it out loud, in an official setting, brought home the reality he'd be forced to leave the ranch, his family, Jesse…

He'd done the crime and now must do the time.

Cowboy up.

Judge James lifted a mug to her lips, her expression shuttered. A tea bag string dangled over its side. After a long sip, she lowered the cup then circled the rim with her index finger. "Carbondale is now fortunate to have a rehabilitation and mental health facility, Fresh Start."

A low grumbling broke out in the back of the courtroom. He glimpsed Brielle's chin lift a notch. The facility's opening had stirred up some recent controversy. He'd heard James mention the townsfolk worried about the kinds of "elements" a place like Fresh Start would bring to their little corner of the world.

Judge James banged her gavel, scowling, and the room quieted. Justin yanked his starched collar and tie, more loans from his brothers, from his hot neck.

"As we now have a top-notch facility in our community—" The judge shot a fleeting smile at Brielle before continuing, "The defendant may admit himself to this facility for the next six weeks in lieu of incarceration. I trust that would be acceptable to you, Ms. Thompson?"

"Yes, Your Honor," Brielle said heavily after a moment's hesitation.

Justin shot her a quick glance but failed to catch her eye. After their heated exchange in the hall, did she not want him as a resident at the facility?

If so, that went double for him.

He didn't have a drinking problem, unless you considered knocking back a few to fall asleep an issue, which it wasn't. How else would he escape his thoughts long enough to get a few hours of shut-eye?

As for his daytime drinking, he always waited until after work. Who didn't want a few beers while watching the game? Harmless. Normal.

A twelve-pack a night isn't normal, a voice inside him piped up.

He shook off the nagging thought. He didn't go through that amount every day, mostly just on weekends, which lately also extended to Fridays…and Mondays… Because who could face Mondays sober? But still, he was not an addict.

That'd been Jesse's label.

Not his.

Plus, Jesse had attended plenty of those kumbaya programs and they'd never done a darn thing except dash his mother's fragile hopes. Justin glanced over at a stone-faced Brielle. She didn't look like the type to sing folk songs and shake a tambourine. In fact, her militant bearing suggested she'd carry a gun easier. Interesting. He'd never met a woman who'd served in a war before.

And he wouldn't meet her now, hc vowed, no matter how much she intrigued him.

"Your Honor," Justin said quickly, "I don't need time to deliberate. I'd like to—"

"Consult with his attorney," interrupted Mr. Sloan. He tapped his pencil on a piece of paper with the writing: *Don't act rashly.*

Rash?

It was practically Justin's credo. Better to act than think too hard, since thoughts cut deeper, bruised harder and never healed the way physical injuries did. He couldn't imagine a worse place than a rehab program that'd force him to think too hard and feel too much.

"But I—" Justin began.

"Appreciate your generous offer," Mr. Sloan cut in again. "My client will give this the serious consideration it deserves."

He slid another sheet at Justin, the words *Think of your mother* scrawled on it.

Justin gritted his teeth. He *was* thinking of his family. By going to jail, they'd be free to lead their happy lives without him spoiling it. Behind bars, he couldn't get into much trouble. No more barn brawl matchups, dirt bike races or the other kinds of hell-raising that gave his mother palpitations.

He swung around and met his ma's watering eyes. James jabbed a finger at him while

Jared's eyebrows nearly hit his hairline. Jewel tapped her teeth with her nail, eyeing him the way she sized up runaway heifers. He bet she'd like to truss him up right now.

They didn't know how much happier they'd be without him. His gaze drifted to Sofia. She smoothed a hand over her belly and shot him an encouraging smile.

"I appreciate your advocacy for your client, Mr. Sloan," Judge James said. "However, I'd like to hear from Mr. Cade."

Ma clasped her hands together and mouthed "please" while James's eyes said something less polite and a lot more threatening. Big brother asserting himself. Justin bristled. Clearly, they wanted him to wait on a decision. He let out a breath and unclenched his hands. Fine. He hated delaying the inevitable, but if they needed more time to adjust to the idea of him going to jail, then so be it.

"I'll give my answer at next week's hearing."

His mother's relieved sigh made him gulp hard. She'd cried too many tears over Jesse to have him add to the count. The sooner he disappeared, the better. Eventually they could move on like they had after Jesse died.

"Before you're dismissed, I also encourage you to express your gratitude to Ms. Thompson. She prevented you from going into shock while awaiting EMTs, a move that might have saved your life."

Justin's back teeth ground together. No. He was not grateful to Brielle Thompson for saving his sorry excuse for a life. In fact, he wished she'd run him over flat. Then this would all be over. The pain gone.

Judge James waited a minute then banged her gavel. "This court is adjourned and will reconvene next week. Dismissed."

A moment later, Justin stood outside with his family, blinking against the strong afternoon sun. His head throbbed and his bruised muscles ached. He needed a drink.

"So," drawled their local sheriff, Travis Loveland, his smug smile practically begging to be smacked off. "You and me. Looks like we'll be spending lots of time together for the next six months."

Justin's hands clenched at his sides.

Six months shut up with a Loveland? His family's neighbors and rivals? Misery. His family had feuded with the condescending Lovelands for over a century. While they'd fooled the community with their constant volunteering, the Cades knew the Lovelands for who they were: kidnappers, murderers and jewel thieves…and those were just the actions which had started the feud. It continued to this day with water access disputes and missing cattle.

Not to mention their cash-strapped patriarch, Boyd Loveland, now courted Justin's ma for reasons that had more to do with her bank account than her heart. Least that's how he and Jewel saw it. James and Jared's improved love lives seemed to have softened them some on the relationship.

"He's not going to jail," Jack insisted. He worked as a deputy sheriff in Denver where his wife, Dani, managed a dude ranch.

Jack should have stayed home. Justin didn't need him, or anyone else, sticking his nose in his private business.

"Can't say I'm excited at the prospect of a Cade being underfoot…" Travis drawled, tipping up his hat and squinting the famous Loveland blue eyes that made the ladies swoon. Justin couldn't see what was so special about them. "But behind bars…that might make you a mite more palatable. Enjoyable even."

He couldn't spend six minutes alone with a low-down Loveland, let alone six months. Fury blasted Justin off his feet at arrogant Travis. Officer or not, he'd rip his darn head off. Arms grabbed Justin around the waist, checking his momentum.

"Hey!"

"Watch him!"

"Quit it, Justin!"

His siblings hollered, holding him fast as he thrashed and flailed.

"Time for you to move along now," James spat, glaring at Travis.

Travis only hooked his thumbs in his uniform pants and looked, if anything, even calmer. Travis's siblings, Maverick, Heath and Cole, lined up behind him, mountain tall like all Lovelands, their shadows long. While the Cades were hotheaded and passionate, the Lovelands barely had pulses, their cool, superior approach infuriating.

"You have no jurisdiction here, Cade," Travis told Jack easily, with just a hint of menace.

Ma and Boyd Loveland stepped between their bristling offspring.

"Boys, home!" Boyd barked. He was as tall and lean as his sons, his shoulders unbowed by age. The grooves around his mouth spoke of hours in the saddle, the line between his brows suggesting long nights after, worrying. Rumor had it the local bank had initiated foreclosure proceedings on the Loveland ranch. Without easy access to the Crystal River, they had to drive their cattle miles out of the way to water, stressing and depleting their herds.

"Don't embarrass me," Justin's mother hissed while smiling and nodding at the rubberneckers passing by on their way to the parking lot.

"See you in jail, Cade." Travis pointed at Justin then guffawed with his brothers as they headed to the parking lot.

"Sorry about that, darlin'."

The Cade siblings exchanged uneasy glances as Boyd pecked their mother on the cheek then strode after his sons. Overhead, a migrating V of geese honked.

Were things getting more serious between them?

Justin barely tolerated his mother and Boyd dating…but engaged? Not on his watch. He'd rather eat a rattler than become a relation to the lowlife Lovelands.

Before a despicable betrayal, the Cades had granted the Lovelands passage to the river. Now, if they weren't vigilant, their families might become entangled again. So far, Ma and Boyd seemed content to simply date. Yet Justin and Jewel speculated Boyd's financial predicament would prompt him to ask for her hand in marriage, gaining him the funds and water he needed.

How could Justin keep an eye on the situation from behind bars?

"Ms. Thompson!" his mother shouted, waving. "A moment?"

The lithe young woman halted then turned, her movements efficient and crisp. She wore a navy suit jacket with a matching skirt ending just below her knees, a white shirt buttoned tight around her throat. Despite the covered-up look, attraction spiked through Justin, taking him by surprise. Something about Brielle Thompson's good-girl image challenged the hell-raiser in him. A red cape before the bull. A sudden urge to unpin her hair, remove that straitjacket and kiss off her immaculately applied lipstick seized him.

He shook away the wild thought.

"I'm afraid I'm running late for a meeting. Another time?"

"Justin just wanted to thank you and apologize."

"The heck I do," he muttered, unable to pull his gaze from Brielle's arresting face. She wasn't beautiful, exactly, but only because that was the wrong word. Lots of people were beautiful. They blended with the scenery. Brielle's direct gaze and firm stance demanded attention. Out in the hall, she'd been aggressive, combative and lovely.

One by one, he admired her features. They weren't remarkable. An upward tip spoiled the straight line of her nose. A heaviness lent her square jaw a stubborn look. Her generous lower lip dominated her mouth, making it uneven. And her eyes, a distinct green color resembling new leaves, oddly contrasted with her darker lashes and brow.

Yet it added up to something unique, compelling—something that made him look twice.

"Not necessary, but thanks." She waved and turned to leave, the dismissive gesture getting under his skin.

"Wait!"

His call jerked her to a stop again. When her piercing eyes swung to his, his throat closed around whatever he'd been about to say.

Idiot.

Let her go.

"Yes?" She arched a brow, the provocative move sending a current of awareness sliding over his skin.

"I should have said it earlier. I'm sorry for hitting your truck."

To his surprise, she strode forward and paused only a foot away. No one ever got this close to him anymore. Not even his ma, yet tough Army Chaplain Brielle Thompson had no problem getting right up in his face.

"Are you?" she asked, skeptical.

Jewel's gasp turned into a surprised chuckle his brothers echoed.

"She's got you figured out," Jared guffawed.

"Shut it," Justin growled without taking his eyes off Brielle.

"Let's give these two some privacy," he heard his ma murmur, then the group tromped away.

"You were saying?" Brielle prompted, her prim tone and serene nature revving him up. She didn't fool him. He'd glimpsed the shadows in her eyes, witnessed her swift burst of anger, and knew she ran deeper, darker, wilder than she appeared.

"I'm sorry I hit your van."

"I don't believe you."

He shifted in his boots, uneasy at her direct, unrelenting gaze. She sure didn't tiptoe around delicate subjects. "I don't care if you believe me."

Her jaw jutted. "Yes, you do."

His mouth dropped open. She'd just called him out. No one dared do that, other than his family, and even they trod lightly.

A breeze rustled the dry leaves of a nearby maple, sending a few spiraling to the ground. "Why would I care?" he asked, forcing a nonchalant tone.

Her mouth ticked up in the corners. "You're still here talking to me."

He pressed his lips together to stop an unbidden smile, amused despite himself. She wasn't scared to give offense, and he liked that. "I'm doing it for my ma."

"Not yourself then?"

He stared at her, mute. What was she driving at? A trio of crows alighted on the telephone line running to the courthouse, bobbing their sleek black heads.

"Did you let go of the handlebars before you hit me?"

His head jerked back as if she'd slapped it.

"You saw me in time to avoid me," she pressed. "Why didn't you slow down or turn?"

He shoved his hands in his pockets and hunched his shoulders, defensive. Her questions pummeled him, pinning him on the ropes. "I was drinking. You heard…"

"Point oh nine?" Her eyes narrowed, a hard street stare, the pain he'd glimpsed the other night now settling into their corners. "That's just barely over the limit. No. Alcohol didn't have much to do with it."

His eyes dropped to his boots. He scuffed a line in the graveled parking lot, alternately wishing himself away and enjoying this dustup with her. "Then what did?"

One of the crows cawed, a rough, harsh, nasty sound voicing the writhing blackness rising from the base of his skull.

"Why don't you come to my clinic and find out?" she challenged, then turned neatly on her heel and marched away.

He watched her hop into a Jeep with temporary plates and peel out of the parking lot.

No shrinking violet there.

His mouth curved. He liked having a sparring partner.

She made him feel alive, a stinging rush like the return of blood to a limb that'd fallen asleep.

Except he liked—no, needed—to stay numb.

He didn't want to wake and face reality.

Did he?

CHAPTER THREE

"My FAVORITE PIZZA toppings are pineapple and jalapeño peppers," pronounced one of Fresh Start's patients during their first group therapy session later that week. Brielle jotted down the unusual pairing on a stand-alone whiteboard then turned back to the speaker. He'd introduced himself earlier as Paul, a former artilleryman who'd served in Mosul. Per his intake, he suffered from PTSD and depression.

Paul took up most of one of the chairs circling the center of the converted ranch house's living room. In his midthirties, he had wide ears, a round, expressive face and a stooped posture that seemed to be apologizing for the sheer size of him. Six inked names scrolled across his forearm.

Lost brothers in arms?

Names of fallen soldiers spun in Brielle's mind then stopped on one, the thought like an ice pick to her brain.

"Dude. That's the worst pizza topping combination ever," a slouchy teenager said.

Maya. She was a skelctal, black-haired girl with bruise-purple skin underlining eyes that looked up from the bottom of a deep well. She hailed from Denver and, according to her mother, had spent most of her life in facilities that'd failed to manage her bipolar and eating disorder.

Hopefully Fresh Start would succeed where others had failed. With its real-world immersion program through ranching experiences, it was designed to build confidence and end self-defeating behaviors. The clinic now housed fifteen residents, half its capacity, with eight more expected at the end of the week.

"This is a judgment-free zone," Craig, the group leader, intoned, mock serious.

Brielle crossed one leg over the other and smiled encouragingly at her latest hire. At fifty-eight, Dr. Craig Sheldon brought decades of experience as well as a deep personal understanding of what it was like to survive a war after his service as a gunner in the second Gulf War. He sported a pointy goatee, long sideburns and thinning hair he'd pulled into a ponytail at the back of his neck. An enamel yin-yang symbol on a leather cord appeared in the open neck of his golf shirt.

"Lame." Maya flicked her hand. A shower

of tinkling silver bangles slid down her forearm and revealed a freshly healed wrist scar.

"Do we get pizza here?" asked a man with white hair that looked electrified. Stew's children had tracked him down in an Aspen homeless shelter last week and admitted him for heroin addiction treatment. He'd stopped taking his mental health medications and had been suffering from hallucinations.

"Every Friday," Brielle supplied and the group slowly turned her way, their eyes wary. She hadn't spoken this whole hour save for a brief introduction. While Craig took the lead and built rapport, she'd stayed at the whiteboard and jotted down group responses while taking mental notes about her charges. "We'll make them, so you can have any toppings you want."

Pizza night was one of several activities she and Craig had brainstormed to build trust, confidence and self-esteem. Yet Fresh Start needed to add ranch skills to reach the potential envisioned by its owner. Thus far, no one had responded to her ad seeking a cowboy to run those activities. Did her lack of applicants stem from the disapproval locals had expressed about the clinic?

"Sweet!" Paul quirked an eyebrow at Maya. "If you're lucky I'll let you try mine."

She rolled her eyes. "I'd kill myself first."

An appalled silence descended. First-time group therapies needed to stay light and upbeat as the clients learned about each other and built trust; Maya's statement was anything but that.

"Kidding. Jeez," she muttered, then slid even farther into her seat. Her stick-thin arms crossed against her chest.

"Hey, if you can't joke about suicide here, where can you?" Craig put in, a twinkle in his hooded blue eyes.

A twentysomething woman with Tourette's syndrome giggled then clapped a hand over her mouth. Paul mouthed "what?" and guffawed. Stew joined in with an infectious belly laugh that got the rest of the group going, including Maya, who perked up enough to resume picking the rubber soles off her Converse sneakers.

Brielle stood, crossed the room and shot Craig a thumbs-up at the door. Very nice. Exactly the right touch of levity and reality, she thought as she strode back to her office. Her plans were finally coming together.

During the last three weeks, she'd fallen into a comforting routine with predictable schedules and specified activities. Now that she'd inserted order in her world, she'd begun to feel, for the first time since her discharge, she fit in…at least within these walls. Her days flew by at breakneck speed as she conducted staff interviews, oversaw patient admissions, supervised daily operations and provided individual therapy sessions to lighten Craig's load.

She rounded a corner and her receptionist, Doreen, a petite redhead wearing oversize glasses, waved at her. Half a bologna sandwich dangled from her fingers.

"Call," she mumbled around a mouthful, then pointed at Brielle's office. "Mayor."

The mayor?

Brielle hustled around her desk and snatched up the handset. Outside her open window was a domed blue sky, the mountains crystal clear around the valley. A light wind carried the scent of wild sage. "Hello, Mr. Cantwell. What can I do for you?"

"Hi, Ms. Thompson. I hope your first week's going well."

She thought of the missing paper supply order and the wrong-size bedsheets that failed to fit their overlong mattresses.

"Couldn't be better." Her eyes wandered to a picture of her parents from a cruise they'd taken during her first deployment. They stood barefoot in sand, their faces red and their smiles wide. She'd been surrounded by sand, too, back then. It hadn't been a photo op, though. Not that she needed a picture to remind her. She could still see, feel and taste that sand. Grains of it clung and scraped inside her, out of reach.

"As you might have seen in the paper, some of our residents have raised concerns about your facility."

"I've read them." The one delivered to her house, the one delivered to the center, even the one sitting on the diner's counter when she ordered her coffee this morning—each one reminding her of how unwelcome her facility was in this close-knit town.

Doreen appeared and set a glass of iced tea and a pile of mail on Brielle's desk. She smiled her gratitude, passed Doreen completed applicant forms for data entry and picked up the welcome refreshment.

"The town council has taken an interest."

The iced tea sloshed over the side of the glass and splatted her desk blotter. "And what does that mean exactly?"

"They're calling a meeting to allow residents to air their grievances."

"Grievances?" she echoed. "I don't understand. We haven't caused any problems..."

"You haven't, and believe me, Carbondale is happy to have you," the mayor soothed, then— "Hold a moment, I've got to get rid of this other call."

"Not all of Carbondale's pleased," she muttered under her breath, thinking of Justin Cade as she awaited the mayor's return. A sip of her sweet, lemony caffeine jump-started her jittering knee.

Despite her burgeoning responsibilities, she found herself thinking often about her dark rider, as she'd begun calling Justin after one particularly blushworthy dream. He'd taken her on a moonlight motorcycle ride to a secluded spot and then… She'd woken up.

Luckily.

Her full-to-bursting life, one she needed to succeed at, didn't allow for romantic fantasies about some tragic Brontë-esque hero in cowboy boots. Her attention and focus needed to be on the clinic and its patients, not an angst-ridden bad boy with possible suicidal tendencies…especially one who might soon be a resident here.

Would he accept the challenge she'd issued after the hearing?

"Sorry about that," the mayor said, back on the line. "More business about this year's Halloween parade. Some are requesting a costume ban because they may scare the children. A Halloween parade without costumes? Can you picture it?"

She made a sympathetic noise, and the man

continued, "Anyway, if you would attend the town meeting and present your case...?"

"Is Fresh Start on trial?" Her fingers traced a cross pattern in the condensation beading her glass. She'd expected a bit of pushback from a few of the old-time residents and figured it would just blow over in a few months...a town meeting was way more than she'd bargained for.

"No." The sound of rustling papers crinkled in her ear. "But Fresh Start's charter is conditional and can be revoked. It'd be helpful if you'd discuss the good work you do to help some of the more—" he cleared his throat "—cautious community members understand there's no reason to fear your patients."

"They're just trying to get their lives back together. The only harm my clients pose is to themselves." Her eyes swung to the dog tags stowed in a paper clip holder beside an overwatered spider plant. A discolored ring encircled the pot's bottom.

"I know. But keep in mind this isn't a big city like Chicago. We don't have those sorts of problems here..."

They had those problems everywhere, she thought wearily. Carbondale just might be a bit too close-minded, too proud, too much in denial to acknowledge it. Maybe they believed a problem wasn't a problem until you identified it.

"What about Jesse Cade?" she blurted, her mind zooming back to Justin.

Neither he nor his family had contacted her about admission. Given his impending sentencing tomorrow, did his silence suggest he'd chosen jail over the clinic?

Clearly, he wasn't ready for therapy's hard work. He'd refused to thank her for helping him or admit he'd endangered his life. And with more protest letters to the editor appearing in this morning's paper, the last thing she wanted were resistant, negative residents during her center's opening. He didn't see the program's benefit and refused to be saved.

So why did she still yearn to do just that?

She'd helped save his life already. The night on the side of the road, when he'd stared up at her dazed and confused, his body bloodied and battered from the impact. In that moment he'd reminded her of the soldiers who'd arrived at her army base on stretchers, crying in pain, asking for their mothers, their girlfriends, their kids. Yet Justin had requested no one, a lone wolf like her, without someone to turn to who'd understand the pain. Was their collision a sign she should help him, despite her reservations?

Her mind whirled, circling a dark hole; she

made it stop and tuned back into her phone conversation.

"I believe he's precisely the reason some locals are concerned," the mayor said.

"They'd rather act like problems don't exist than get people the help they need?"

"I'm sure it's not as drastic as that. More a lack of understanding."

She sighed. *Lord. Give me the strength.* "When is the meeting?"

"Next Wednesday at 8:00 p.m. in the town hall."

"I'll be there. Thanks."

Brielle hung up and drummed her fingers on the side of her glass, making the ice cubes clink, her mind in overdrive.

Would her tenure at Fresh Start end before it began? Her chance to help others cut off again? The questions twisted in her stomach. She pressed her palms together, rested her chin atop her fingertips and eyed the dog tags. This time she wouldn't leave quietly. Or easily. She was stronger now, able to bottle her dark emotions and fight for those who couldn't stand up for themselves.

She'd made little headway with Justin Cade, but she'd do everything in her power to sway the rest of Carbondale.

No matter what it took.

"PLEASE, JUSTIN. GO to Fresh Start."

Justin pulled his mother close in a quick hug. Her scent, lilac mixed with something powdery, rose from her neck and made his nose itch. He breathed in the familiar fragrance then forced himself to let her go. She had better things to worry about than him.

"I've made up my mind." He dropped to the living room floor beside the family's obese tabby, Clint, and rubbed his round belly. A fire, the first of the season, crackled in the floor-to-ceiling, two-story stone hearth. Javi's train set and miniature village, once his and his brothers', dominated a corner of the open living space.

"Wanna play with me?" Javi waved a piece of track.

"Sure." He crawled over to join his nephew. "Looks like you've got some major remodeling going on, bud."

"Yeah. I'm making room for the Halloween parade." Javi ripped up more track.

"Like the one here in Carbondale?" His mother perched on the edge of the couch, her knees pressed against their glass-topped wagon wheel coffee table.

Javi nodded; his tongue poked through the gap between his front teeth the way it did when he concentrated.

Justin grabbed a handful of tiny plastic pumpkins and set them in front of the miniature buildings. "Are you going to change it up this year or go as Batman again?"

Javi's dark eyes rolled up at him, exasperated. "Everyone expects me to be Batman."

"You don't have to do what people expect." Justin balanced a couple of pumpkins on some church steps.

Javi pointed a connecting track piece at Justin. "Yes, you do."

"Why is that?"

Javi shrugged. "So you don't hurt anyone's feelings."

"What about your own feelings?" Justin grabbed a couple of musty, pint-size hay bales from a Ziploc bag and stacked them in front of the town hall building.

Javi frowned. "I like Batman."

"Got it."

"You're gonna break Grandma's heart if you go to jail," Javi said offhandedly as he realigned the tracks to circle his tiny town.

"Javi," cautioned Sofia, joining them.

Justin stole a quick look at his ma and caught her wiping her eyes with her sleeve. The sight struck him like a punch in the gut. Sofia stopped at the edge of the sofa, pinwheeled her arms, then collapsed onto the cushions with an *oof.*

"I'm as big as a whale," she laughed.

"A blue one," Javi shouted. "Because they're the biggest! Mrs. Penway told us."

"Tell Mrs. Penway thanks," Sofia observed drily.

"And she's hugely beautiful, too," James called from the kitchen. He shed his coat and hat, strode around the granite island, then paused to kiss the top of Sofia's head.

"Emphasis on the huge." Sofia exchanged a tender smile with James that filled Justin with a strange sense of longing. He'd never be loved like that. Not that he'd let anyone close. He'd had and lost his better half. No one could occupy that spot again.

"What's that behind your back? Is it a present?" Javi abandoned the train set and flung himself at his stepfather. James dropped a bag and caught Javi in a bear hug.

"More dresses for our little one?" Sofia passed Javi a light-up Batman mask then held up a glittery pink garment.

Something twisted in Justin's gut. He'd miss seeing her and James's child born while he was behind bars. A couple months ago, they'd revealed the baby's gender—a girl, rare in his male-dominated family. Jewel, who could outride, outrope and outshoot any of her brothers, was the least feminine of any of them, especially pretty-boy Jared.

Since then, James had compulsively bought tiny dresses, flowered headbands, ruffled hats and lace socks with ribbons, each item frillier than the one before. The nursery resembled the inside of a Pepto-Bismol bottle, the walls practically oozing pink. The house hummed with hope and joy, leaving Justin feeling at odds whenever he entered it. He no longer fit in with his family—if he ever had. His head drooped.

"This one has rhinestones," James protested.

"So do about twenty of the other dresses you've bought her." Sofia smoothed a hand over her stomach.

"Those were sparkles and some had sewn crystal beads. Big difference."

Justin had to give it to James—he considered himself the absolute authority on just about everything, from bioenvironmental engineering down to the trimmings on a child's dress.

Sofia and his ma exchanged amused glances, and Justin's throat constricted. What did happy feel like exactly?

He couldn't remember.

"Yeah, *big* difference," exclaimed Jewel as

she swept down the open spiral staircase from the loft above the living room. She'd freshened up some from this morning's cattle drive, her hair tucked back into her usual braid and her dusty Wranglers swapped for a cleaner pair. "Don't know why you're trying to ruin your daughter with all this girly-girl stuff. Good thing she'll have her aunt Jewel to set her straight."

"Oh, her father's going to spoil her rotten." Sofia sighed.

"Am I spoiled?" Javi, wearing his glowing Batman mask, bumped into his miniature village then tumbled to the wide-planked pine floor.

Justin snatched him close before he hit the ground, protecting Jesse's son the way he should have shielded Jesse. "Never. You care too much about everybody."

Javi pushed up his mask and peered at Justin. "How come you don't?"

Justin shook his head, feeling his family's judgmental eyes on him. "I do."

"Then how come you're gonna break Grandma's heart and go to jail?"

"Javi," Sofia warned again.

"You told Daddy that," Javi huffed.

"The decision might be out of his hands anyway." James settled on the couch beside

Sofia and draped an arm around her shoulders. "Heard the town's holding a meeting next week to discuss revoking the facility's conditional charter. Place might close."

"Why?" An image of Brielle flashed in his mind's eye. He could tell she was committed to Fresh Start, and it bugged him that she'd lose it. Darned if he could say why exactly, but it did.

"Just what we read in the paper. Folks are worried property values will go down, and crime rates will rise from attracting the wrong kinds of people." James dropped his ear to Sofia's belly.

Javi joined them and placed a hand next to his father's cheek. "What makes people the wrong kind?"

Sofia slid her fingers through Javi's hair. "Some people don't like drug addicts or people going through tough times."

"We had bad times, and the shelters let us stay. Why won't they let them stay?" The color blanched from Javi's normally tan skin. "Does that mean people don't like Mama and me?"

Justin felt a lasso cinch his chest and squeeze. Javi had a point. "Everyone loves you, bud."

James pulled Javi onto his lap. "You have a home now. A family. No more troubles."

"But Mama was an addict," Javi continued,

his voice rising. "And my first daddy, too. They needed help. How come people won't help them like they did for Mama and me?"

"Because they're idiots," Justin bit out. He wanted no part of the facility personally, but the idea of the town shutting it down irked him. Places like Fresh Start gave people hope, a second chance, a refuge. Jesse had sobered up before he'd been gunned down for an unpaid drug debt. Who knew how long he would have stayed clean that time? Each period of sobriety extended Jesse's life. If not for the murder, he might be here today, setting up a train set with his son... Of course, that'd mean James and Sofia wouldn't have a baby on the way, but...

Did it mean Jesse's death was one of those "meant to be" curveballs life threw at you? He'd bet the godly chaplain Brielle Thompson would think so.

"Thought you hated clinics like that," Jewel drawled. She passed him a beer on her way back from the kitchen.

"Hate's a strong word." His thumb traced the tab's sharp, metallic outline. "Just don't see it helping me."

"They're dragging Jesse's name into this," James put in, grim.

"What? How?" his mother exclaimed.

"Javi, go to your room," Sofia ordered.

"But—" he protested.

"Now." James pointed at the stairs, and Javi scurried up them.

When they heard his bedroom door shut, James said, "They blame Jesse for bringing those murderers to town and claim the Fresh Start residents might do the same."

Justin swore a blue streak, finishing with, "Of all the small-minded, hypocritical, overreactionary talk I've ever heard. We need to stop this." His thumb twitched over his beer's tab, but didn't bend it back. It felt like a grenade— pull the pin and *boom*.

He needed to be alert for this conversation. Not numb.

"We'll speak at the meeting." James swept Sofia's swollen feet onto his lap and rubbed them.

"That might help, but I'm not sure it'll be enough," worried Ma. "The lady who's running it—what's her name?"

"Brielle Thompson," Justin supplied, thinking of the saintly warrior he'd gone toe to toe with days ago. She was a fighter. He set the beer down on the coffee table.

"Right." His mother pulled off her glasses and polished them with the bottom of her yellow shirt. It coordinated with the polka dots in her headband and on her socks. Some people collected dolls. Some were into antique cars. His mother obsessed about matching her outfits, her furnishings, even her car accessories right down to the ocean-blue air freshener in the same shade as her sedan. She called it a lifestyle choice. "As a stranger," she continued, "and a city girl, I'm not sure our neighbors will listen to her."

Fired up, Justin bolted to his feet. "I'll make them listen to her."

"How are you going to do that?" Sofia asked, her eyes closed as James kneaded her insoles.

"I'm going over to Fresh Start to figure that out. Can anyone give me a ride?"

"Me." Jewel bussed their ma on the cheek then hustled to join him. "I have plans in town anyway."

"Wouldn't be to hear Heath Loveland play at the Barnsider?" James teased.

"I'm going for the wings," she huffed, then grabbed her coat and flounced out the door.

Justin and James grinned at each other. They loved tweaking their tough, tomboy sister about her supposed crush on one of their archrivals. Dubbed the "sensitive cowboy" by swooning ladies who flocked to his local gigs, Heath was the youngest in his family, like Jewel. Sometimes, given her extreme defensiveness, Justin and his brothers wondered if they might be right about Jewel liking Heath after all, crazy as that'd be.

"Take care now," he heard his mother call as he jammed on his hat, shoved his arms in his jacket and flung himself out the door. Beer forgotten.

Fifteen minutes later he tromped up the steps to the old Greyson place. Its owner had raised a few cattle as a hobby and stabled horses, until recent years when hard times forced him to sell. The new owner, an investment banker looking to shelter money, rumor had it, had bought the place lock, stock and barrel. And it most recently had become the home of Fresh Start.

"Anybody here?" he called, opening the front door when no one answered his knock. He stepped inside just as Brielle emerged from a room to his left.

"What are *you* doing here?" Then— "Was the door unlocked?"

For some contrary reason, her hostile tone slapped a wide smile on his face. He swept off his hat and bowed slightly, all old-school, country-boy charm. "Yes, it was. And it's nice to see you, too."

"Can't say the same, but come in. Doreen, please contact maintenance to have them check and reset the security keypad," she called then turned back the way she came.

He followed her into a small, sterile-looking room, admiring the sway of her trim hips beneath a modest skirt that flowed nearly to her ankles. Today, the silky lavender material of her shirt buttoned at each wrist and twisted into a bow at her neck. With all this covering up, maybe it was a wonder he found an inch of her to be attracted to. Yet his eyes stuck to her like she was flypaper. He stroked his beard, his own form of concealment.

"Please. Sit."

He folded himself into a chair and watched as she strode behind her desk and sat, her back so straight, he bet he could plumb an entire building off it. A hectic red colored her cheeks and brought out the mint of her magnetic eyes.

"What can I do for you?"

"It's more what I can do for you."

Her lips quirked, and he found himself mesmerized by the fuller bottom lip, imagining its softness…its taste…

"And what would that be?"

"Heard about the town hall meeting next week, and I wanted to help."

She tilted her head and narrowed her eyes. "Why?"

"Why?"

"Seemed like you thought the clinic was a waste of time last time we talked."

He dropped his eyes at her piercing gaze. With one look, she turned him into glass, see-through and potentially breakable. It was a damn uncomfortable feeling.

"It is for me. But other people…"

"If you don't believe in what we do, how can you convince others?"

"I—I do believe you can make a difference. Just—you know—not with me."

"And you're in the habit of pronouncing judgments on things you know nothing about?"

His mouth dropped open. No. That was know-it-all James. "Look. I'm just beyond help is all."

Her expression softened. "No one's beyond help unless they put themselves out of reach." He followed her eyes to a set of dog tags stowed in a paper clip tray.

"Are those yours?"

Suddenly she hurried from the room, rubbing her eye as if she'd gotten something in it. He glimpsed the anguish, the inner torment he'd spotted the night of the accident. It stirred his protective instincts. What kept her up at night?

Curiosity overruled politeness, and he

leaned forward, grabbed the metal discs and read the inscription.

Pelton
William R.
4763888912
O Pos
Protestant

A brother? Friend? The need to know seized him.

"Who's William?" he asked when she returned, blowing her nose.

"No one." She snatched the tags from his hand, yanked open a drawer and dropped them inside.

"My brother Jesse died almost four years ago," he heard himself say.

What was he doing? He knew better than to talk about Jesse. Yet something about Brielle's pain made him want to share his.

Her stiff expression slackened. "I'm sorry. I heard he was your twin?"

"Identical. We even liked the same mustard. The brown spicy kind, not the yellow stuff." He nearly kicked himself. Why was he telling her this nonsense?

Her smile revealed two enchanting dimples on either side of her mouth. "I hate the yellow kind, too. Much too watery. What else did Jesse like?"

"Kids. No mother was safe around him." His shoulders lowered as he relaxed into the tale. No one ever talked about Jesse except in tragic terms, if they spoke of him at all. His family tiptoed around Justin's grief like it was a land mine.

Yet undaunted Brielle waded right in without hesitation. It felt good to have an unbiased ear, someone who'd let him focus on positive memories, unfiltered by the bad. "Jesse begged to hold babies every time he came within fifty yards of them, and he had to be bribed to give them back."

"He sounds like a special guy."

Justin's eyes burned for a moment. How long since he'd cried over Jesse? He hadn't allowed himself tears at Jesse's funeral nor a day since, and he'd be damned if he was going to start now, in front of a beautiful woman whom he never wanted to view him as broken. "He wasn't a bad element like they're saying." He jerked his head toward Carbondale, visible through her window.

She nodded. "I know."

Two words. Simple and direct. They carried such conviction that they reached inside and stirred his heart.

"So that's why I want to help you."

"You won't be able to do that from jail."

He let that sink in. She was right. He'd be behind bars when the meeting took place and couldn't speak up for Jesse.

"Unless…"

He leaned forward, hands on his knees. "Unless?"

"You came here instead."

When he opened his mouth to object, she held up a hand. "Hear me out. I know you don't think we can help you, and maybe we can't, but you could do *us* a lot of good. I haven't found someone to lead the patients' ranch activities yet. You could take that over temporarily, as a volunteer, while you're staying here to fulfill the court ruling. It'd help my case and impress the local ranchers at the meeting. Plus, I'd have more time to recruit another cowboy to take on the job permanently. What do you say?"

The room spun around him for a moment. "I—I'd have to think on it."

"What's to think about?" she challenged with that same give-no-quarter directness that backed him up and kept him off balance. "What are you afraid of?"

That snapped his spine straight. "Nothing."

"Then prove it. I dare you to spend the next six weeks here."

"Dare?" Was she joking? This wasn't kid stuff...it was life or death. And the way Brielle got under his skin, opened him up, was downright dangerous. If he accepted, he'd need to keep his distance. "I'm not going to any group talks."

She pondered that a moment then sighed. "Fine. Go only if you want to, which I'm betting will be plenty."

"You're pretty sure of yourself."

"I am."

He found himself smiling. When was the last time he'd smiled for no reason? He liked Brielle's gumption.

"So," she pressed, looking so flushed and vibrant he wagered touching her would be like grabbing hold of an electric fence. He could feel the spark from where he sat. "Do we have a deal?"

He shoved back his chair and held out his hand. "Dare accepted."

As he left the facility to meet his sister for a ride home, thoughts ran through Justin's head. He hadn't been able to save his brother, but perhaps it wasn't too late to make some sort of amends and help others, even though he had little faith it'd make a difference with him.

And deep down, he had to admit that the choice between spending the next one-plus month with Brielle Thompson versus Sheriff Travis Loveland wasn't exactly hard to make.

His lips curved as he pictured her fired-up expression.

Nope.

Not a difficult decision by a long shot.

CHAPTER FOUR

"HE'S HERE. HE'S here!" Doreen stage-whispered, fluttering in Brielle's office door the following day. Her gravity-defying bangs quivered like antennae.

Brielle cocked her head and raised an eyebrow. "Who?"

"*Him…* Justin Cade. He's filling out his contact and insurance information." Doreen waved a hand before her scarlet face. "And he's wearing his dark leather jacket and black cowboy hat with the brim low over those eyes of his and…"

"Decorum, Doreen," Brielle chided gently, knowing herself to be a flat-out hypocrite considering she craned her neck to glimpse the dark rider just feet away.

Anticipation fired her synapses, lighting her up inside. She'd nearly given up on Justin showing today, given the hour—4:55 p.m. A clear indicator of his reluctance, and his nerves, she suspected, no matter how tough and gruff the grizzly bear of a cowboy appeared.

"Send him in when he's finished, please."

"Can I offer him coffee?" Doreen bit her lip and shot a sideways glance over her shoulder. "Tea…some Twizzlers…?"

Brielle tucked back a smile at her smitten secretary. Justin Cade was a tall, dark, dangerous drink of water. No wonder he had Doreen spinning in circles.

"Whatever you like, but don't stay past five, okay? You've put in too many extra hours as it is." She shot her employee a grateful smile. They'd all been slaving, double time, to get the facility up and running. With her resident cowboy now on location, the final pieces fell into place…

Except community buy-in.

She clamped a hand over her jittering knee. In a few days, she'd face the town members who'd written complaints to the local paper's editor. They'd air their grievances, and she'd settle their concerns. Simple, right? So why did she feel as though she was preparing to trundle down an IED-riddled road? One wrong move, one careless word, could destroy everything.

Just this morning, a letter had appeared in the paper labeling Fresh Start a "Dangerous Den of Druggies." She appreciated the alliteration—the sentiment, not so much. She'd defend this facility to her last breath just as she'd stood by her soldiers.

Until she hadn't…

And look where that got you…

Got them…

The dog tags by her spider plant drew her eye, and she dumped the rest of her water into its dark soil. Mud flowed out the bottom and seeped onto her desk blotter. A yellow frond caught her eye. Was it dying? She scrutinized the rest of the greenery as she pinched it off, dropped it in her wastebasket then sopped up the wet with a tissue clump. Her fumbling hands knocked over her tea, and the scalding liquid shot onto her lap.

"Mary, mother of Jesus!" She hopped in a circle, dabbing at the material. It burned a hole in her flesh—well, her skirt at least. What'd Doreen put in there?

"Is this a bad time?" a man's low bass voice rumbled.

Her head snapped up, and the heat radiating down her leg paled in comparison to the firestorm of her cheeks. She pressed her hands to them and nodded, her eyes drinking in Justin Cade.

In worn Wranglers, scuffed boots and a black hat that contrasted with his light hazel eyes, he pulled a sigh right out of her. Ragtag as all get-out, he still commanded attention. Hers, at least. He sauntered into her office, lanky, wiry as an apostrophe, his square-shouldered, loose-limbed gait oddly graceful, his dark beard a little menacing. Her heartbeat tripped into double time.

"What gave you that impression?" She swept a hand toward a chair across from her desk, inviting him to sit.

"Thought I interrupted some religious ritual." He slouched into the chair and crossed his legs at the ankles. With his lids half lowered and the corners of his mouth hidden by his beard and mustache, she couldn't tell if he was serious or teasing. "Any more saints you plan on summoning? Should I be worried about fire and brimstone, preacher?"

"We'll see how things go," she replied wryly. "I've got ten thousand more to call on if need be."

"Jesus," he muttered, slipping a toothpick into his mouth.

"Technically, that's the Lord's son, but always a good go-to."

That drew a sputtering chuckle out of Justin, a rusty sound like an old engine starting up for the first time in years. It did something strange to her chest, expanding it so her lungs drew in more air, thin and heady.

Or was the response Justin's effect on her?

"If you'll tell me where I'm bunking, I'll go on up." He jerked a thumb over his shoulder. "Leave you to your tribal dance."

She smiled. Beneath Justin's glower lurked a bit of a comedian. "Once I complete your intake, we'll get you settled."

"Intake?" His lids lifted. "Thought I filled out all the paperwork."

"Some, but we need more information before we can admit you."

Justin tugged at the collar of his black T-shirt then pulled off his leather jacket. "How much more?"

"Not much." She crossed her fingers beneath the desk and tried not to admire the way his shirt stretched across the wide V of his chest. *Tried* being the operative word. "I'll be asking you a series of questions. Your answers will be confidential."

"No, they won't." He dropped his leather jacket on the floor beside his duffel.

"Yes, they will."

His broad shoulders lifted and fell in a shrug. "You'll know them."

"I don't count."

His eyes lasered into hers. "Says who?"

She blinked at him. As a counselor, she served as a conduit for patients, channeling their fears, their rage, their despair. Justin's comment solidified her somehow. He made her feel present and alive in a way she hadn't in a long time. "The counselor you're assigned can't help you without this information."

"I don't want help."

She counted backward from ten then said, "We can't admit you without a completed intake, and you accepted the dare."

"To volunteer teaching your patients to tend cattle. Ride. Rope…" Justin folded his arms over his chest, mutinous.

"You had the option, here or jail, and you chose Fresh Start. Whether you go to group sessions or not, you're still a patient."

"Not so's I see it," he grumbled. Behind him, Doreen strolled past the doorway, rubbernecking.

"Would you please close the door, Doreen?" Brielle called.

"Can I get you two anything?" she asked, her eyes sticking to Justin like he was made of flypaper.

"A beer?" Justin drawled.

"That'll be all, Doreen, thanks."

Once the door closed, Justin lifted his eyes and studied her. The slanting sun glinted on the gold flecks in his jewel-tone depths. "What kinds of questions?"

She clicked on her keyboard and brought up his Addiction Severity Index sheet. "Medical, employment/support status, alcohol, drug, legal, family/social and psychiatric."

One thick eyebrow rose. "You said this'd be quick."

"We'll be as fast as possible. All clients partake in this interview. The information helps us provide you with the right care for your needs."

"I don't—"

"Need anything," she finished for him, an edge entering her voice despite her effort to stay neutral. He wasn't used to the tough, blunt talk she'd adopted with her soldiers. Sometimes it was the only way she'd gotten through. "Got it."

Justin waved a hand. "Let's get this over with," he mumbled around the toothpick.

She squared her shoulders.

Lord, give me strength.

"You also have the right to refuse to answer any question."

"Now we're talking." He tipped his hat down so low it covered his eyes. His chin dropped to his chest. Her hands clasped each other, and it took all her self-discipline not to flick that blasted hat right off his head. She knew avoidance when she saw it. Knew how to handle it, too…so why was he getting under her skin?

He's a client.

Yet she struggled to see him that way.

"If you're uncomfortable," she continued as if she hadn't heard him, "or if it feels too personal or painful to give a response, then don't answer."

His nostrils flared. "Are you calling me a coward?"

"Some things are hard to talk about."

"I'm private. Big difference." He spread his large hands, and she noticed his scraped knuckles. A boxer's hands. A fighter, like her. Now she squared off against him, circling the ring, trying to pin him on the ropes. She didn't want to beat him so much as break him down until his hard shell cracked. Until then, she couldn't reach him—who he really was inside.

"Private or just hiding?"

He flipped up his hat brim and stared at her, aghast. "Is this part of your script?" He waved a hand at her computer.

"Nope. My own improvisation. Oh, and when answering, please try to be as accurate as possible."

He angled forward in his seat. "You think I'm a coward *and* a liar?"

"I don't know you well enough to tell," she

said bluntly, though she felt as though she did know him, on some deeper level. She sensed the parts he hid because she concealed them, too.

He shook his head and leaned back in his chair, turning the tables on Brielle. "What rank were you before you left the army?"

She shifted in her seat. "This isn't about me."

"How about this?" His eyes bored into hers. "For every question you answer, I'll return the favor."

A sheen of perspiration popped out on her brow. She crossed to the window and cranked it open, letting the cool early October air flow over her. How personal did Justin plan on getting? If she started talking about her past, she risked triggering her PTSD. She'd fall into the same depression that'd forced her to abandon her comrades during her last tour of duty when they'd needed her most.

One especially...

She wouldn't risk failing her current charges. Fresh Start had to succeed, for her patients and herself. And that included a recalcitrant Justin Cade, who awakened her inborn need to help.

Was she a fraud for refusing to open up while expecting others to share their secrets?

Absolutely.

But right now, it was about survival. Just like the airlines directed, you had to put the oxygen mask on yourself before you secured it on others. If she thought too hard—or at all—about her time in Kandahar, she wouldn't be able to breathe.

"How about I'll answer one question for every section you answer completely. And I was a captain."

Justin saluted her. "Ask away, Captain."

She refreshed his chart on her computer screen and spied the general information Doreen had added before leaving for the day.

"How many times have you been hospitalized for a medical condition?"

"Lost track."

"Ballpark."

"Twenty."

Wow. She filled in the box. "How long ago since your last hospitalization for a physical problem?"

"You know the answer to that as well as me."

Keeping her eyes locked on the screen, she hid her wince. She'd never forget the thud of his body as it crashed into her truck. Did this near tragedy fuel her compulsion to help Justin? Or was she just another good girl trying to convert a bad boy?

All her life, she'd sought to bring light to those in the darkness. Now she fumbled in the gloom, lost, too. She had to find her way, or she'd never lead others to that light again.

"Any chronic medical conditions?"

"Nope."

"Injuries in the past month?"

"Fifteen, give or take."

She stopped typing and peered at him. He gnawed on his toothpick, unfazed by that whopping number. "Fifteen?"

"Give or take."

"How…?" He didn't live in a war zone.

"I ride dirt bikes. And bulls. Cliff dive in summers. Oh. Then there's barn brawls."

"Barn brawls?"

"Cage fighting, country style." He cracked his reddened knuckles.

"And you engage in these high-risk activities because…"

He shrugged. "They're fun."

"Risking your life…"

"What's it matter?"

A shadow fell on her heart, making her shiver. She held out her palms. "See these?"

He jerked his chin in acknowledgment.

"They held the hands of mortally wounded soldiers, and you know what they all had in common?" Her voice shook ever so slightly.

His eyes narrowed.

"Life mattered to them. They fought for it, begged for it, wept for it..."

Justin's callused hand reached across the desk to cover hers. "I'm sorry."

Warmth exploded up her arm at his rough, tender touch. "Don't be sorry. Be grateful."

"Where were you stationed?" he asked a moment later, releasing her.

"Kandahar."

"My brother James served in Kabul."

"Where's he now?"

"Waging war against our neighbors the Lovelands. Much more dangerous." The quirk of his lips siphoned her attention from her dark memory. Was he trying to settle her down? That was her job, not his.

She forced a light tone. "Sounds serious."

"Our feud goes back over a hundred and twenty-five years." Justin dropped his arms so they hung at his sides and faced her full on, his features relaxed. "It began when a Loveland kidnapped Maggie Cade to steal her dowry, a fifty-carat sapphire named Cora's Tear."

"What happened to her?" Brielle asked. If following this tangent loosened Justin up and helped build rapport, she'd play along.

"Murdered. Thrown off a cliff, and her jewel stolen."

Brielle shuddered and glanced at the dramatic vista beyond her windows. Soaring mountaintops glistened in the now fading light. She imagined falling from one, the absolute terror of such a plunge. "Did your family get Cora's Tear back?"

"Nope, but we strung up the Loveland lowlife who killed Maggie Cade, and we've been feuding ever since." Satisfaction rounded out every syllable. Clearly Justin relished the ongoing tension, and no wonder...it provided an outlet for the anger she'd glimpsed inside him.

What fueled his rage?

"That's quite a tale."

"And now my ma's dating the head of the Loveland clan." His boots clomped heavily on her wooden floor as he crossed to her wastebasket and tossed away his toothpick.

"How does that make you feel?"

He wheeled around and wagged a finger at her. "Uh-uh. I don't want any of that psychobabble. Are we through yet?"

"We're just getting started."

A whistle of air escaped him. "Didn't think so." He dragged himself back to his seat.

After going through his employment and education history, she followed up with, "No dreams of leaving the ranch?"

His gaze flitted out the window, and his lips pressed into a straight line.

"Justin?" she prompted, sensing she pressed a sore spot.

"Kilimanjaro," he muttered.

Her eyebrows rose. "You want to climb mountains?"

"Was more Jesse's idea."

"Not yours?"

"I just wanted see what was beyond there." He pointed at the horizon.

"What's stopping you now?"

"My brother's dead," he said flatly, his voice shutting the door on her follow-up question.

Did Justin believe he didn't deserve a life without his twin? Survivor's guilt? She'd seen it often in squad members who couldn't wrap their heads around why stopping to sneeze meant they survived an ambush that killed their platoon members. Random acts of destruction—life was full of them.

Justin squinted at her. "Why'd you leave Kandahar?"

"I was discharged."

"Why were you discharged?"

She clenched the linen material of her skirt, the black tide of shame, remorse and grief crashing inside her. "We agreed to only one question."

He stared at her from beneath lowered brows. "Fair enough."

She unfurled her fingers. Hopefully, he'd forget the question…

"Have you consumed any alcohol in the last thirty days?"

"Just beer."

"How much in the past month?"

He shoved his hands in his pockets. "Around a couple a day or less."

"Cans or six-packs?"

He blinked at her. "Six-packs…but not every day."

She tabbed to the appropriate box on her screen. "How many days do you drink a twelve-pack?"

"Just on weekends, and Mondays."

Her fingers curled over the keyboard, waiting. "Fridays, too?"

He nodded.

"So how much do you drink Tuesday through Thursday?"

He shifted in his seat. "I don't have to drink every day."

"But do you?"

His mouth scrunched side to side, then he nodded. "But it's by choice."

Right…

"We're a dry facility here," she underscored

as she filled in his alcohol intake. "No drugs, no alcohol."

"I don't do drugs," he growled.

Beyond her door, footsteps and voices heralded the start of dinner. Her stomach growled at the beefy scent of stew. She should have snitched a square of corn bread earlier. Was Justin hungry? He appeared so formidable, so hard-bitten, it was difficult to imagine him wanting—needing—anything. "How often do you drink to intoxication?"

"I don't drink to get drunk. I drink to fall asleep."

She nodded, understanding. Justin drank to shut his brain off completely, often a way to avoid the nightmares that plagued people with PTSD. She typed in a note to their physician about assessing Justin for a Prazosin prescription, the medication that allowed her to unplug every night. "Do you have trouble sleeping?"

"Not when I drink. Look. Are we through this part? Wouldn't mind getting a plate of whatever's cooking."

"Dinner's served for the next hour, so there's plenty of time." She glanced at the digital clock on her desk then continued. "How many years have you been drinking like this?"

"This much? Don't know. It's crept up on me..."

"Since…"

"Next question." He snapped his mouth shut.

"Okay, then. Next section—"

"We agreed you'd answer my question first," he chided. "Why'd you get discharged?"

"You didn't answer everything. That was the deal. So, when'd you start drinking so much?" she demanded, holding her breath.

They stared at each other for a tense moment. In the strained quiet, a flock of migrating geese honked furiously overhead, the sound desperate, hectic, as though they ran for their lives. It mirrored her wish to escape Justin's question, just as he sought to dodge hers.

"Next question," he said at last, his voice low.

She released her breath and smoothed a hand over her tight bun. A couple of strands dangled by her temple, and she tucked them behind her ears, her fingers shaking slightly.

"How many times in your life have you been arrested for the following?" She ran down a list of charges.

"Only the DUI."

"No assault charges?"

Justin's grin was more grim than humorous. "We settle scores between ourselves around here."

"No weapons offenses?"

"Nope."

"Do you own any weapons?" Brielle persisted. Laughter rose and fell following a crash from the distant dining room.

He rattled off a list long enough to arm a small militia: handguns, rifles, knives, crossbows, even a grenade launcher.

"Why do you own so many?"

Justin shot her an inscrutable look. "Lots of people own more," he said, dodging the question. "Is that the end of this section?"

At her nod, he asked, "Why'd you get discharged?"

Sheesh. He wasn't letting up. She rubbed the back of her tense neck. "You didn't explain why you own so many weapons."

At his exasperated sigh, she tapped her keyboard, finished entering the information, then scrolled to the family/social section. "Are you married?"

"Do I look like someone's husband?"

She studied the scruffy man, one eyebrow raised. He had the strong, silent type nailed. Rough as he might be, she suspected he cleaned up nice… "There's no accounting for taste."

That pulled a hard crack of laughter out of him. "Guess I'm no one's taste, then."

Not entirely true, not when it came to her,

she admitted to herself, drawn more and more to this opaque man.

"Do you want to get married?"

"Are you improvising again?" he drawled, sounding amused.

"It's on the list," she rebutted. The question intrigued her, and she was curious about the answer, about Justin…just not for the right… the professionally appropriate reasons.

Once she finished his intake, she'd assign his case to Craig and step away from Justin Cade's dangerous allure. His recklessness, his need to throw himself needlessly into harm's way, could get him hurt or worse, thereby triggering her PTSD.

"I'm never getting married," he pronounced, emphatic.

"That still doesn't answer whether you want to or not."

His eyes slid out from under hers. "Next question."

"Do you live with your family?"

"No."

She scrolled back up to his contact information. "But your address says—"

"I have a cabin on the property."

Interesting. Despite living on his family ranch, he considered himself alone, not a part of their family unit.

"Are you satisfied with that arrangement?"

His gaze darted to the window again, and the yearning she glimpsed on his face made her ache. "It'll do."

She noted her low confidence in the honesty of his answers and moved on. It wasn't that he was being untruthful with her. More likely he didn't realize that he lied to himself. "Do you live with anyone with an alcohol problem or drug abuse issues?"

"Not anymore."

"Jesse was an opiate addict?"

"He was a hell of a lot more than that." A muscle jumped just above the line of his beard.

"I liked hearing about him the other day."

Justin's tense features relaxed, and she blinked at the transformation, his handsomeness snatching her breath. "It was the first time I've talked about him since he passed."

"I'm honored you shared him with me."

Their eyes locked for a moment, then she cleared her throat. "Justin, who do you spend your free time with?"

"No one."

"Are you satisfied spending your free time alone?"

"Glad not to be making anyone else as miserable," he muttered, more to himself than to her. An honest admission. One she connected to.

He avoided social situations so he didn't bring others down...a classic move for a person suffering from depression. Sometimes it was situational, induced from a traumatic event. In other cases, it was a chronic, biological condition. She couldn't determine which type of depression Justin suffered from...not yet, anyway, not with him being vague and semitruthful with his answers. She'd leave that diagnosis to Craig, but she hoped they'd be able to help him. To do that, though, he'd have to want to help himself, too.

"No close friends?" she asked.

"Jesse's gone." A bleak note entered his voice, and she wondered at the unique bond between twins. How devastating it must be to lose someone so close to you.

"Are we finished with this section?" Justin asked.

"Yes." She braced herself. How to explain her discharge without giving too much away?

"Are you married?"

She released her grip on the sides of her chair. "No."

"Do you want to get married?"

"That's two questions," she protested, turning on her brisk, military voice. No chink in her body armor...no sign of just how much she longed for a partner in life. Like Justin, she hadn't the stomach to get close to anyone…

The dog tags gleamed in the corner of her eye.

After Justin denied any history of abuse, she asked him if he had any serious conflicts with family.

"They're happy. I'm not," he said offhandedly. "That's a conflict."

"It's hard being around people who don't understand." She commiserated with Justin. Hadn't she moved out to this remote part of the world for the same reason? She wanted a fresh start, one that'd buffer her from her PTSD, and part of that came from distancing herself from personal interactions that only reminded her of her past. "How much does that trouble you?"

He shrugged. "You can't change what you can't fix," he quoted.

"That's a cop-out."

He whistled, rolling his shoulders. "You sure don't mince words."

"Fixing yourself is hard work."

"I'm not afraid of hard work." He bristled.

"Guess we'll see. We've got a group session tonight if you've got the guts to attend."

He stared at her, slack-jawed. "Thought ministers were supposed to be nice."

"I'm called to help. Nice isn't always required." She bit back a smile at his shocked expression, enjoying catching the hard-nosed cowboy flat-footed. Maybe too much. "Ever been hospitalized for a mental illness?"

"Now you're saying I'm a nutjob?"

Her jaw tightened. "We don't use those kinds of terms. Have you ever been diagnosed with depression?"

"Do I look like I sit around and cry all day?" he blurted. "I'm not sad."

"What emotions do you feel most often?"

"Nothing." He scrubbed a hand over his face. "Except when I'm dirt biking or scrapping."

"I see." Her fingers flew across the keyboard. Justin's behavior fell into the self-harm category. To feel something, he went to extreme lengths. Some cut themselves. Justin barreled directly into moving vans at ninety miles an hour.

"You never feel happy? Excited about things?"

"What's to be excited about?" he asked through a yawn.

"How about anxiety, compulsion, trouble concentrating?"

He shook his head, his eyes lowering to half-mast again. If she didn't know better, she'd think he was about to fall asleep. But she did know better. He was hiding, ducking behind his wall, a strong indication her questions cut too close to the truth.

"Trouble controlling your anger? Episodes of rage or violence?"

"Comes with being a Cade."

Her fingers stilled. "Excuse me?"

"We're known as the town hotheads."

She cocked her head and recalled how he'd lunged at Sheriff Loveland in the courthouse parking lot. In the comments section, she jotted down a note to Craig to assess for anger management.

"Any thoughts of suicide?"

"No," Justin said quickly. Too fast.

"Have you ever attempted suicide?"

"No."

"What about when you hit my van?"

"That was an accident," he insisted.

"You said you weren't a liar."

His hands clenched in his lap. "It's more like a dare."

"To who?"

He studied her for a long moment then blew out a breath, his jaw working. "Death."

Outside, a wind rose and howled off the mountain peaks. "I don't understand."

"It came for Jesse."

"So?"

"Why hasn't it come for me?" The vein of anguish in his voice was even more powerful for its restraint. It pulled at her.

"Should it?"

He nodded.

"Why?"

"Jesse was the good one."

And had been given the halo effect from his grieving brother, she added silently. "And you're not?"

He shook his head, his face a heartbreak. "I'm nothing but trouble. Always have been. Always will be."

She studied him closely, absorbing his words, frustration rising at seeing him give up on himself so easily. He'd anointed his departed brother with sainthood while labeling himself a sinner, someone who deserved the bad in life or no life at all. "Then do something about it."

"Like?"

For the first time, in a long time, she found herself getting angry. And it felt good to replace the hopeless despair that'd dogged her. "Something worthwhile. You're volunteering here to help the facility. How about helping yourself while you're at it?"

His expression grew guarded, and he stood. "Are we finished?"

She ducked her head and ran her eyes over the screen to hide her irritation. So much for neutrality, for professionalism, for avoiding personal involvement. "Yes."

He headed to the door then stopped at her voice. "The dining room's just down the hall to the left. I'll have your counselor, Craig, show you to your room."

"You're not eating with the group?"

"No."

"Guess you're not much of a joiner, either," he said then let himself out, shutting the door softly behind him. Quiet descended, and her shoulders sagged. She met her restless eyes in her computer screen's reflection.

Justin Cade *was* trouble…to her. He saw too much. Made her feel too much.

But how to keep him at arm's length now that they'd be living together for the next six weeks?

CHAPTER FIVE

JUSTIN HUNCHED OVER a plate of stew and mopped up gravy with his buttered bread. With his hat pulled low, his isolated seat in a far corner, he tuned out the dining room babble and rehashed his conversation with Brielle.

She dished out a lot of questions, but she couldn't take them. Why was she discharged? Why didn't she want to get married? Her vague answers, her deflections, piqued his curiosity, and he found himself interested in something—in someone—for the first time since Jesse died.

She was full of vim and vinegar, as his gram used to say. Tart tongued and strong as all get-out. He respected her irritating directness. The vulnerability he glimpsed attracted him, too. What was she hiding?

And why was *she* hiding?

These were her patients, but she lurked in her office. Why? As a director, he'd have thought she'd be in the thick of things. She was direct. Bold. Her audaciousness kept him on his toes and woke him somehow, a stinging, uncomfortable sensation…like walking on feet after they'd fallen asleep.

Since Jesse's death, he lived in suspended animation. He believed Brielle when she'd warned him therapy was hard work. If he needed it, he'd put in the time. One day. But right now, his comfortable numbness insulated him from the feelings she'd mentioned.

Depression? Crazy.

According to his brother Jack, his wife, Dani, had cried for a month straight after they'd had their baby. Postpartum depression. That wasn't Justin. In fact, none of this mental health stuff applied. He should have just gone to jail. He'd barely gotten through thirty minutes of Brielle's pointed questions without crawling right out of his skin. How would he survive six weeks of *feelings*?

They inflicted more damage than any dirtbike crash or knockout punch.

A chair scraped across the polished wood floor, and he spied a reed-thin teenage girl slumped in the opposite seat. Blond roots shone at the crown of her shoulder-length, uneven black hair, and purple circles pouched beneath sunken eyes. Her bony fingers fidgeted with her fork as the tines chased peas around on her plate. Silver scars dragged from her wrist up along her forearms.

Suicide attempts?

How old was she? No more than sixteen, he'd wager. Too young to cash in. She hadn't even been dealt her full hand yet.

"Stop staring," she snapped without tearing her eyes from her plate. "It's creepy."

"Don't recall inviting you to sit here," he said easily, her irritability relaxing him more than his family's cheer.

"You were the only one I didn't think I'd have to talk to," she grumbled.

He felt a grin come on. "Good. I hate talking."

"Good."

Stony silence settled between them. As he polished off his plate, she jabbed her beef chunks with short, vicious stabs.

"What'd that meat ever do to you?"

"Trying to eat here," she grumbled. Dark eyes rolled up to his from beneath thin brows.

"Didn't know you could do that without putting any food in your mouth."

Her mouth rose in one corner, then the other before she clamped her lips flat again and dropped her gaze to her plate. "The food here sucks."

He buttered another piece of freshly baked corn bread and passed it to her. "No one can mess up bread. I'm Justin, by the way."

"Maya." She sniffed the slice, dropped it to her plate, then sprinkled pepper on it.

"Haven't seen that combination before."

"I hate pepper."

"And you added it to your bread because…"

Maya groaned and half rose from her seat before he held up a hand. He didn't want her to leave. Something about her agitation aroused his protective instincts. She was just a kid, and around the same age as Jesse had been when a sports injury got him hooked on painkillers. "Hey. I get it. No talking. Or eating."

With a sigh, she plopped down again. "I just don't know why I have to be here. I'm not hungry."

"Is it a rule?"

"Yeah. We have to attend all meals. You didn't get the list?"

"Nope."

She rolled her eyes. "We can't do anything, and they took my phone."

Justin pushed aside his empty plate and grabbed a sundae glass containing a swirl of chocolate whip. "Thought you didn't like talking."

"I like YouTube."

"That's videos, right?"

"Yeah." She eyed his dessert.

"What do you watch?" His first spoonful of

the sweet, rich cream dissolved on his tongue. His eyes closed in satisfaction. He admired James's wife, Sofia, but her experiments masquerading as meals left a bit to be desired. At least Fresh Start's food was tasty. He guessed Maya's scorn had more to do with her unwillingness to eat than a true dislike of the food.

"Animals. Horses, mostly." Maya's eyes clung to the extra dish of chocolate mousse he'd grabbed off the buffet line.

"You ever ridden?"

"No. I've wanted a horse since I was little, but my mother says if I can't take care of myself, I can't take care of a horse," she bit out, half the meat on her plate pulverized into flattened, brown discs. "She's so stupid."

"Why's that stupid?"

"Because I love horses!"

"And not yourself?"

Maya glowered at him. "Why did I sit here?"

"Beats the hell out of me." Justin shoved his extra dessert at her. "I can teach you to ride."

Her eyes brightened and met his, full on. "Here?"

"Yeah. I'll be teaching everyone about ranching, which includes horses and cattle."

"You're not a patient?"

"Well…I'm just helping out." He grabbed a sliding maraschino cherry and popped it in his mouth. Brielle had challenged him to help himself while he helped others. Did she have a point?

Maya grabbed her spoon. "Will I have my own horse?"

"Yep."

She dipped the tip of her spoon into the mousse, brought it to her nose and sniffed. "I want a white one."

"I'll see what I can do."

Her tongue flicked out and caught the tiniest bit of chocolate. "Can I name her?"

"They have names already." Justin pictured the horses he'd inventoried when he'd toured the stables before ringing Fresh Start's buzzer. "There's a pretty gray mare with a white mane and tail called Starburst. She's also got a white star, right here." He tapped his forehead.

"She sounds beautiful." Maya scooped up a spoonful of dessert and swallowed it down. "Is she friendly?"

"She's got a sweet tooth like you."

He grinned, and to his surprise, Maya grinned back, dimples appearing in her hollow cheeks. "I want to meet her."

"Tomorrow. I've got to settle the schedule with Ms. Thompson, but horse riding is at the top of my list."

Maya's spoon flew until it rattled the bottom

of the cup. Worried eyes rose to his. "Will you tell me more about Starburst?"

"I don't know much about her yet."

"Make something up, then."

"Why?"

"Because I really, really don't want to throw this up, and if I leave this table, that's exactly what I'll do."

His heart swelled at the trust she'd placed in him. Opening up to a stranger took guts. More guts than he had. Brielle seemed offended by his silence, and maybe that was a cop-out like she said. But she hid her entire self in her office, more damaging in the long run than clamming up. At least he was *here*.

With Maya's expectant eyes on him, he said, "Starburst's a little shy at first. Didn't stick her head out like the rest when I first wandered into the stable."

"I'm shy, too."

He tipped his head back and lifted one eyebrow. "I thought you just hated everyone."

"That, too," she mumbled around the empty spoon clamped in her mouth. "What else about Starburst?"

"When I held out my last sugar cube, she came right to me. Ate it from my hand, and then sniffed for more."

"Poor Starburst."

Justin gulped milk then set down his glass. "She found something else she liked."

"What was that?"

"A package of Skittles my nephew Javi gave me. She ate them all except orange."

"Ugh. Why do they even have that flavor?" Maya's eyes sparkled, and her broad smile hinted at the trouble-free teen she might have been…could be again if Fresh Start…if he could help her.

Maya's gaze skimmed over the group as they lugged dishes up to the kitchen window and ambled out the door. "I'm glad I sat here."

"Same."

They rose, gathered their plates and strolled across the emptying room. "Since you're not a patient, guess you're not coming to group tonight, huh?" she asked, wistful.

He cleared his throat, feeling like a fraud for holding back his own troubles in the face of Maya's honesty. "Some other time."

"See you tomorrow!" She waved her fingers then passed through the door, her shoulders back and her head high.

He stared after Maya, marveling. They'd connected through something simple yet powerful: horses. Besides meeting Sofia, had Jesse ever bonded with anyone at his other rehab stints? Could one person, even someone as rough around the edges as Justin, make a difference? It was a weighty responsibility, a chance to do for others what he wished he could have done for his brother.

He gazed at the stragglers filing out of the dining room. How many of them had family at home, hoping that this time, this facility would make a difference? He could be that difference. His stay at Fresh Start wasn't just about getting through this time for himself, but also for real people with families back home.

He could help others, just like Brielle said.

Was she right about her second assertion?

Could he also help himself?

BRIELLE WIPED DAMP palms on her navy dress, greeted Carbondale residents and projected competence as the town hall filled later that week. The session began in five minutes, yet residents continued piling into the large, utilitarian room. Many leaned against the walls when the folding chairs ran out. She eyed the line running out the door. Where did it end? Speculative stares peppered her, a firing squad of accusation that drew blood. All around her rose babbling voices, and she caught disturbing snippets—"not in these parts," "psychopaths," "bad influences."

How could she win them over?

She fingered the metal cross pinned to her lapel.

Please give me the words.

And don't let me sound like an idiot.

She considered the frowns pointed in her direction, the surreptitious glances, the crossed arms and mistrustful expressions. Not exactly a welcome wagon. In some ways, they reminded her of her restless flock in Afghanistan, the comparison increasing her dread. Most soldiers attended services seeking reassurance, absolution and hope, while others demanded answers to one simple yet impossible question. Why.

Today the stakes felt just as high.

Fresh Start was a fledgling enterprise. Like the army, it couldn't withstand doubts and morale dips, fears that might halt their critical, life-saving business.

And she stood alone to defend it.

She could not fail.

"Order. Order," pronounced Mayor Cantwell, taking his seat beside Brielle at the long table traversing the front of the room. City council members occupied the rest of the chairs.

Mayor Cantwell leaned into his microphone. "Order!"

The crowd quieted, save for a fussing baby. A sneeze followed a man's dry cough.

She opened her mouth to say "God bless you" then snapped it shut. From the corner of her eye, she spied the mayor's tight smile. It appeared painful, as though someone had tacked it to his face. He was a portly man with silver temples and a thick head of ginger-colored hair that made him resemble a jolly elf, more suited to ribbon-cutting and tree-lighting celebrations than a disgruntled constituency.

"We've called tonight's meeting to introduce you to Fresh Start's director, Captain Brielle Thompson, a former army chaplain who served two tours of duty in Afghanistan. Captain, we thank you for your service."

Brielle inclined her head and jerked her mouth into a smile at the applause. No doubt the goodwill would evaporate when the mayor stopped waving her stars and stripes.

"Thank you," she said into her microphone. "It's a pleasure to be here tonight."

Liar.

She wished herself back at Fresh Start, alone in her office, out of this scrutiny. If the locals looked hard enough, they'd know her for a fraud. A broken bird couldn't lead a flock.

"Ms. Thompson is aware of your concerns regarding Fresh Start," Mayor Cantwell said through his rigid smile. "And she's kindly agreed to provide information and answer your questions."

The baby's fussing rose to a wail, and Brielle waited for the mother to exit before she spoke.

"I'll be happy to take questions once I've shared Fresh Start's mission and goals."

The clinic's psychologist, Craig, gave her a thumbs-up from his front-row seat. Beside him, Doreen swung a crossed leg, her mouth working overtime on a large wad of gum.

Brielle drew in a deep breath and met Justin's light hazel eyes. The rangy cowboy propped his shoulder against an exposed beam, his posture nonchalant, one boot crossed over the other, his thumbs hooked in the loops of his jeans. As a staff member/inpatient, his privileges allowed him to leave the facility when accompanied by his counselor. According to Craig, though, he'd neither attended a one-on-one nor group therapy session yet. Still, she'd glimpsed Justin working with the patients in the corrals and pastures. Some interaction, at least, for the loner cowboy.

Was he here to support her? The thought slowed her rushed breathing and filled her with warmth.

"Fresh Start's mission is to—is to—" She shuffled her papers, unable to find her talking points. "Is to—"

A couple of men exchanged eye rolls as she faltered. Justin shot them a hard look then gave Brielle a firm nod, bolstering her confidence.

Bullet points be darned…she knew what her mission was.

"Fresh Start's mission is to provide exceptional physical, spiritual, emotional and mental health care to individuals and families needing treatment for addiction, eating disorders and trauma/mood disorders."

She paused, and her eyes swept over the restless crowd. They fidgeted in their seats, some staring at her, openmouthed or narrow eyed, while others checked their cell phones or whispered to one another behind raised hands.

Her gaze landed on Justin, and his take-no-prisoners expression was a clap on her back, propelling her forward. "We're a freestanding residential facility that provides twelve-step, evidence-based treatment combined with an integrated traditional and holistic component. We provide humane, compassionate and expert care, always emphasizing the dignity of the individual."

A chilly gust accompanied the returning mother and curled through the packed room.

Brielle cleared her throat and continued. "Our integrated system of addiction medicine, nursing and counseling services is based on a balanced program of patient care, education, performance measurement and real-life experiences designed to build self-esteem and confidence while reinforcing positive behavior and the acquisition of lifelong coping skills."

She stopped to sip the lukewarm water beside her microphone.

"We greatly value our community and will contribute positively to Carbondale by providing support to your local hospitals and community centers currently working with addiction and mental health outpatients through direct services and resource sharing, as well as knowledge."

A grumble swelled from the unconvinced crowd, and stinging heat crept up her neck. "Our capacity is twenty-five inpatients and fifteen outpatients. We're currently employing a psychiatrist, Dr. Bill Fulton, who couldn't be with us tonight, and two psychologists, one of whom, Dr. Craig Sheldon, is here."

She pointed to Craig, who stood and waved, his short gray ponytail, goatee and peace sign–patterned shirt not winning him many smiles from the conservative crowd.

"We've also hired four food and housekeeping workers and an insurance billing specialist, as well as our receptionist, Miss Doreen Bell."

Doreen popped out of her seat then belatedly

tugged down her short tube skirt so it hit her midthigh—barely. A couple of women raised their eyebrows as Doreen smiled wide enough to show off her tonsils.

"Thank you, Doreen," Brielle prompted when Doreen remained standing, oblivious to the judgment raining down on her. As for Brielle, she wanted to duck and take cover.

Doreen slid back into her seat and waggled her fingers at a straw-hatted cowboy farther down the aisle.

"And finally, we're fortunate to have Justin Cade volunteering his time to lead our real-world skills program, teaching our patients ranch work basics."

Heads swiveled in Justin's direction then whipped back at his scowl. His mutinous expression dared anyone to say anything negative…to even think it.

"We greatly appreciate the town's cooperation." She paused to smile at the councilmembers sitting on either side of her. "And Fresh Start is proud to be a part of, and to serve, Carbondale. Thank you."

Doreen's wild clapping echoed in the silent room. Brielle gulped more water, but it failed to soothe her dry mouth, her constricted throat. The water's surface shook as she carefully set down the glass.

"Thank you, Ms. Thompson." Mayor Cantwell beamed, rising to his feet. "Now, if there are any questions, please line up at one of the microphones." He pointed to stands on either side of the seating area.

To Brielle's horror, about a fifth of the crowd stood and jostled for position.

She pointed to the first in line, a small man with large ears that stuck out perpendicular to his bald head. "Brent Jarvis, Carbondale's Home Owners' Association."

He extricated a piece of paper from his jacket pocket, unfolded it and began reading aloud. "We're a cooperative community that is expressing our opposition toward a locally owned business that is trying to establish a for-profit venue in our residential neighborhood. We ask that the town revoke Fresh Start's conditional charter because it will impact property values and the overall effect a commercial business would have on a primarily residential zone."

He slipped his prepared statement back in his pocket and stepped back from the microphone.

Revoke the charter? Panic whipped through Brielle with hurricane force. Her fate, all her patients' fates, might be decided within the hour and by this man.

Mayor Cantwell spoke. "Worries about declining property values cannot be used by a city as a reason to reject an application for such facilities."

A heavy breath blew past Brielle's lips.

The crowd exploded into chatter. A steel-haired woman, local elementary school principal and city councilmember Miss Lillian Grover-Woodhouse, tapped on her microphone until the room hushed.

"May I remind you," Miss Grover-Woodhouse intoned, "that Fresh Start is a nonprofit agency. Had you attended Ms. Thompson's open house, you would've known that. Remember, knowledge is power and ignorance weak." At her quelling remark, several waiting in line seated themselves. Mr. Jarvis knocked over the stand as he fled.

"Next question," pronounced Mr. Cantwell.

"I'd like to address Mr. Jarvis's question as well," Brielle said.

At the mayor's nod, she continued. "There's been extensive research to show that treatment facilities in residential neighborhoods can operate without complications or difficulty. The zoning area is one of the main reasons why the location was chosen, as certain patients heal better in a residential setting rather than an institutional setting."

"Better for them, but not for us," someone muttered, and a smattering of cheers greeted the gibe.

Brielle's eyes burned, but she refused to show a flick of the fear raging inside her. Once she trusted her voice, she continued. "Research shows that people struggling with addiction do better in recovery in a residential setting. The federal government recognizes this research, which is why the Americans With Disabilities Act allows for treatment facilities to be set up in residential areas that aren't originally zoned for them."

"I'd like to see that research!" declared a middle-aged woman at the opposite microphone. She held hands with two identical towheaded toddlers.

"Copies will be coming around to you." Brielle nodded at Doreen and Craig, who began passing out the sheets they'd prepared for tonight's meeting. "Next question, please."

"Just a comment," said a man wearing a Rockies baseball hat. He turned to the crowd. "Would you like this in your neighborhood? Perhaps you should speak with the parents who have their children playing outside near one of these centers, which is filled with people who've shot, smoked and snorted all kinds of drugs. I'm not saying that even half of these people are bad, but there are those select few who'd be walking out and trying to sell drugs to those neighborhood kids. I'm all for these drug centers, but in a neighborhood where children play? That shows a huge lack of common sense."

The crowd roared its support, and one of the city councilmembers, Doug Rowdy, a hardware store owner who hadn't shaken her hand earlier, said, "Thank you for that enlightening comment."

An enormously pregnant woman pulled the microphone from its stand. "Rory Masters. As a recovering alcoholic, I wish the best for my brothers and sisters in recovery. I've been clean and sober for almost ten years, and thank all of those who helped me. God bless Fresh Start."

A few in the crowd applauded. A very few.

"Larry Spaulding," said a square-shaped man next. He wore a tie too short to cover his paunch and a John Deere hat perched high on his head. "Was wondering how you're gonna keep them crazies from escaping."

Brielle sputtered on her water, and it splashed over her hand as she placed it back on the table.

"Please refrain from using negative language," instructed local judge and councilmember Charlotte James. "It's disrespectful to Fresh Start's clients, who, I remind all of you, are our guests…and we have a long tradition of hospitality in Carbondale."

To Brielle's relief, several in the crowd nodded, and a few more in the question lines sat.

"As to security," Brielle said, "we have a system that will alert us if anyone leaves the property without our permission."

"What about when they're out doing their ranching and stuff?" a tall man challenged from the opposite microphone.

Justin straightened, flipped back his hat and glowered at the assembly. "*I'll* be with them." The curt words were delivered with such authority, such finality, that a few more people fled to their seats. "Y'all are a disgrace, acting like cowards, too afraid to help folks just because they're outsiders, because they're different. I bet most of you are religious, but you obviously don't treat people as you're taught on Sunday. The people in Fresh Start are bettering themselves. Which is not something any of you are doing."

"Ain't seen *you* in church in a long time," crowed a black-garbed man now at the head of the question line. "Not since your brother's—"

A woman's gasp cut him off, and Brielle's eyes flew to a row of enormous dark-haired men, a petite redhead and a lovely silver-haired woman Brielle recognized from the courthouse. The Cades.

"Not since my brother Jesse's funeral," Justin growled. "What of it?"

"Ain't that the point here?" demanded a woman wearing a sweatshirt with an enormous screen image of a pug. "We're a peaceful community. I'm a Christian, but I'm also no fool. Drugs bring trouble. That gang came right here for Jesse Cade. Who knows who else they might have hurt."

"Ma'am," Brielle interjected, "our patients are seeking to break their drug habits."

"So was Jesse," she rejoined, her chin jutting. "Now I'm sorry, Joy, you're a good, God-fearing woman, and I know you did your best for your son, but we don't want trouble in Carbondale. Can you guarantee we won't have it, preacher?"

"And won't some of your patients be ordered by the court to seek treatment? They won't be voluntarily trying to clean up their vices," chided a suited man with polished hair that reflected the fluorescent overhead light.

"That's true," Brielle admitted, her eyes cutting to Justin as a flurry of chatter erupted. She waited for it to die down then said, "Nothing in life is guaranteed, but I urge you to have faith. I believe this understanding—that God suffered greatly to face off against the evil in our world—can give these men and women hope as they wrestle with their own wounds. More than anything, I want them to know that they are not alone. Not only do they have fellow soldiers who are also struggling, but they have a God who has personally faced the horrors of combat and will stand with them in the battles they go through. Will you stand with them, too?"

"We will," boomed a deep voice from the back of the room, no microphone needed. All heads swiveled to a line of mountain-size men with piercing blue eyes. They took up the entire back row—the entire room, it seemed. An older man in the group hurried down the aisle to Joy and knelt beside her on the aisle, patting her shoulder.

"Cole Loveland speaking," the man who had spoken continued. "A program like Fresh Start could have helped our mother. If she'd attended one, she might still be with us."

The Loveland clan roared their agreement.

Mayor Cantwell leaned over and whispered in Brielle's ear, "Suicide." She nodded, her eyes on the family Justin had labeled murderers and thieves. They looked like good folk to her. Their staunch support was a finger under her chin, lifting it high. "Any further questions?"

The Lovelands and the Cades, united in this, at least, cracked their knuckles and glared at the murmuring crowd.

"I say we take an up-or-down vote to revoke the conditional charter," cried the pug-loving local.

The group hollered a resounding "Yes!" and Brielle's heart leaped to the base of her throat, clogging it.

A vote? Now? Given the group's questions, she sensed which way the winds blew…and it was not in her favor, despite the Loveland and Cade support.

"Do y'all even know who you're running out of town?" Justin spoke up, stopping the momentum dead. "Do ya? One's a little bitty thing. Just sixteen years old. She tried to kill herself, twice, because every time she looks in the mirror, she sees a girl she hates. But now she's got something she's wanted all her life. A horse. I'm teaching her to ride and care for one so she'll learn how to love and care for herself."

Chairs creaked as residents shifted in their seats, leaning forward, listening to the usually taciturn cowboy. The benefit of seldom talking, Brielle mused, was that when you did, folks paid attention. Thankfully Justin seemed to know better than to use patient names to protect confidentiality.

"Another is a vet. National guardsman. Served our country in Iraq. His whole platoon came under fire while they were clearing a section of Mosul. This guy's a decorated hero for risking his life to grab his pinned-down buddies. Yeah. That's the kind of person Carbondale's too good for," Justin said, the accusation met with a wave of head shakes.

A man wearing a leather jacket with an American flag patch limped over to Justin and clapped him on the back.

"Then there's a grandfather who couldn't afford his medication and started hallucinating. When he wandered from his home one Christmas Eve, he went missing for a long time. When his children found him, he was homeless, nearly dead of hypothermia. This is the first home he's had in over five years, and you want to take it from him."

A mumbled chorus of noes broke out.

Brielle gaped at Justin, moved at his knowledge of her patients, and shamed by it, too. He'd scolded her about not interacting with them, something he'd clearly been doing the past couple of days.

She'd urged him to help himself. Perhaps she needed to heed his advice as well. Justin made her patients real, not just threats to her teetering emotional stability.

"May I propose an alternative to tonight's vote," she blurted, thinking fast. "A fact-finding mission by a city council–appointed group. They can tour the facility, prepare a report and share their findings and recommendations at next month's meeting. That way you'll have the information needed to make an informed decision that will affect not just Fresh Start's patients, but the community's ability to serve locals with addiction and other social-emotional problems."

"We don't have none of those," called an anonymous protester.

"That's a lie!" cried a pretty blonde sandwiched between the Loveland brothers. A sister.

Brielle considered a stone-faced Justin. No wonder he failed to recognize his own depression, his alcohol dependence. The town lived in the same denial he did.

"Order, please," pleaded Mayor Cantwell. "The council will confer and relay our consensus to you momentarily."

Brielle's heart thudded as the city council

members huddled, murmuring in low, indistinct voices.

Was this the end of Fresh Start?

CHAPTER SIX

JUSTIN ZIPPED HIS leather jacket against the cold October night and eyed an empty beer can beside the town hall's recycle bin. In two strides, he reached the container, brought it to his nose and inhaled.

His eyes closed and his throat constricted at the faint scent of hops. Nothing ever smelled so good. He needed a drink. Bad. How long had it been? Three days…and five and a half weeks to go unless the approved fact-finding mission recommended revoking Fresh Start's charter.

"What are you doing?"

Justin whirled at the sound of his sister's voice, tossed the can in the bin and shoved trembling hands into his back pockets. The parking lot behind him hummed with activity; headlights blared, engines cranked.

"Darn litterers," he muttered.

The pug sweatshirt–wearing attendee halted and shook her finger. "Why don't you start with cleaning up that mouth?"

Justin's lip curled into a snarl, and her husband threw an arm around her shoulders. "We don't want no trouble." He hurried his protesting wife after the chattering crowd streaming toward the parking lot.

Jewel planted her boots wide and angled her narrow, freckled face up at her brother. An oversize Stetson covered most of her unruly red hair. "Didn't know you were so civic-minded."

He shrugged and her hazel eyes, bright beneath the streetlight, probed his as she spoke. "How's it going?"

"Taught the residents how to saddle a horse, and they walked them around the corral yesterday."

"I meant *you*. How are you doing?"

He scuffed a pile of dead pine needles with his boots. "No complaints."

She ducked her head and caught his eye. "We miss you."

"Yeah, right," he scoffed, picturing their happy evenings without him bringing everybody down. "Like a hole in the head."

A choking sound snapped his head up. Jewel blinked, hard and fast, her features scrunched into a tight mask of grief. "Don't ever joke about that."

He laid a hand on her arm. "'Bout what?"

"Shooting yourself."

"I wasn't—" he protested, her ferocity taking him by surprise. Jewel was tough as nails and rarely sentimental. Growing up in a house of rowdy brothers, his petite, rough-riding sister learned fast how to survive in a testosterone-filled world. Truth was, she had more guts, more grit than any of them.

"All I'm saying is I already lost one brother. I'm not losing another, even if you are a miserable grouch."

"At least I've got my looks," he teased, tugging on his beard.

That coaxed a grin from Jewel. "If you think a werewolf's good-looking."

"To each his own," he intoned, and her chuckle soothed the ache inside. He hated causing his family pain or concern. Despite what Jewel thought, they'd all be better off without him.

"Listen to this." Jewel lowered her voice and moved closer. "Jared heard someone spotted Boyd Loveland shopping for a ring."

"What kind?" He whipped his face toward the town hall's door as Jared emerged. He cupped Amberley's elbow as her guide dog led them down the concrete path to the parking lot.

"A diamond."

"For Ma?"

Jewel nodded. "Got to be."

He smacked his forehead. If there ever was a reason to go back to drinking, the thought of his mother marrying Boyd Loveland sure was a good one. "Where's he getting the money?"

"Beats me."

"You two talking about Boyd's ring shopping?" Jared asked, joining them.

Justin scratched Petey's notched ears, and the former cattle dog's tail thumped. He'd come a long way from the stray who'd shown up in their barn a couple years back. With Jared's training, he'd become Amberley's service dog when she lost her sight. "Yeah. Who'd you hear it from?"

"Sheila," Amberley piped up, her eyes swerving in Justin's general direction. "She waited on Boyd at Jay's Jewelers."

"No secrets in small towns," Jewel observed.

Justin swore under his breath. "He's just gonna up and marry her, and we've got no say?" His eyes cut to the Loveland crew as they tromped from the meeting hall. Justin's muscles wound tight when he glimpsed Cole Loveland stopping to talk with Brielle. The family already had his mother wrapped around their fingers—he'd be darned if he let them have Brielle as well.

"We've got plenty of say in it," James said as he neared.

"How's that?" Justin's gaze stuck on Cole and Brielle. What were they talking about?

James fastened his work coat's top button. "According to Jack, he wants all of our support before he'll pop the question. Won't do it otherwise."

Heath Loveland halted beside his pickup and cranked his head at Jewel's startled laugh. "That'll never happen," she exclaimed. "We won't be related to them."

"Not a snowball's chance in hell," Justin vowed, though he didn't breathe any easier, not with Brielle now touching Cole's arm and smiling up at him. Justin's hands balled and he swallowed the urge to walk over there, yank Cole away from Brielle and lay him out.

"He's got Jack's support." James pulled on a pair of black gloves and retrieved his keys from his pocket. They clanked together, the metallic clash matching Justin's jangling nerves.

"How'd he get that?" Justin exclaimed. Cole's hand now rested on the wall behind Brielle, and the cowboy leaned close. Justin took an involuntary step forward. If it wasn't for this conversation, he'd break up whatever was going on over there.

James blew his nose then tossed out the tissue, along with the contents of his pocket: broken animal crackers, a worn-down crayon and a Popsicle stick. "Boyd called him."

"And Jack just said yes?" Jewel's eyes flashed when a blonde gal approached Heath Loveland then hopped into his truck's passenger side before he reversed out of his spot.

James nodded.

"Traitor," Justin growled. Tension bubbled inside at Brielle laughing up at Cole. What was so funny?

"He's got a right to his opinion," James said mildly. "Same as me." James's cell phone rang, the shrilling sound echoing through the parking lot. He pulled it out and scanned the screen, quickly typing back a reply to the text that had interrupted their conversation. "Guess I'm off to find chocolate-banana-coconut ice cream. Sofia's got a craving." He clapped Justin on the shoulder. "You did good in there, little brother."

Jewel shook some wintergreen Tic Tacs into her hand then offered them around. "You think he's gonna give Boyd his support?" she asked once James moved out of earshot.

"Doesn't matter if he does." Justin dropped the mints on his tongue. "Boyd said he's not proposing unless we all support him, and the three of us won't, at least."

"Well. We'd better go." Jared gave Justin a one-armed hug, and Amberley smiled his way. "Amberley's got an early race in Denver tomorrow."

"Don't show up those sighted barrel racers too bad, girl," Jewel called after them. "Not like you do to me."

"You do just fine," Amberley chided over her shoulder.

Jewel cupped her hands around her mouth. "Didn't know you for a liar," she hollered.

Amberley's laugh floated back to them, followed by the slam of Jared's truck door and the rev of his engine.

"You reckon Jared might say yes, too?" Jewel questioned.

"Better not. Either way, there's still two of us," Justin answered, grim.

Cole pointed to his truck, and Brielle shook her head. Was Cole, a recluse since he and his ex-fiancée called off their wedding a few years back, actually offering Brielle a ride? Maybe looking to date her?

Not on Justin's watch.

A tight-lipped, stubborn, arrogant Loveland was the last guy Brielle should get involved with.

Not that he had a clue who she *should* see.

But it sure as heck wasn't a Loveland.

"Can I ride back with you?" Justin called to Brielle. The rest of the Fresh Start crew left earlier, so she must have driven herself.

She twisted his way. A dark wool coat, buttoned over a navy dress, contrasted with her bright hair and fair skin. His heart did a strange flip. Brielle was as pretty as the porcelain dolls his gram had collected. She'd kept them perched on a high shelf, just beyond his reach.

"Sure," she called.

Cole scowled in Justin's direction, and he smiled back, baring his teeth at his longtime rival, happy to come between whatever plans Cole had for Brielle...

Jewel threw a hug on him then pecked his cheek. "Looks like you've got a hot date," she whispered in his ear then released him. "Like that song...what's it called? 'Hot for Preacher'?"

A chuckle rumbled out of him. "Teacher, idiot. Least I'm not hankering after a Loveland."

Jewel jerked away as if stung, and he caught her hand. "Kidding. We're just tweaking you about Heath. You hate them as much as any of us." He thought of Jack and James... "Or me and Jared, at least."

She mumbled something indistinct and fled

just as Brielle joined him. "I was looking for you."

"Not too hard." An irritated edge ruffled his voice.

Her long eyelashes blinked fast. "Excuse me?"

"I saw you talking to Cole."

Now why did he sound accusing?

A line formed between her brows. "He was asking about volunteering at Fresh Start."

Justin's eyes flew to the full moon engulfing the purple-ink sky. "He just wants an excuse to be around you."

She rubbed her hands together and blew on them. "He wants to help."

"To help himself to more time with you." He caught her hands between his and rubbed them, the sensation of her soft skin against his callused flesh a trip wire to his pulse. It rushed headlong through his veins, tumbling over itself.

"You sound jealous," she accused, her words a bit breathy, misting the air white.

"Jealous? That's crazy." It took every bit of willpower to release her. Her touch banished the dry burning in his mouth, the pounding in his head. Being around her, holding her hands, settled him somehow.

"Thank you for before."

He raised an eyebrow.

"What you did in there. Talking about the patients. I couldn't have done it."

"If you knew them, you could."

She ducked her head and pushed her hands into her coat pockets.

"Besides," Justin continued, "You came up with the plan for the fact-checking group."

"I did," she half groaned. "And now they're planning to show up unannounced to look us over. What if we get a bad report?"

Between his ranching program, the group sessions, counseling and fitness and diet regimens, the patients received exactly what Brielle described, a real chance to make permanent life changes. Any committee failing to see that would be blind, stupid or just plain biased. "We won't."

"Let's hope. Are you ready to go?" There was a brief catch in her voice as he tucked her loose scarf into her coat collar.

"There's something I want to show you first."

"Maybe another time." She twisted a cross pinned to the lapel of her jacket. "I've still got work to finish and—"

Her words cut off as he laced his fingers in hers. "Work will be there in the morning. This won't."

An exclamation of white blew from her lips. "Why's my seeing this important to you?"

He cupped her chin. "Don't know, it just is. Will you come?"

Her wide eyes probed his, her teeth worrying her bottom lip. "What are you going to show me?"

"The moon."

She peered up at the sky. "I can see it just fine."

"Yeah. But can you touch it?"

Her lips curved as she shook her head. "You're being silly, you know that."

"It's part of my charm," he drawled, and her smile widened, her ease around him filling him with warmth. He was used to pushing people away. Brielle, however, refused to be budged. She just kept coming for him, and he liked that about her. A lot.

"Okay. Let's go," she said. "Must be I'm crazy, too."

Something he couldn't identify, light and sparkling, spun through his chest as he led her up a path through dark woods. What was he doing?

Darned if he knew.

He just didn't want to let her go so quick. Not when a large orange moon hung low and heavy in the sky, flooding the world with magic, filling a lonely man's heart with longing for what couldn't be…except on a night like this.

BRIELLE'S SENSIBLE HEELS didn't seem so practical now that she hurried along an uneven dirt path in the shadowed woods. Overhead, the moon's rays streamed through the pine canopy, illuminating the dark. They failed to enlighten her, though. Why had she agreed to this crazy jaunt? Good girls didn't run off, heedless, into the night with bad boys like Justin Cade…

And where was he taking her?

Her skin shivered over her bones at the brush of his arm against her shoulder. He prowled through the forest like a predatory cat, sure-footed and graceful. When her toe caught on a root, Justin snaked an arm around her waist and held her tight, guiding her forward without breaking stride.

For such a scruffy man, he sure smelled good: leather, soap and an earthy musk, a wild, masculine scent. If it was bottled, they'd name it Untamed. It howled at the part of her that had grown up following schedules, attending planned events and adhering to predetermined routines.

As a military brat, she'd been taught unquestioning respect for authority and expected discipline for infractions. As an army chaplain, she'd understood the safety provided by rules and procedures. Yet here she was, stumbling through the dark with a man who cared little for his life—who courted danger…welcomed it, even.

All her life she'd walked the straight and narrow—until she'd stumbled. Fresh Start was supposed to help her regain her bearings. Yet Justin pulled her down another path into the unknown, and something inside her thrilled at this impulsive detour, even as a voice inside whispered, *run*.

The path grew so steep she clawed at dirt to keep from toppling. Justin hoisted her over rocky outcroppings and loose-pebbled inclines, her breath quickening, her body warming from the exertion. An owl hooted then swooped by in a white flash. Scrub brush rustled with skittering animals fleeing their approach.

"How much farther?" she huffed as Justin lifted her over a downed tree.

He set her down gently. "Almost there. Doing okay?" The rich timbre of his voice, the note of concern deepening it, vibrated inside her.

She'd dedicated her life to helping other people, both as a chaplain and a counselor. How long had it been since she let somebody help her? "Yes."

Fifteen minutes later, the trees thinned then ended. She and Justin glided from the forest onto a grassy plateau where the world fell from a distant edge to a shadowed valley. Overhead, the orange moon bore down on them as crickets sang dirges in the crisp fall night. The wind rustled through dry leaves, a crackling, papery sound, and the faint scent of hickory smoke carried on the breeze.

She breathed deep and drank in this glorious moment. "What is this place?"

"Miracle Point." Justin tugged her closer to the precipice. "We race dirt bikes up here."

She glanced back at the narrow, treacherous path. All the injuries he'd described in his intake report now made sense. "That's insane."

"And fun."

"I don't call throwing your life away fun."

"I wouldn't call not living life fun, either."

"What's that mean?" she demanded.

"Holing up in your office. Taking your meals alone. Working until after everyone's headed to bed…that's not living."

"It's working."

"It's hiding," Justin insisted, his jaw jutting.

She jerked her hand away. "I didn't come up here to be insulted."

He gripped her shoulder, and the moonlight spun in his green-gold eyes, a kaleidoscope of shades. "It's the truth. Not an insult."

"Not true at all."

"Name one fun thing you've done all year."

She opened her mouth, but nothing emerged. The wind's lonely moan carried her back to Kandahar, to a card game...

"Come on, Chaps, just one hand. We won't play for money this round," Private Stan Dobbins had begged her as she passed through the mess hall. Desert gusts flapped the edges of the thick canvas tent and howled through its seams.

"What's the game?"

"Twenty-one," piped up a newly arrived marine, his hair buzzed to the scalp. Private Kevin Maloney, according to his name tag. Peach fuzz sprouted above his upper lip. Had he even had his first shave yet? She marveled at the strange sequence of events that'd put an assault rifle in his hands before a razor.

"Sounds like gambling to me," she'd teased, wanting to join, but needing to put the final touches on her Easter Sunday sermon.

"Plus, guys..." Private Michael Jennings flashed the deck that was decorated with scantily clad women before he dealt them. "Don't think Chaps wants to touch these."

"We shouldn't touch 'em, either, considering whatever you done with 'em in private," mocked an older soldier, an enlisted man on his fourth and final tour of duty. He pinched his cards between his thumb and index finger and wrinkled his nose.

"Hey. Show some respect," Jennings scolded, one side of his mouth hitching up. "They're a family heirloom. My great-grandfather had 'em in WWII. My grandfather in 'Nam. Dad in the first Gulf War. They're good luck."

"Good for something, anyway," the older soldier chuckled.

"I'm heading out tomorrow," Private Maloney said to Brielle as he surveyed his cards, his knees pumping fast beneath the table.

"Popping his combat cherry," a wire-thin soldier mumbled, his body taut and electric as he huddled over his cards. Puffs of smoke erupted from the cigar clamped between his teeth.

"That's not the only cherry he needs to pop."

A howl rose from the group at Private Jennings's jab. She'd wandered away, laughing on the inside, until the following evening when she'd found him writhing on a gurney outside the crowded triage tent.

"Am I gonna die?" he'd asked her.

She slipped her hand in his and her heart

tumbled, landed and shattered at the ice-cold feel of his flesh. "No."

"I'm gonna die," he gasped. A wheezing sound rattled from his red-soaked chest.

"Medic!" she hollered, panic filling her, rising along with her dread. Using her sleeve, she'd wiped the blood bubbling on his lips.

"Used to be a pretty good shortstop," he rambled, his unblinking eyes burning into hers.

"You're going to be all right," she'd insisted, sending up a silent prayer, then turned and shouted, "Medic!"

Her eyes landed on a motionless, staring body a few feet away. Private Maloney. A nurse pulled a sheet over his blackened face, the one he'd never get to shave. No!

"The cards," gasped Jennings. A tear rolled from the corner of his eye and streaked his red cheek. "Give them to my kid brother. They're his now."

"You're going to be okay," she promised then silently begged, *Lord, save him.*

Lord?

"I want my mom." He coughed a red stream. "I want...my..." And then he'd stopped speaking. Stopped breathing. And she'd stumbled away, forsaken, as a nurse checked his pulse then covered him, too.

Anger burned through her, a firestorm charring her inside out. *Where are You, Lord?*

A hand squeeze pulled her back to Miracle Point. To Justin.

"You okay?" he asked.

"Fine." Her voice, when it emerged, scraped over her tight throat, raw and gritty.

"Liar." A rough thumb brushed the damp from her cheeks, the gesture achingly tender. Were those tears? She never cried. Never allowed herself to be vulnerable, not in private or in public, not around others.

Only…Justin didn't feel other. His shadows called to her own.

"I haven't had fun in a long time. I—I'm not sure I know what it feels like anymore."

"Come on." Justin led her to a large, flat-topped rock and helped her up. He lay on his back beside her a moment later and propped his ankle on his opposite, raised knee. "Put your hands around your eyes like this." He circled his fingers around his eyes, cutting off his peripheral vision.

She stretched out beside him, copied his move and stared up at the enormous moon, her blood swarming, rising along with its tidal pull.

"Can you feel it?" he asked.

"Yes. It's beautiful," she murmured, her

fears dropping from her like sandbags cut from a launched balloon.

"Beautiful," he echoed, and she felt his eyes on her. "What were you thinking about back there?"

"Kandahar," she admitted after a moment. The moon, this moment worked its magic and loosened her tongue.

"You never told me why you were discharged."

Her breath evaporated in her lungs.

"You don't have to say if you don't want."

Silence descended, the only sound her heartbeat knocking down her eardrums.

"It was Easter," she murmured, wanting to speak, at last, in what felt like a safe space. "We'd lost twelve men the night before when a daisy chain of IEDs hit their caravan. One of them was just eighteen years old. I'd never seen so many soldiers at service. Some were enraged, others grieving, the rest oscillating between the two. I asked them to bow their heads and began one of the Divine Office's morning prayers, Psalm 144. 'Blessed be the Lord my strength which teaches my hands to war, and my fingers to fight.'"

Her voice faltered. Justin's hand curled protectively around hers, his warmth seeping into her chilled bones, steadying her.

"'My goodness, and my fortress; my high tower, and my deliverer; my shield, and he in whom I trust; who subdues my people under me,'" she continued. "'Lord, what is man, that you have taken knowledge of him! Or the son of man, that you make account of him!'"

She stopped and stared up at the glittering sky.

"What comes next?" Justin asked.

"I couldn't remember." She pressed her lips together to keep them from shaking.

Justin released her hand and wrapped his arm around her shoulders, pulling her close.

"I couldn't say anything else."

He tucked a loose hair strand behind her ear, his fingers grazing her sensitive lobe. "What'd you do?"

She squished her eyes shut. "I walked out. Never went back."

"To church?"

She shook her head. "To any of it. To the army, the soldiers I'd vowed to minister to."

His fingers skimmed her jawline, a touch so gentle it could have been a moonbeam.

"I abandoned them when I should have had their backs. It's a morally bruising battlefield."

"You weren't on the battlefield with them," Justin argued.

"Wasn't I?" she cried and opened her eyes

to meet Justin's burning gaze. "I caused my share of casualties."

"What do you mean?"

She bit the inside of her cheek, unable to say more, the chasm inside her yawning wide, threatening to swallow her whole. "I asked God to protect the battalions from further harm. I knew He wouldn't. I asked him to spare the innocents caught in the cross fire. I knew He wouldn't. I asked Him finally for grace."

"And did you receive it?"

"Not yet. I'm still trying to find my way back."

When he turned on his side, she angled her face and their noses brushed. He slid a finger down the side of her cheek, and the wind fluttered strands of her hair between them. "You're here now," he said, his voice deep.

Their eyes clung.

"Yes, I am."

He cupped her cheek, and her heart beat hard enough to burst from her chest. His lips lowered to hers and hovered a breath away. "That's why you avoid your patients."

"I've been working," she insisted, but her conviction evaporated in the face of raw truth.

"You don't want to lose anyone else."

This close, she could smell his minty, warm breath. "No," she admitted.

"Then get to know them. Come to my ranching workshop tomorrow."

"I don't know if I can," she confessed. "It's not easy for me…like it is for you."

His short laugh rushed across her cheek. Their eyelashes tangled. "You think it's easy for me? I hate talking to people."

"What about me?"

His eyes blazed into hers. "You're different."

"How?" she breathed.

"Don't know. You just are. You get me to say things."

She stared into his gorgeous eyes, and she touched his beard. It was softer than she expected, almost silky. "Like?"

His eyes closed, and a low groan drifted from his throat. "Things I don't want to say."

"You never told me when you started drinking so much."

His lids lifted, and he flattened her palm against his chest. Through the leather of his jacket, she felt the faint beat of his heart. "I'll tell you if you promise to come to my workshop."

"I will if you'll consider attending Craig's group therapy session."

He whistled. "You don't let up, do you?"

"It's part of my charm," she teased, lobbing his earlier words back at him.

He laughed. "Guess we're a regular pair of charmers then." He fell silent and then— "I drove straight from Jesse's funeral to the liquor store," he said, his voice breaking slightly. "Bought a twelve-pack of beer. Finished it that night. Went back the next morning and bought another. Haven't missed a day since."

"How are you managing now?"

"Not sleeping much."

"If you'd see Dr. Fulton, he could prescribe something to help."

"I don't need help."

"What do you need?" she challenged, slightly breathless at his intense perusal. Oh… she should have known not to go into the forest with the big bad wolf…

"This." He leaned closer. Then, as light as a butterfly's wing, as imagined as fairy dust, his lips brushed hers. The brief contact drugged her senses, sapping her strength so that she melted into him, ready for more.

A twig snapped, loud as a gunshot, and they broke apart. Justin swept a protective arm around her as she scrambled to her knees. From the tree cover, an enormous creature emerged. Dark, tall and majestic.

"Moose," she breathed in Justin's ear.

"And baby," he murmured as a calf peeked from the brush then trailed after its mother.

The pair gamboled into the grassy area then froze when the wind blew Brielle's hair forward, carrying her scent. In a flash, the pair turned and bounded back into the murky forest.

"That was—" Brielle began then ran out of words, the wonder of the moment beyond her ability to capture.

Justin's eyes searched hers. "A miracle."

Yes, it was, she thought as they trekked back to the parking lot. As beautiful as the moon in the night's sky had been, as wondrous as a sighting of the large animal and her child, divine intervention had stopped their near kiss. She needed to be more careful around Justin than ever.

Next time, she might not be so lucky.

CHAPTER SEVEN

BRIELLE TROMPED THROUGH tall grass to Fresh Start's corral. She leaned against its white-slatted fence and waved, the dry blades tickling her ankles.

"Good morning," she called. The group inside fell silent. Despite her rolling stomach, she smiled and clutched the top rail. It anchored her so she wouldn't flee.

"Howdy." Justin's white teeth flashed between his dark beard and mustache. A pair of dusty jeans and a fitted black thermal shirt hugged his lean, lanky frame. His wide-brimmed rancher's hat shaded his handsome face. Her heart lunged against her rib cage, throwing itself at him.

Shameless hussy.

Her eyes lingered on his mouth, and the remembered feel of his lips on hers, the soft scratch of his beard against her cheek, snatched her breath. "Thought I'd join you today."

At their murmured approval, she ducked through the fence, started forward then jerked to a stop. She peered over her shoulder and spied her shirt hem snagged on a nail. A horse nickered, and a titter wove through the group.

Great.

Her first attempt at getting to know her patients outside their individual therapy sessions, and she was making a mess of it, had them laughing. Even the fence thought her coming out here was a bad idea.

Justin hustled over.

"Let me." He brushed her hand away, and the brief contact breathed fire into her cheeks. This close, she could touch the beard now fascinating her, kiss the mouth she'd been dreaming of when she woke.

Justin had laid her bare last night. While it'd be easy to blame it on the moon, the man, the wild outdoors, deep down, she knew where the fault lay…with her. No one had forced her to confide in Justin and briefly kiss him, a reckless man capable of destroying the peace she sought in Carbondale. She'd made that choice on her own.

Worse.

She wanted to kiss him again.

Worst of all…he was a client. Technically he wasn't a patient in her direct care, so she hadn't violated any ethical codes, yet she needed to maintain a professional boundary between them—for her own sake.

"You're free." Justin released her shirt, winked, then strode back to the attendees, leaving her to stare after him.

Why was he in such a good mood?

Didn't he regret last night, too?

If not for her promise to attend his workshop, she'd have buried herself behind piles of paperwork today, avoiding him entirely. Yet here she stood, her focus on the last man she should be thinking about...especially with the town's fact-finding group waiting for their chance to pounce. Imagine if they caught Fresh Start's director mooning over a client?

Talk about bad optics.

Speaking of which... She surveyed the patients, noting they wore helmets. Justin considered others' safety, at least—just not his own.

"Want to ride?"

She started to shake her head then stopped when Justin led out a saddled, glossy bay by its halter.

"She's soft." She stroked the horse's velvet nose and warm, moist air rushed over her fingertips. "What's her name?"

"Ted." Mischief dialed up the gold in Justin's hazel eyes, setting them aglow. "Not sure if Ted likes being called she."

"Dr. Sheldon said we're a judgment-free zone," hollered Stew, whose adult children Brielle had spoken to this morning about his progress. He'd put on weight, she observed with satisfaction—physical healing which, for the formerly homeless man, was as needed as the emotional and mental work he'd been undertaking.

"Sorry, Ted," she chuckled. "Guess I should have—uh—checked. You're a handsome boy, though, aren't you?"

Ted bobbed his head and snuffed her empty pockets. Justin passed her a green candy strip.

"What's this?"

"Green apple licorice. His favorite."

Delighted, she offered the treat, and Ted slurped it like a spaghetti strand. "You little piggy," she crowed, her mood lightening, as fluffy as the white clouds erupting in the broad blue sky. No wonder her dark rider resembled a white knight today. Being outdoors, surrounded by majestic mountains and the endless, rolling sky lifted the weight from your shoulders.

"Are you riding with us, Ms. Thompson?" called Paul, the former artilleryman she'd also met at the first group meeting. His tree-trunk legs angled off the sides of a brown mare, his large frame covering most of his saddle.

Her fingers tapped on her thigh as she considered her answer.

"She's scared," giggled Pam, a patient with Tourette's. She clapped a hand over her mouth and spoke through her fingers. "Sorry."

"No. It's okay," Brielle rushed to reassure her. "It's just, I've never ridden before."

"Me neither," Maya put in. The teenager had her arms looped around a gray mare's neck, her cheek resting against the horse's silver mane. "It's not hard. Even Paul can do it. Mostly."

"Hey," protested Paul. His weary-eyed mare flicked her tail. "I only fell once."

"Twice," Maya sniped good-naturedly.

Brielle scrutinized the faces surrounding her. Their expressions were open, calm, much different than the creased brows and crossed arms from their first group session. The horses relaxed them, just as she'd envisioned when she'd agreed to direct this unconventional treatment facility.

"Need a hand up?" Justin plunked a wood block down beside Ted.

"Okay." She tried to ignore the delicious feel of Justin's chafed hand against hers, but the sensation steamrollered through her anyway, heightening all her senses. Everything intensified: the loud chirping of sparrows, the bright splashes of sunlight, the tart scent of green apple licorice and especially the rub of Justin's palm against hers. It turned her insides to liquid.

Once in the saddle, she gazed around her. This height somehow diminished her crowded, pressured world, lifting her from it. She breathed and her lungs moved freely, the band that'd been tightening since the town hall meeting easing.

Justin stepped on the block and reached around her, placing his hands atop hers on the reins. "Tug on the right rein to go right. Left goes left. A gentle kick gets him walking. Pull back and say 'whoa' to stop. Got it?"

She nodded, impressed at Justin's straightforward explanation. It lessened her anxiety, though her pulse refused to slow given he practically hugged her from behind. And oh, he smelled so good. A delicious woodsy-apple combination. It made her want to sink her teeth into him. "We're just staying in the corral, right?"

Justin hopped down and tilted his head so his hat brim shadowed one side of his face. "For now. And you can leave the group any time you want to, though Ted might be sorry about it."

"Just Ted?" she murmured, low, her inappropriate question jumping off her tongue as the preoccupied group chattered among themselves.

Justin squinted at her, intent. "Who else?"

"Forget it." She reached down to pat Ted's silky neck, hiding her burning face. "Stupid question."

"No. I'm glad you came. Hope you stay." His admission snapped her head up, and she stared straight into his unguarded eyes, the naked vulnerability pulling her back to last night's intimacy. "Will you stay?"

Pleasure, bright and sweet, bloomed inside. She smiled. "Okay."

A slow grin began on his lips and rose to his eyes, lighting them. "Okay." He pivoted. "Circle your horses," he called, and the group walked their mounts toward the center of the corral.

Empowerment flowed through her as she nudged Ted and he responded, walking forward, following her direction as she guided him to the right. When they reached the group, he stopped when she ordered him to halt.

"Dr. Sheldon suggested we talk about what we want to focus on today before we ride." Justin tugged at his beard then shoved his hands in his pockets. "But I'm not much for talking."

No surprise there.

He lifted his hat and waved it in front of his flushed face. A few strands of damp hair plastered to his forehead lifted. "Let's keep it to one word."

"One word?" Maya asked, stroking her horse's neck. "That doesn't totally suck."

Justin nodded and resettled his hat.

Pam's horse sidestepped as she wriggled in her saddle. "Anything we want? Like…"

At Paul's stream of expletives, Maya belly laughed, a huge, whooping sound that spread like a flu in church till everyone howled with her.

Even Brielle.

Justin had asked her to name the last time she'd had fun…if he asked her again, she'd have an answer. Today. He was right about her mingling with the patients. They weren't a threat to her emotional stability, though the jury was still out on Justin…way out…like permanent recess out.

"Cut that down to one word," Justin drawled, "and you'll be fine."

Paul scratched at his red, peeling nose. "We don't have to tell you what it means?"

"Nope."

Brielle bit her tongue to keep from jumping in and correcting him. Justin was a client, not a licensed practitioner. His job was to provide real-life experiences to build confidence and self-esteem, not delve into the issues that'd brought her charges to Fresh Start. But plenty of psychotherapy awaited the patients inside, hard work that took its toll. Downtime like this was critical. Plus, she had no intention of saying anything revealing, either—not when her patients needed a strong role model, not someone lost like them.

Although, strangely, despite sharing one of her blackest memories with Justin, she'd fallen asleep while reading last night. Without medication. When her alarm blared at 7:00 a.m., she'd stared at it, dumbfounded. It was her first unmedicated eight-hour sleep in almost a year.

"We'll go around clockwise," Justin said. "Who'll start us off?"

The white-haired man beside Justin lifted his arm.

Justin nodded at him. "Okay, Francis, you're up."

Francis lifted his horse's reins. "Riding."

The group's snicker died down, then a middle-aged woman missing a front tooth startled. "Oh. My turn. Um…suntan." She angled her face to the sky and smiled, eyes closed.

"Sleep," yawned a young guy in his twenties, drooping in his saddle. Brad Timmons. A former college basketball star whose failed drug test and heroin addiction fast-tracked him here rather than the NBA.

"Cheerios!"

Everyone turned at Pam's exclamation.

She shrugged. "You said I could say anything."

"Guess we hoped it'd be a bit more interesting," Justin observed wryly.

"I'll do better next time," she vowed, and the group groaned.

Brielle's smile faded when the group turned her way. "Oh. Um…" she delayed, and her eyes landed on Justin. He jerked his chin at her, almost a dare, and she said the first word that leaped to her tongue. "Redemption."

She pinched her mouth shut. Why had she said that? Out loud. In front of her clients? In front of him? She'd thrown her heavy issues over this light, fun therapy break, smothering it like a blanket.

"What's that mean?" Maya stage-whispered.

"A second chance," Justin informed the teen without tearing his intent gaze from Brielle.

"Loneliness," declared a thirtysomething woman beside Brielle a moment later. A court-mandated patient, Mary had lost her children to foster care because of a drug-related felony. She was also being treated for severe anxiety and, according to Craig, had been extremely uncooperative thus far.

Had Brielle's slipup inspired Mary to speak openly? Bravely?

Mary patted her palomino's side and made a shushing noise when it tossed its head. "Loneliness."

"Dinner," Maya stated when it was her turn. She peered around at the puzzled group, her chin jutting at their tilted heads and scrunched foreheads. "I haven't eaten one in four and a half years."

Brielle nodded at her, her heart stirring. She'd sparked two of her clients to consider their goals. Justin's one-word session was working…even on her.

"Paul?" Justin prompted.

The veteran raised his head and two wet tracks wound down his cheeks. "Forgiveness."

Justin raised his eyebrows a fraction of an inch at Brielle, an *I told you so* written all over his face.

Yes. He had told her so. And she was glad she'd listened, happy she'd come and relieved to have spoken her deepest wish out loud. The sky hadn't fallen, and she hadn't tumbled, either. He'd urged her to connect with her patients, and at least one, maybe two, had had a breakthrough because of it.

Plus, her.

"What about you, Justin?" Maya asked.

"Only one word comes to mind. It's not an easy one. In fact, someone said it'd take a lot of hard work to get it. And it's already been said."

Paul lifted his arms and brushed his cheeks with his sleeves. "What is it?"

Justin ducked his head then rolled his eyes up to meet Brielle's.

"Redemption."

JUSTIN HEAVED AN ax over his shoulder then swung it down to a log perched on a chopping block. It cleaved the wood in half, and he scraped the pieces onto the pile he'd begun a half hour ago for tonight's bonfire. Despite the chilly temperature, sweat dripped in his eyes. The bare skin exposed by his muscle tank steamed. His hat rested beside his shirt on the seat of the facility's front loader. He tried swallowing but his mouth was too parched.

He needed a beer.

He released a sigh, grabbed another log and set it on the block. If he wasn't trying to avoid Brielle, he'd head in for a water break. But being outdoors, always his preferred element, soothed the beast she'd unleashed when she'd briefly returned his kiss beneath a moonlit sky.

The afternoon sun flashed on his blade as

it whooshed through the air and sank into the wood. He flicked away the pieces, set another log in their place and hefted the ax again.

Why had he kissed her?

Because you wanted to, dummy.

A moment later, he jerked the blade free of the chopping block after a hard stroke. It'd sunk in a good inch. He placed another log in the center of the chopping block, split it and repeated the maneuver, his mind turning back to Brielle.

He couldn't stop thinking about her. Brielle had this way of looking at him, like she knew him and wasn't intimidated or put off by his snarky attitude and gruff mannerisms. A strange feeling, considering most folks switched sides of the streets or avoided making eye contact when they saw him coming. She made him feel appreciated. Wanted. Not because of anything he tried to be, but because of who he was, scars and all.

Worst of all, he was starting to like hanging around her too much. He'd enjoyed having her company during this morning's horse therapy. She showed real character by following through on her word to attend. More impressive was her honesty with her patients in confiding her own goal.

Redemption.

She wished for a second chance to undo the mistakes she thought she'd made. He wanted another chance to save his brother, to stop Jesse from throwing his life away and carrying Justin's with it.

He paused his wood chopping and rolled his aching shoulders. His arid throat clenched. The desperate craving for a drink clawed at him, a nonstop occurrence since he'd stopped drinking cold turkey earlier this week.

Brielle had asked him about his habit during her intake, and he'd assured her he didn't need to drink. Now he wasn't so sure. When he'd admitted last night to buying and drinking a twelve-pack a day, every day, since Jesse's funeral, he'd questioned himself.

Was he an alcoholic?

He propped the ax on the chopping block and leaned on it, breathing heavily.

No.

He'd never let a substance get a hold of him and he rarely drank recreationally. In fact, drinking alone, night after night, was the loneliest thing in the world. Not a drop of fun spilled from one of his beers.

Addicts hankered for a fix, a temporary high. Not Justin at all. If anything, drinking brought him down, the opposite of a buzz. He only gulped enough brew until his grief fizzled and he snuffed out like a spent candle, no longer sputtering in the dark.

And why was he thinking about all of this? He lifted the ax, swung it, then stared at it half buried in the chopping block. He'd forgotten to set a log on it.

He pressed his eyes closed and listened to his thundering heart. This was Brielle's doing. She pricked him like a needle to a fingertip, squeezing, squeezing, squeezing until unwanted emotions bubbled up, red and stinging.

He'd promised he'd consider attending a group session, and he supposed, since she'd kept her word to him, he should do the same. Just maybe not right away… With his head pounding nonstop, he could barely hear his thoughts, let alone speak them.

Except with Brielle.

Yes.

She was different. She made him think, feel, want and dream…all things he'd stopped doing after Jesse's death. He needed to halt his growing feelings for her. To her, he was probably just another case, a patient at her facility in need of help. Once he left the program, she'd move on to the next client, and he'd be left pining for her.

His tendons strained as he hacked at the chopping block again, belatedly noting he'd forgotten the log again. The pain of losing someone he loved as much as Jesse made it impossible to imagine ever letting himself feel close to another person again. He couldn't give in to his budding emotions for Brielle.

"Strange technique," a man drawled behind Justin, and he whirled, ax in hand. "Never seen anyone split wood without wood before." Cole Loveland stood beside the front loader and eyed the cut-up chopping block with raised eyebrows.

"What are you doing here?"

Cole nodded at the heap of uncut logs. "Volunteering. Question is, what are *you* doing here?"

"Chopping wood."

"Right…" The ax hanging by Cole's side caught Justin's attention. "Lucky for you I'm here to lend a hand."

"Don't want your help." Justin turned away from Cole's irritating, cocky expression and dropped another log on the block. Typical Loveland.

"Wasn't asking for permission." Out of the corner of his eye, Justin spied Cole grabbing a hunk of wood and placing it on a tree stump. He halved it in one smooth move, chucked the pieces to the ground and picked up another log.

Justin clamped his back teeth and set to

work, one eye on Cole's fast-growing pile. He heaved, he swung, he cleaved, yet his rival began catching up to Justin's heap. Like all Lovelands, Cole was mountain tall and built like a Mack truck, his trunk-size arms moving effortlessly as he chopped piece after piece without breaking a sweat.

Was this guy a machine?

"Shouldn't you be up at the house with Brielle?" Justin grunted as he smashed through another log.

"I will be when I finish this," Cole said easily, not a hint of strain in his voice as he cut through more wood then tossed pieces on his stack. "I'm going to the Al-Anon meeting."

An ironic laugh escaped Justin. "That's a piss-poor excuse." Al-Anon was a support group for friends and family of addicts.

"For?" Cole slammed down his ax, breaking apart another log.

"Seeing Brielle." Justin's hands tightened around his ax handle to keep from smacking off Cole's smug smile.

"That'd be a bonus, but I'm here for the meeting."

"You don't have any addicts in your family," Justin accused, calling out the hypocrite. If Cole wanted Brielle, he had another think coming...namely Justin's fist.

Cole returned to his work without bothering to answer, and Justin finished up the last of his stack. The satisfaction at scoring a point on a Loveland eluded him, though. Something about the rigid set of Cole's shoulders, the clench of his jaw, left Justin uneasy.

"My mother drank," Cole said at last when he split his final log. He pulled a can of pop from his knapsack and offered it to Justin. When Justin shook his head, Cole tossed it to him anyway, forcing him to catch it before retrieving one for himself.

"Didn't know." Condensation rolled down the side of the cold can and Justin popped the top, unable to resist. A sweet fizz bubbled from its opening, then splashed down his throat in one long pull.

Cole's lifted can paused in midair. "It was in all the papers. News shows. The talk of the town—the state, even—how my supposedly abusive father drove Colorado's favorite senator's beloved daughter to drink, go insane and then take her own life."

"Don't pay much attention to rumors." Justin tossed back another cold swallow and softened a touch for Cole. Justin's father had mentioned the Loveland tragedy only once, referring to it as a suicide, and Justin never knew his father to lie. "Everyone trash-talked Jesse. They only had it half right."

Cole nodded as he polished off his pop then stowed the empty in his bag. "Heard them yammering about him at last night's meeting. That's why I decided to volunteer."

Justin lowered his can to the truck bed's open gate and blinked at Cole. "Because of my brother?"

"And my ma." Cole grabbed split wood from the pile and tossed it into the front loader's bucket, the heavy clanging sound punctuating his admission. "She had depression. A place like this could've helped her."

Justin joined Cole in transferring the firewood. "She might be alive, and our parents wouldn't be dating."

Cole nodded slowly as he hurled another piece. "Can't change what we can't fix, though."

Justin's mouth dropped open to hear one of his own phrases from a blasted Loveland. "We can stop it," he muttered, thinking of Boyd's crazy vow not to propose until all the Cades agreed. Boyd had to know he'd never succeed.

"And keep our parents as lonely and miserable as us?" Cole countered. He scooped up an armful of wood and dumped it on the growing mound. "How's that fair?"

"I'm not…" Justin faltered. Okay. He *was* lonely and miserable. He recalled Cole's hastily called-off wedding. It looked as though Justin and his rival had more in common than he'd thought. Both were solitary, unhappy bachelors. He shoved down the budding sense of camaraderie and grabbed more halved logs. He would not make friends with a Loveland.

"Focus on your own happiness instead of trying to stop theirs." Cole stopped and his unusual Loveland eyes—some called the color sapphire blue—bored into Justin's.

He threw down a bundle of wood without tearing his gaze off Cole then picked up his drink for a last swig. "I'm trying to save Ma."

"You're holding on to old grudges. Anger." Cole chucked the last of the cord into the loader.

"I've over a hundred years' worth of reasons to be pissed at you Lovelands." Justin's hand clenched around his can, crumpling it in his fist.

"We're not the ones you're angry at."

"Then who am I angry at?"

Cole studied Fresh Start's main house. "Come to Al-Anon and find out. Could be someone closer than you think. Someone besides yourself. Trust me. I've been there, buddy."

Without another word, Cole turned on his heel, leaving Justin agape.

No question, he was angry at the world, at fate, at death and, most of all, at himself.

But he wasn't mad at anyone close to him… was he?

CHAPTER EIGHT

"READY?" JUSTIN ASKED the rope-holding patients gathered around him.

Overhead, heavy gray clouds blotted out the sun and obscured Mount Sopris's peak. A misty wind rushed across the grassy space like a cold, wet slap. The grim weather matched Justin's oppressive mood. Carbondale's fact-finding group had arrived unannounced this morning, and he'd gnawed over their whereabouts ever since. What were they seeing? Thinking? He wished he could be with Brielle, defending the program instead of teaching a workshop on tying and circling a lasso.

"Wait a minute." Francis chuckled and kicked at the hemp tangled around his boots, ensnaring himself further. "Looks like I figured out how to hog-tie myself, anyway."

Maya crouched to free him. "Don't go hurting yourself, Grandpa," she grumbled with a twitchy smile.

Francis ruffled her hair. "Ain't been called Grandpa in a long time. Thank you, darlin'."

Maya rolled her eyes, looking pleased none-theless.

"The first step in tying a lasso is to make a simple overhand knot," Justin began, demon-strating. "An overhand knot is the basic knot you're familiar with. Just make a loop, then pass one end of the rope through it. Keep it loose and give yourself lots of slack to work with. Your rope should now look like a large O with the loose knot at the bottom."

He strode to Mary, loosened her knot a touch, then grabbed his rope again.

"Next up, take the shorter tail end of the rope in your hand. Pull it around and over your O loop."

"Can you do that again?" asked Francis.

"Yes, sir." Justin replicated the move, watch-ing Francis until he'd completed the step. "Now thread it between the outside of the O portion of the overhand knot and itself. Pull the rope about six inches through. This'll form a new loop, which'll be the base of your lasso."

"How, how, how," Pam muttered. She flexed her wrists and flicked her fingers repeatedly as she struggled with the cord.

"Like this." Justin guided her through the motion slowly, working around her tic, care-ful not to pressure her.

"You have nice lips," Pam blurted, then clamped a hand over her mouth.

When Mary tittered, Francis wagged his finger at her. "Judgment-free zone."

"Thank you, ma'am." Pam's forehead smoothed at Justin's easy smile and neutral tone.

He backed up a few paces, his lips still curled, and it struck him, full on, just how much he'd been smiling lately...more than the three and a half years since Jesse's passing combined. By a mile. By light-years, even. In his family, he stood out as the sad, lonesome one. Here, everyone struggled, including Brielle. And this camaraderie redistributed the weight of their burdens because they carried them together.

"Pull on the slack end of the rope, the part you'll hold on to when you throw your lasso, and the new loop you just made." He tugged the line taut then paused for the group to catch up. "Be careful not to pull the tail end back through the knot."

"Wrong!" Pam exclaimed.

Justin inspected her handiwork and adjusted the line slightly. "You've got it."

"You're doing better than me." Francis held up his knot. "This looks like a cat toy."

Pam's wrists and fingers stilled and a fleeting smile whisked across her face. "Mittens." Then— "Thank you."

"When you finish," Justin continued when Maya jumped in to aid Francis again, "you should have a tight knot at the base of a small loop. The tail end of your knot should extend from the knot, too."

"This is a honda knot, right?" Paul held up his rope. "One of my buddies showed it to me in Mosul."

"Is he a cowboy?" Mary asked.

"Was." Paul's face contorted. "Did rodeo. Promised to teach me how to rope calves when we got out. Ride bull."

"He's dead!" Pam shook her head. "Oh, no. I'm sorry, Paul."

Paul hung his head. "Me, too."

"What was his name?" Maya asked as her nimble fingers freed Francis's knot.

"Tyrone. Tyrone Johnston." Paul's face lifted.

"We'll rope some calves for him, then," Justin vowed. "In his honor."

Paul blinked up at the sky. "Yeah?"

"Heck, yeah."

"Cows smell like—"

"Hello!" Brielle called, interrupting Pam. Her stiff smile and high shoulders, along with the pinch-faced crowd surrounding her, told

Justin everything he needed to know about how the fact-finding mission was going.

"Howdy." He glowered at Brent Jarvis, the Carbondale Home Owners' Association member who'd called for a vote to revoke Fresh Start's charter. How did such an idiot get on the committee?

"We don't mean to interrupt." Mayor Cantwell beamed at each patient with a wide, toothy smile.

"Good," Justin bit out. His gaze swerved to Doug Rowdy, the hardware store owner who'd helped rile up the locals against Fresh Start.

Another idiot.

"It's the feds!" Pam warned.

"What? Where?" Francis dropped his rope and Maya slung an arm around the older man's thin, shaking shoulders.

"That looks like a honda knot," observed Judge James, aiming an admiring look Pam's way.

"Dead," Pam whispered, nodding in Paul's direction. "His friend is dead."

Paul dropped his rope and lumbered away, his shoulders hunched, his hands shoved deep inside his parka's pockets.

"What's wrong with him?" shrilled Dana Stoughton. She owned a convenience store about a half mile down the road and had lost her son to a drunk driver a few years back.

"As we mentioned at last week's meeting, Justin's teaching our residents ranching skills," Brielle said, her tone brisk as she deftly switched subjects to avoid revealing confidential information about her patients...something she'd warned him, and the rest of the staff, about in advance of the visit. If she was intimidated or nervous, she wasn't showing it.

"What have you learned so far?" Justin's elementary school principal, Miss Grover-Woodhouse demanded. She pinned a stern eye on, of all people, Maya, an authority-resistant teenager.

Justin bit back an oath.

"Who?" Maya looked around her. "Me?"

"Yes, young lady. What have you learned?" Despite the steady, waterlogged wind, Miss Grover-Woodhouse's clipped gray hair lay perfectly flat, her lipstick not daring to stray from its borders. She was an uncompromising woman, stern and exacting, but also fair, Justin recalled. He'd clocked a lot of hours in her office...more than in his actual classrooms.

"Nothing." Maya dropped her rope, flipped up her hoodie and tugged its strings tight.

"I'm sure that's not the case," Brielle jumped

in. "They're all just beginning, gaining basic skills."

"And they're attending meetings and therapy and dealing with withdrawal," Justin added, feeling like a hypocrite since he hadn't done any of those things, even after Cole's prodding the other day.

"Still looks more like a vacation to me," grumped Doug Rowdy as he glanced at the assembled group.

"Our residents are working quite hard," Brielle insisted.

Justin's gaze skimmed over the residents, imagining what the committee saw. Pam flicked her fingers and flexed her wrists, Francis managed to tangle himself in his line again, and Paul stood apart, shoulders shaking. Maya had disappeared inside her hoodie, and Mary swung her lasso like a jump rope.

Anger flared inside as he pictured the negative words they'd write in the report, words that didn't apply to Fresh Start's patients.

"Ms. Thompson's right. Everyone here's working hard on themselves. On what's inside. You feel it more than you see it." A muscle jumped in Justin's jaw as he stared down Doug, daring him to criticize one more thing. From the corner of his eye, he spied Brielle's slightly open mouth and still form. He'd surprised her—heck…he'd surprised himself—but he meant every word.

"Paul," Justin commanded. "Report for duty."

The word choice worked. Paul squared his shoulders, marched to his rope and grabbed it from the ground. Maya shoved back her hoodie and Francis managed to organize his rope—somewhat. Pam's hands stilled, and Mary stopped twirling her rope.

"Next step. Pass the slack end of your rope through the honda knot." He modeled the maneuver, his attention solely on the students in front of him. "Then pass the long slack end of your rope through the small loop in your honda knot to create a functional lasso."

"I got it!" cackled Francis.

"Don't have a heart attack, Grandpa." Maya mocked then glared at Dana, who pressed her hand against her chest, eyes wide. "If you can't joke about death here, where can you?"

Justin bit back a smile at Doug's outraged sputter.

"Thank you all for your time." Brielle's shadowed green eyes settled briefly on Justin then skittered away. "We'll leave you to your work."

"And miss the last few steps?" he insisted, galvanized to defend Fresh Start, its residents and Brielle, who, despite her own issues, was doing a good job. If Fresh Start shut down, she'd leave Carbondale. He had to sway the committee's opinion and ensure they voted to keep the facility open. Then Brielle could stay here, where she belonged. "We're learning to rope next."

"I'm a proponent of lifelong learning," Miss Grover-Woodhouse declared. She unzipped her purse, pulled out a plastic square, unfolded it, then placed the rain bonnet over her head. As if on cue, the clouds began dripping, light cold sprinkles.

"I'd like to see it," added Judge James, opening her umbrella.

"It's settled, then." Mayor Cantwell yanked his hood over his head.

Justin held out his rope. "By pulling on the slack end of the rope, you can tighten the lasso to grab onto objects. See?"

A waved of affirmative murmurs rolled around the circle.

"Tie one more basic overhand knot at the end of the tail to keep the knot from coming undone and ruining your lasso."

"That's a stopper knot," Paul announced. Water droplets glistened on the tips of his short, spiked hair.

"Right. Now here's how you hold your lasso.

Grab on to the slack end of your rope and start to swing. The tension in the rope will pull the loop in your lasso shut before you can throw it. So it's important to use a grip that keeps your lasso wide-open as you twirl it and build momentum."

Justin peered through the water dripping from his hat brim. The bedraggled group approximated his directions. Francis grabbed the loop without letting most of it fall, and Pam compensated for her hand tic by alternating her grip.

Did the committee understand the effort, the courage, the grit the Fresh Start residents showed? They darn well better. "I need a volunteer." Then, since he'd already picked his victim, Justin pointed at Brent Jarvis, the Home Owners' Association rep. "You."

"Me?" the weasel squeaked.

"You. Justin jerked his chin to the left. "Over there. Nope. Farther back. Now take ten more steps backward. Do it again."

"You'll never rope him from there," Doug Rowdy exclaimed between the scarf folds wrapped around his neck and face.

"Wanna bet?"

"Betting's not Christian," Doug chastised, pious as a TV preacher broadcasting from jail.

"Neither is turning your back on people who

need help, but you're certainly doing it," Justin replied.

"The weather's worsening. Let's head back," Brielle urged.

"What's your bet?" Doug demanded, as though he hadn't heard Brielle.

"If I get this rope around Brent, you lose your vote in the committee."

Doug licked his lips and peered at Justin, then Brent. "What do I get if I win?"

"I'll let you leave here on two feet."

"Justin!" Brielle gasped.

He shot her an apologetic look. "How about, I won't speak at the next town council meeting?"

"Or her." Doug pointed at Brielle. "And Brent steps back five more paces. You do that, I won't cast a vote on revoking the charter."

"Deal," Justin said, then turned toward Brielle. "If it's all right with Ms. Thompson."

Brielle studied the soggy ground then raised blazing eyes to Justin. "Rope him, cowboy!"

"Yeee-haaawww!" hollered Paul.

"Whoop!" cried Pam.

When Brent took his place, Justin lifted his arm and circled the rope overhead, each pass making a familiar whoosh as it revolved around his hat.

"Point your index finger down the shank

toward the honda knot for added control," he instructed the patients. "Holding the rope at the end of the shank, begin to twirl it in a circle above your head. Be careful not to hit your head or to catch yourself by the neck."

He kept his eye on a squirming Brent, while judging the distance, the wind, the force he needed to truss Brent up and lock down Doug Rowdy's vote.

"Swing fast enough to keep the loop roughly horizontal, but not so fast that you struggle to control it."

"Ah!" Francis cried, and Justin glimpsed Francis's lasso as it fell around his shoulders and arms.

"Roped yourself again." Maya dropped her rope and assisted him. "What are the odds?"

"Hula-Hoop!" Pam exclaimed.

"I'm getting the hang of it!" Mary shouted, then laughed when her lasso fell. "Nope."

"Release the rope as you feel its momentum swing forward. Throwing a lasso isn't the same as throwing a baseball—it's more a matter of releasing the lasso at the right time than of propelling it forward," he continued, stretching out the tense moment, torturing a fidgeting Brent. The rain now fell in earnest, and Justin's hands slipped on the rope as it slashed through the air.

"Let go of the lasso as you feel its weight swing forward—this isn't necessarily when the loop's in front of you. It's most likely when the loop is to your side. Oh, and keep your hand pointed down for better control," Justin added, spying Paul struggling to maintain a consistent swing.

"Are we going in yet?" Dana griped. "We're likely to catch pneumonia out here, and I've got things to do."

"More important than Fresh Start?" Miss Grover-Woodhouse demanded. "If so, then leave and give up your vote."

"N-no," Dana blustered then subsided.

"When you throw the lasso," Justin forged on, ready to end this dog and pony show, "let go of the loop but keep control of the rope so that you can tighten your lasso. Like this." After two more swings, Justin tossed his lasso. It zinged through the air then dropped neatly around Brent's thick spare tire.

Applause broke out, as well as cheers. Brent's fierce scowl pulled a grin out of Justin. "Tighten the lasso to grab your target. Once it's around whatever you're trying to lasso, pull hard on the rope. This will pull the slack in the loop through the honda knot, tightening the lasso around the object inside it."

At Justin's yank, Brent stumbled forward, his feet slipping on the wet, dead grass.

"Never use a lasso on people or animals unless you're an experienced roper—unsafe lassoing can cause suffocation or damage to the throat."

He tugged again, harder, causing Brent to skitter and slip to all fours. "It's also difficult or impossible for someone to remove a lasso without help, so don't run this risk unless you know what you're doing." Brent rolled on the ground, thrashing.

"He looks like a dog!" Pam exclaimed, cackling.

Brielle rushed to Brent's side and helped him to his feet.

"You!" Brent stormed, his face as red and glistening as a washed tomato. "You did that on purpose!"

"It sure wasn't no accident," Justin drawled, easy.

"I'm owed an apology," Brent sputtered, shaking with outrage. Justin's hands fisted when Brent roughly brushed Brielle aside.

"Doug owes me a nonvote on the committee." Justin forced himself to speak calmly.

"But—but that's not fair," Doug protested. "Justin's a ringer. He set us up."

"The deal stands," Judge James weighed in.

"You entered a verbal agreement, which was witnessed by others."

Francis waved his hand. "I heard him!"

A chorus of yeahs rang out.

"Fine!" Brent fumed as he stomped toward the main house, the rest of the committee following. "But I'm not the only no vote!" he threatened, an ominous warning that sobered Justin quick.

Brielle paused beside Justin and laid a hand on his arm. Her light touch jump-started his heart. "That was wrong," she said loudly, though her laughing eyes communicated something else entirely: fierce pride and unfiltered admiration.

"But it sure felt good," he countered, covering her hand with his.

"I'd better get back," she said, breathy. "I've got to see them off, then I'm running this week's Al-Anon meeting for Craig."

He laced his fingers in hers and squeezed. "Good. I'll see you there."

"You will?" She pulled her hand back slowly, and her large eyes searched his.

"I talked up the program so much to the fact-finders, I'd be a hypocrite not to follow through myself."

She considered him for a long moment, then

nodded. "You're a lot of things, but a hypo-crite isn't one."

"What am I, then?" he shouted after her, ad-miring her straight-backed, confident stride. It beckoned him to follow. Challenged him to chase.

"Come to the meeting and find out!"

CHAPTER NINE

BRIELLE SIPPED HER tart lemonade, eyed the clock above the converted living room's entranceway, then set the wax cup on the table behind her. The musty-stale smells of wet wool, cigarettes and sweaty anticipation wove through the thick air. To cover the goose bumps rising on her skin, she shoved her arms through her sweater's sleeves.

Five minutes past three o'clock.

Time to start the Al-Anon meeting. She smoothed a trembling hand over her hair and listened to the steady rain tapping the roof overhead. Where was Justin? He'd vowed to attend, and he always kept his word.

Attendees chatted, fidgeted or zoned out in the folding chairs occupying the large space. A few watched her with expectant eyes. They stuck to her like tentacles, a dragging, pulling sensation. She hadn't led a group since Kandahar, hadn't felt the weight of their needs, their hopes, their fears in months. It shoved her shoulders forward and down, her chin to the floor, especially after a nail-biting afternoon with the town council's fact-finding committee.

They'd peppered her with questions but given few clues to their thoughts…verbal cues, that was. Dana Stoughton, the local chamber of commerce president, seemed to have been sucking lemons all day. Brent Jarvis, the Home Owners' Association president, had scribbled notes while shaking his head. And Doug Rowdy jumped every time he spotted a patient, as if he expected to be offered drugs, get mugged or both. Judge Charlotte James and Miss Grover-Woodhouse had seemed neutral, at least, but gave little away.

What if they voted to revoke Fresh Start's charter? An ice pick of fear slammed into her brain. Thanks to Justin, she'd begun opening up, finding her footing…maybe even rediscovering the column of strength that'd crumbled in Kandahar. She didn't want to be forced to abandon another post and leave Fresh Start.

Or Justin, she admitted to herself.

Speaking of whom…where was her dark rider?

He'd been in rare form today at the roping workshop, obstinate, defiant and defensive of Fresh Start, the memory calling up a smile. He cared about the facility.

Did he care about her, too?

Did she want him to care about her?

And would any of it matter if Fresh Start shut down?

"Did you want to get started, Ms. Thompson?" Doreen called from the doorway. She rolled out the pocket door to close off the archway.

"Um—I believe we're still expecting one more person."

"Justin!" Doreen's face flamed red, and her skyscraper bangs stood at attention.

"No—I mean," Brielle fumbled then blew out a frustrated breath. *Come on. Snap to it, girl.* "There might be—"

"He's here!" Doreen swept a frosty pink wand over her lips then tucked it down her blouse just as Justin stalked by her. In two strides, he reached a chair in the back row, flipped it around then straddled it. His hazel eyes swept the room then stopped on Brielle. His tough expression changed just a fraction, his eyes softening as though about to smile, before he shuttered them again.

Doreen mouthed "hot" then fanned herself with her hand.

"Please close the door, Doreen," Brielle requested, or imagined she did, since she couldn't hear anything over the thrumming of her heart.

Justin pulled off his black hat and leather jacket then dropped them on the seat beside him. With his dark hair flattened around his skull and curled at his ears, his beard glistening with rain, his skin ruddy with his farmer's tan, he'd never looked more ruggedly appealing.

And was she ever glad to see him.

Tonight was a breakthrough for them both. His first group meeting and her first time back at the helm.

How would they do?

"Hello, everyone," Brielle called, quieting the group. Her lips cracked into a quarter smile to cover her jitters. "Welcome." She waited for a few stragglers to grab treats before continuing.

"As some of you know, my name is Brielle Thompson, and I'm the director of Fresh Start. Dr. Sheldon is away tonight at a symposium, and he sends his best wishes for a great meeting."

Please let this be a great meeting.

She stared out at the assembly, noting the curved shoulders, the crossed arms, the downcast eyes. They'd only had one Al-Anon meeting at Fresh Start so far, and, according to Craig, had been a quiet group.

"Tonight, we're focusing on anger and the forms it takes when someone we love is an addict. We're fortunate to have a guest speaker."

Justin twisted around to eye Cole Loveland in the back of the room then half rose in his chair. For a moment, Brielle worried he'd bolt before Justin subsided, resting his chin on his chest, his lowered lids obscuring his eyes.

"Before Cole speaks, I want to thank you for coming tonight. This is a safe place, a place to go where you know you're not alone. Where you can share what's in your heart, your mind, your soul and you're not going to be criticized for it or judged. Where it's okay to love an addict, okay to learn how to love yourself and how to keep the focus on you because you're worth it."

Justin's lids lifted, and the profound sadness she glimpsed in his eyes caught at her heart and squeezed. Despite his swagger and bristle, he didn't believe himself worthy. How could he not know how incredible he was, see the difference he made with her patients? With her?

Somehow, she needed to convince him without revealing her growing feelings.

"Cole, please come on up."

"Thank you, Ms. Thompson." Cole's blue

eyes crinkled down at her, and he bowed his head slightly, a respectful, old-fashioned gesture. It reminded her of a bygone era when men held open doors and believed going Dutch meant a trip to the Netherlands. "I'm glad to be here again," he said, turning to the crowd.

Brielle scooted down the aisle and sat beside Justin. This close, she could smell the rain on his clean male skin and the sweet hay and cornmeal he must have fed the horses. He moved his hand a fraction so that it rested on his thigh, right beside hers, and the urge to reach for it seized her hard.

"I was the son of an alcoholic," Cole began, his hands laced behind his back. "I say *was*, because my ma killed herself on my sixteenth birthday."

Someone gasped while another muttered, shaking his head.

A band tightened around Brielle's chest, crushing the breath from her as she pictured the dog tags beside her spider plant, the soldier they'd once belonged to…

"It was supposed to be a big night. We'd planned a bonfire. Got a guitar player and a fiddler. Strung lights from trees and had a pig roasting in a pit. A real shindig. I'd even invited a pretty girl to the party, Katie-Lynn Brennon, and couldn't believe she'd said yes.

My pa taught me how to fasten a tie that night, and I'd shaved for the first time."

He paused and stroked his chiseled jaw. Silence reigned as the patients listened closely, spellbound, while steady rainfall drummed on the tin roof. Justin leaned forward over the back of his seat. Every muscle in his body looked clenched, from the biceps curling from his shirtsleeves to his tight jaw.

"The band swung into something slow, and I asked Katie-Lynn to dance. I remember how scared and excited I was, how grown-up I felt, how normal…'cause normal wasn't something I felt often—if ever—growing up with an alcoholic parent."

Murmurs of agreement circled the room. Outside, the wind whispered, rustling leaves and flattening a few against the rain-slicked windows.

"I grew up stuffing down everything in my life, whether it was family secrets or my feelings. It was uncomfortable to be who I was. When I wasn't in school, I rode the range, spending every minute outdoors, only coming home at night. As Ma's alcoholism got worse, I stopped inviting friends over because I never knew what was going to happen, some chaos, drama, petty arguments or flat-out fighting. It was confusing and scary growing up in such an environment."

Heads nodded and patients released their crossed arms, opening themselves up to hear this strong man become vulnerable. Did Brielle dare reveal herself so completely? The dog tags swung before her mind's eye, and she shuddered.

No. Too dangerous.

She dug her nails into her palms to remind herself never to let her thoughts slip that way again.

"But Pa promised my party would be different. He'd raided Ma's 'secret' stashes, hidden her car keys and gotten her to promise not to make trouble. I remember her saying how proud she was of me. It was the first time she'd ever told me that...and the last words she ever spoke to me."

He cleared his throat, twice, while staring up at the ceiling. A few sniffles and a muffled sob erupted in the quiet pause.

Cole's blue eyes glistened when he leveled them on the group again. "I'd never kissed a girl before and I hoped, badly, that I'd get to kiss Katie-Lynn when we strolled in the woods. We stopped in a clearing, and I remember the moon, how big it was, how pretty Katie-Lynn looked in her yellow sundress. When she put her arms around my neck, I thought, *this is it*. Then we heard the screams, and I knew…I knew it was my mother."

He reached behind him for his glass of lemonade, drained it, then continued. "We high-tailed it back to the party and found everyone crowded around our pool. My dad had filled it with these floating candles in plastic globes, and I remember thinking…I remember thinking that Ma looked like a fairy drifting among them…her white nightgown and her long blond hair fanned out around her… I'd never seen her look so peaceful. It wasn't until my father jumped in that I realized she'd drowned—drowned herself, according to the police. They determined this after I turned over the suicide note she'd left in my birthday card."

When Cole fished a folded paper from his pocket, Brielle's heart seized. The sight of it yanked her back home, a week after her discharge when she'd opened a similar letter from a soldier in Kandahar that'd also contained his dog tags…

"'Happy birthday, son,'" Cole read without looking up, his voice full of gravel. "'I know I've hurt you. Disappointed you and let you down. I wish I had something better to say on your special day, but I don't. Truth is, I've never felt like a mother, never felt like

I belonged anywhere, least not on this earth. I thought hard about what I wanted to give you, my eldest boy, and then I realized I had nothing to give—never have, never will. I'm sorry that I did this. I don't want to die, but my heart can't take the pain anymore. You've always been a loving son, a good boy and I know you'll grow up to be a better man without me. I'm going to miss you so much, and I can't wait till the day when I see you again at the pearly gates. Until then, I love you, always. Ma.'"

Cole carefully refolded the note, smoothing each worn edge, before tucking it back into his jeans pocket. The rain pounded the windows, and the wind scraped a branch on the glass.

"She killed herself on your birthday?" blurted Maya. She'd shoved both hands in her black hair, making the uneven strands sprout between her fingers. "That witch!"

A surprised titter erupted at Maya's impolite comment, and tears stung Brielle's eyes.

A bitter laugh escaped Cole, dark and full of pain. "This *is* a meeting about anger."

Was Cole's mother a witch? Surely not; she'd needed help, just like…

Brielle's brain flipped the breaker on that dangerous thought, closing it off completely before she shut down, too.

Justin laced his fingers in hers, his touch gentle and reverent, although his expression remained as hard and unreadable as stone. "You all right?" he asked. He was so close his breath caressed her ear.

"Fine," she assured him, her voice a hoarse whisper that hardly reached her own ears. She didn't lift her eyes to look at him because the tears hadn't gone away yet.

Justin's bulletproof exterior hid a sensitive man. He was the last person you'd want on your bad side, but she couldn't think of anyone she'd want by her side more…at least right now, at this moment, she hastily amended.

Cole ran a hand over his thick, clipped brown hair. "Ma's death created a publicity storm. Her father was a prominent senator at the time. He called press conference after press conference, was sure the sheriff back then—my uncle—was covering up a homicide, since his daughter would never kill herself. He even accused my father of drowning her for her inheritance and said so in all the papers and broadcasts. My father…who'd devoted his life to running a ranch, building a family and taking care of his struggling wife all on his own… The injustice of it nearly broke him."

Justin's fingers tightened around Brielle's. He hated the Lovelands, especially Boyd, who now wooed Justin's mother. Did any of Cole's story soften Justin's opposition?

"Our lives got turned upside down." A deep line appeared between Cole's brows. "I went from hiding everything to being photographed and hounded by reporters every minute. They wanted me to answer questions about my ma, but I couldn't. I was numb. Then I was angry. Then furious. I hated what she did. Hated *her*…something I believed was wrong to think or feel, let alone say. You're not supposed to hate your family, your mother, or God would strike you down for it."

As if on cue, a flash-pop of thunder and lightning brightened the world outside the windows with a rolling boom. The group laughed, tentatively at first, then louder when Cole spread his hands and said, "See? And with the anger came guilt. She was dead, and if I hadn't had that party, she might have still been alive."

"That was her fault!" cried Maya.

Justin shifted in his seat beside Brielle, restless, Cole's words unsettling him it seemed. Was Justin relating Cole's admission to his feelings about Jesse's self-destructive behavior, at his anger over his twin's death, a resentment he had yet to admit?

Was she making that connection to her own dark past, too?

"Once I started attending Al-Anon meetings, I learned to face my anger head-on...to accept it," Cole said. "It was a relief to walk into a room and have people nod their head— *yes, I've been like that*, or *yes, I've experienced that*, because I didn't realize how dysfunctional it was until I saw how it *could* be. Coming to Al-Anon was finding some sort of common ground, a feeling of acceptance and learning that addiction is a disease we play no part in causing. We can't cure it, and we can't control it. Your health and happiness are up to you. Control what you can, accept what you can't and attend these meetings. You're not alone in your pain."

He peered at the group, his sober blue eyes revealing his sincerity and humility, a combination as effective as his powerful story. "Thank you for having me."

Applause rang out as Cole strode to the back row, pitched Justin's hat and jacket to another chair then sat on Justin's other side.

"How'd I do?" Cole murmured out of the corner of his mouth.

"It didn't totally suck," Justin grumbled, then tempered the comment with a grin.

"Cade," Cole muttered beneath his breath, quiet enough for only Justin and Brielle to hear.

"Loveland," Justin growled, low.

Sheesh.

Brielle hurried to the front of the room. "Thank you, Cole. We appreciate your courage and your honesty tonight."

Her own story banged on the closed door she'd shut it behind, demanding release.

"Who'd like to share their experiences with addiction and anger?"

Maya raised her hand and stood. Shaking her bangs from her eyes, she turned in a circle until she faced Cole and Justin. "My mother's an alcoholic. Mostly she drinks vodka, so no one can smell it, but I can. I always know. One time she came into my room, slurring her words, reeking of alcohol and knelt by my bed. She said the doctor told her she had cancer, and she wasn't going to make it. Then she took off her necklace and said, 'I've decided I'm going to die tonight, and I want you to have this cross.' I was six years old, lying in my bed, thinking about my mom dying, how she wasn't going to be there in a few hours…it was freaking traumatizing. Now I just hate her."

Maya dropped back in her seat, and Brielle made a mental note to check Maya's family history, dismayed. She hadn't recalled a mention of alcoholism, yet a closely guarded family secret would explain a lot about Maya's struggles.

"I'll go next," said a middle-aged woman with pushed-out front teeth and sunken cheeks. "I'm Sally, and the alcoholic in my family is my brother. The role that I took on as a child was to make everybody happy. To be the best kid that there was. I was an overachiever and I just wanted people to like me. So I bought people things. I never had an opinion. I went along with crowds, no matter where they were going, whether I agreed with them or not. And I also got in dysfunctional relationships—whether it was with men or friends, or on jobs, I was attracted to toxic situations."

Lots of heads nodded.

She pinched the bridge of her nose and spoke through her fingers. "I'd find myself getting angry or screaming or ranting about the smallest thing. I'm even scared, in the privacy of my own thoughts. I'm scared by how much I overreact sometimes."

Sally sat down to a chorus of "Thank you for sharing."

"You can learn ways to move beyond the harm you experienced as a child, Sally," Brielle reassured her. "You were powerless over your brother's behavior, but what you *can* do is change the way you feel about yourself. You can move on and make healthy changes and good decisions for your own life."

Sally nodded at Brielle, smiling despite the tears streaming down both cheeks. "Thank you."

Those two simple words detonated in Brielle's heart, blowing it wide-open. She was helping others again, making a difference in their lives, a blood-stirring sensation.

An older man with narrow, rounded shoulders and bowed legs stood in the front row. He shoved his hands in his pockets and turned to face the group. "Name's Tom, and my wife's an alcoholic. We'll be married thirty-two years tomorrow."

"Happy anniversary," someone said, eliciting a faint smile from Tom.

"It hasn't always been happy. Mostly it's been misery. And work. Why stick with it, I bet some of you are asking."

Several shook their heads, showing their support and understanding about loving an alcoholic, staying with them, regardless of the pain.

"I love my wife, and I resent her, too." Tom stared out at the writhing black night beyond the window. "Being with her is like swallowing poison every day, but I'll never walk away, no matter how much it kills me. So I take that anger out elsewhere. I had jobs where I would work there for three months, six months, a year, then I would lose my temper and lose my job. It's a struggle to make ends meet. I know something's got to change, and I know it's got to be me. That's why I'm here."

"Thank you," Brielle called over the group's roar of a welcome, then closed her mouth when another person got to their feet, then another and another. Before she knew it, the hour-long session was over, sixty minutes full of tears, laughter and commiseration, a potent mix of support and understanding that settled deep into the marrow of her bones, strengthening them. Strengthening her.

She led the group in a short prayer at the conclusion then lifted her head. "Remember, you are not responsible for the world. Let go and take time to restore yourself to sanity, even if it's just for a minute. I hope to see you all here next week."

Justin and Cole exchanged quick, firm nods. Would Justin speak about his experiences next time? Would she?

"Remember that we need people to move through life with, people to *do* life with," she said, her eyes now locked with Justin's, the words rolling off her tongue—no, shoving themselves off her tongue, inspiration rushing through her at long last. She wanted to reach Justin, to reach all of them.

"We need people to tell us we're not seeing this as it really is. We need people to say that we're being too hard on ourselves, or too easy. We need people to say when we're procrastinating. We need people to challenge us and comfort us. To be our life preservers," she said, thinking of these past couple weeks with Justin and how the prickly man had pushed her out of the closed-off world she'd retreated to after her breakdown.

"We need people to do life with," she repeated, her voice rising at Justin's speculative stare. "Often, I think modern culture is very anonymous. You can move through life quite alone, even when surrounded by people. But you need to know and be known. At Al-Anon, we're each other's lifelines, an ear to listen, an arm to hold us up, a shoulder to lean on, to cry on. We're always here," she concluded, fingering the cross pin at her lapel.

If Fresh Start remained open...

Please, please, she pleaded silently, flinging out another request, wondering if this time she'd finally get an answer.

CHAPTER TEN

JUSTIN THWACKED A saddle blanket with a broom, battering it until his muscles ached. Physical pain was better than dealing with the emotions unleashed during tonight's meeting.

His nose twitched at the stable's dust-filled air, and his eyes stung. Beneath his leather jacket, his body steamed despite the autumn chill. He yanked it off, tossed another blanket on the line and walloped it hard. White puffs rose from the woven material. He grunted with every whack, releasing his frustration, confusion and grief.

He should've trusted his gut and avoided group meetings. Tonight's stories didn't apply to him. He was *not* angry at Jesse. He smacked the blanket. Jesse had let him down, sure. Justin swung the broom again. But drugs were to blame. The blanket billowed from another blow. The dealers. They ruined Jesse's life... both their lives.

Justin stopped and leaned against the broom handle, breathing hard, listening to the rain hammer the stable roof, wishing like hell he had a beer—the first time in years he'd gone almost a day without thinking of drinking, he realized with a start. Horses nickered at a distant roll of thunder. They stomped on freshly spread hay, as unsettled as he was.

Why was Cole's story needling him? Raising disloyal thoughts? He and Jesse were blood brothers, womb mates, two hearts that once beat together. He was *not* mad at Jesse.

He swung the broom and whaled on the blanket again. And again. And again.

"What'd that blanket ever do to you?" a soft voice asked behind him.

He whirled and saw Brielle standing in the soft pool of light cast by the stable's overhead dome. His heart lurched as his eyes drank her in with a greedy gulp. There was a simple beauty about her, a down-to-earth appeal that didn't require any decoration. Rain had flattened her loose golden hair, and droplets clung to her lashes. Unlike him, there wasn't a hint of restless energy surrounding her. A quiet sense of purpose emanated from her intelligent green eyes, a force of personality that even her long floral dress and knit shawl didn't soften.

Clearly, she was a woman on a mission. What did she want with him, alone, so late at night?

His body tightened at the remembered feel of her mouth against his and her passionate response to their brief kiss. He turned away. "What are you doing here?" His voice emerged rougher than he'd intended.

"Looking for you."

"Why?" He grabbed the edge of the workbench to stop from reaching for her. She'd called herself a life preserver at Al-Anon… and he was drowning…

"Group meetings can churn up a lot of emotions, especially your first time." When her fingers smoothed over his back, he swallowed back a groan. "I wanted to make sure you were okay."

"I'm fine. And busy."

"Can I help?"

"No."

"But, I—"

"Go away," he barked, his self-control breaking. Brielle was the last person he wanted around when he felt raw and exposed. She saw through him, even when he had his guard up.

"No." She ducked under his arm and wedged herself between his body and the workbench. Their noses brushed. "What do you want?"

"To make sure you're okay."

"Aren't you off the clock now?"

Her eyes flashed, and her generous lower

lip jutted, ensnaring his attention. "You think I'm here because of my job? You're not my patient."

"And I'm not your charity case."

Brielle took a deep breath, squared her shoulders, and looked him straight in the eyes. "I don't feel sorry for you. I'm frustrated with you."

"Huh?" He backed up a step.

"You act like this big—" she shoved his chest "—tough guy—" another shove "—but you always run away. You retreat."

"You just hit me," he exclaimed.

"You needed it."

He shook his head, impressed as always by her brash fearlessness, then jerked his chin at the dangling blankets. "I'm working."

"Not on yourself," she insisted, her warm, cinnamon breath whispering over his mouth as she closed the small distance between them again. "You said it earlier. The real work is on the inside, where you feel it more than you see it. You haven't addressed the real source of your anger."

He closed his eyes and wished for cover. Brielle was a sniper. She always hit her mark.

"I'm not angry at my brother." He sounded surly. It was the best he could do.

"Who then?"

"I'm mad at heroin. At dealers. *Life* for taking Jesse."

She angled her face and a strand of her honey-gold hair whispered across her cheek. "So that's why you're challenging it? Daring it to take you, too?"

His heart beat furiously at her dead-on accuracy. "So far it hasn't."

"You say that like it's a bad thing." Brielle's mouth turned down at the corners, her sorrowful expression burrowing under his skin, making him want to jump out of it.

"It'll get me sooner or later." His emphatic statement jolted Starburst. She bobbed her gray head above her stall door and whinnied.

"Why's that?"

Anger and frustration swamped him. "It got Jesse."

"Everything that happened to your brother has to happen to you?" Brielle's voice rose, challenging. A couple more horses poked their heads out, noses flaring as they blew, investigating the ruckus.

"We're twins. We did everything together until the drugs."

"Until he abandoned you," Brielle asserted, throwing her arms wide. Her shawl slid to the floor.

"No. I abandoned him." His nails dug into

his palms. "I walked away when he refused to get help."

"You set boundaries."

"I shut him out when he needed help."

"He chose to be on his own. He didn't want your help."

Justin could swear his heart stopped beating for a minute. His fingers felt like they were freezing. Then his breath returned to him in a painful heave. "Don't insult my brother."

"I'm not."

"I was the strong one." The muscles in his arms flexed. "I should have protected him better, helped him get sober."

"So he gets none of the blame and you take all of it?" Her eyes were so intensely green they were almost black.

"Jesse was a good guy." A sense of urgency grew in him.

"You can be angry with good people," countered Brielle. "It doesn't cancel out the love. And you can't forgive him until you acknowledge your anger, until you admit Jesse's guilt."

"He doesn't need forgiveness. I do."

"If Jesse were here, what would he say to you?"

They looked at each other without saying anything. He wondered what she saw as she watched him standing beneath the light, exposed, his heart beating outside his skeleton, it seemed. "Jesse forgave everybody."

"What would he say to you?" she repeated, standing her ground.

Air rushed from his lungs, deflating him. "He'd tell me I had nothing to be sorry about."

Brielle reached up, tentatively, and stroked his face, her gentle touch unraveling the knot that had held him together these past three and a half years.

"But me getting angry at him is what killed him." Acid churned in Justin's stomach.

Brielle's eyes widened. "How?"

"Because we fought," he blurted, every bit of his guilt, his shame, his regret infusing his darkest confession. "He came around one night, strung out, looking for money. I caught him going through Ma's things, and I threw him out of the house."

"He's lucky you didn't call the cops."

"We settle scores between ourselves around here."

"You mentioned that. What happened?"

"He tried to go back inside, and I wouldn't let him. He shoved me, I shoved back. When he raised his fist, I walloped him. Next thing you know, we were tussling on the ground, going hit for hit until I busted his nose. I wanted to knock some sense into him, but I drove him off instead. It was the last time I ever saw him. Alive," he amended.

"Oh, Justin, I'm sorry."

He released a ragged breath and pressed her silken palm against his cheek. "Don't be. Like I said. It's my fault."

"But it's not," she insisted. "We can't control other people's actions, and you shouldn't hold on to painful memories."

Good advice…something she didn't follow herself, he mused, thinking of the dog tags by her spider plant. "Who's William Pelton?"

Her skin blanched, and she ducked her head. Her hair swirled around her like flowing honey. The strands shimmered and swayed in the meager light as she moved, robbing her of her usual reserved look. "I didn't come here to talk about me." Her toe caught the edge of a feed bag, and he used both hands to steady her…or to feel her?

But his hands fit right into the notch of her waist as if they were meant to be there. The smooth silk of her skirt seemed to beg for his touch, but he contented himself with gently smoothing the fabric over her hips.

Then he pressed a finger beneath her chin, tipping it up until their gazes tangled. "Stop hiding from me," he murmured, his voice hoarse with the strain of keeping himself in check.

"I'm right here," she whispered.

The enticing scent of raspberries emanated from her, and he nearly groaned with the torment. He traced the outline of her lips with one finger.

She started to pull away, but he halted her by sliding his fingertips over the smooth flesh of her upper arms. Her answering shiver was both rousing and scary. It amazed him that he kept her captive with no more than his touch.

His fingers brushed through her hair, to her heated skin underneath. He curved his palm around the back of her neck, ignoring the niggling voice that reminded him he had no business touching her, an innocent compared to him. He was the kind of bad boy mothers warned good girls like Brielle away from. Who would caution her now?

He told himself he wasn't going to kiss her.

But as he leaned in close, nearing the heady heaven of her soft lips, he knew himself to be a liar. He was going to kiss her because he wanted to, and it'd been a long time since he'd wanted anything…especially this badly.

Her eyes drifted closed, and she slid slender arms around his neck. Her lips tilted toward him.

"Justin." She breathed his name a second before his mouth met hers.

She tasted sweeter than tea on a hot, humid night, and she fired his senses twice as fast. Two weeks' worth of suppressed desire ignited in one brush of her lips. He felt like an engine that had been idling for too long, suddenly revving faster—more erratically—than it should, eager to flex its muscle and test its own power.

When Brielle stepped closer still, he tensed, debating the wisdom of holding her for all of two seconds before he enfolded her in his arms. She moaned low in her throat as he slid his mouth ardently, fervently, reverently over hers. The caress an invocation. Her fingers clenched his shoulders as she swayed on her feet against him, her raspberry scent teasing his nose.

She was like a sensory explosion, swamping every inch of him with tantalizing sensations, leaving him no choice but to sample every bit of her exposed flesh, starting with the column of her neck. He trailed kisses down its silken length as her fingers tunneled through his hair. He paused on her fluttering pulse, his own raging in response.

When she melted against him, knees buckling, he swept her off her feet and lowered her gently to a soft hay pile, his lips moving over hers again, unable to stop. The straw rustled as he cupped her hips, pressing her against him. The full-body contact, even clothed, sapped his brain cells and fired his blood to a painful degree.

When she skimmed a hand down his chest, he groaned and captured her lower lip lightly between his teeth. His heart was on fire, burning out of control. He wanted to kiss her forever. He blocked out all thoughts about what this was, what it might mean, what further mess he might create for himself. *C'mon, live*, he told himself, *just this once*. And he kissed her until reason seeped out through his pores and he became a living pulse, conscious only of how much he wanted to be with her.

A nickering horse was a bucket of cold water to his face. Brielle wasn't some tumble in the hay. She was a chaplain. A woman of God. Way too good for a troublemaker like him. He couldn't, in good conscience, let this go any further without her say-so. *After* she had a chance to think.

"Brielle." He pulled away in slow degrees and kissed her one last time, still holding her hands.

He hadn't counted on seeing her eyes still closed, her lips still thrust forward.

Something inside him turned to mush at the sight. He hoped it was only his brain.

"Brielle?" He squeezed her fingers.

She smiled before she opened her eyes. "Hmm?"

The sound of the wind rattling the stable door reminded him of their rough, rustic surroundings. Not exactly the place for a tryst with a chaplain...if chaplains even had trysts. He had little experience with good girls and wasn't about to corrupt one without her clearheaded permission. He willed his breathing back to normal.

Justin eased closer again. "If we take this any further, I won't be able to stop myself."

"What?" Her green eyes sharpened into focus immediately.

"I mean, do you want me to keep kissing you?"

Justin was surprised to realize he was practically holding his breath. He couldn't remember the last time he'd wanted a woman this badly. Had he *ever* wanted a woman this much?

"No." Brielle touched her lips hesitantly, as if they might have changed since his kiss.

The simple gesture made him want to kiss her all over again. And that kind of thinking could only get him in trouble.

In one motion, he stood and helped her to her

feet before he stopped listening to his blasted conscience and kissed her senseless again. She stirred something inside him he wasn't sure he remembered existing or feeling before—a sense of belonging. A sense that in her arms he was home.

Brielle released his fingers, scooped her shawl off the ground and wrapped it around her. "That was a mistake," she gasped, confirming his suspicion. She'd kissed him on impulse. She didn't really want him. She'd been caught up in the moment. He told himself it didn't hurt…but it did. It did.

Brielle's hands clutched the ends of her wrap as if it were armor. "You're a patient."

"Not of yours. Not technically."

"Still. I can't be seen kissing residents of my facility. The community already thinks the worst of Fresh Start without there being rumors about me becoming romantically involved with clients."

His breath returned, clearing his head in time to form a better response. "You're right. Sorry if I overstepped…"

She rushed to the door. "No. It was my fault as well as yours."

"Hold on." He snatched up his hat. "Let me walk you back."

"I'd rather be alone." She held up a hand

when he started toward her. "Please. I just need some air. 'Night." She strode outside, leaving the door to slam behind her.

Justin snapped off the lights and followed, careful to keep his distance, but close enough to ensure she reached the house safely given the stormy weather.

He stopped beneath a swaying maple and stared up at the gable window to her room. A light flicked on, and he spied her shadow flitting back and forth behind her shade. When she paused, he glimpsed the shape of her hand raise to her face and wondered if she still felt his lips on hers, the indelible imprint now seared on his mouth forever.

He'd never forget how she felt, tasted, smelled—how her embrace had banished his loneliness and given him refuge. Just as she'd advised during the Al-Anon meeting, she'd made him feel known, made him whole rather than a shadow who drifted on the edges of others' lives.

Brielle said people needed other people to do life with. People who'd challenge and comfort them.

He'd only ever considered his twin in that role…but now he wondered. Jesse had always defined Justin—alive and dead. Who was Justin without Jesse? Maybe he needed to start figuring that out.

Could Brielle be his people?

The person he needed to do life with?

BRIELLE FRANTICALLY SCRIBBLED notes while Brent Jarvis reported the committee's findings at the town hall meeting. Justin Cade's brooding presence, just feet away, wasn't exactly helping her concentration.

All week, she'd avoided him. The physical distance, however, hadn't faded the memory of their mind-blowing kiss. In between agonizing over tonight's verdict on revoking Fresh Start's charter, she'd thought of Justin nonstop. He'd made her feel reckless, abandoned and free in the stable. He'd made her feel as if she had a right to the delights he aroused in her—a right to enjoy the life she'd been spared when others had not.

She scrawled the word *please* in the margin, and her stomach clenched as tight as a fist.

"In conclusion, while there appears to be a variety of activities available to patients, some, such as the life skills ranching component, pose a physical threat t-to p-patient s-safety," Brent stuttered when he caught sight of Justin's hard glare.

Brent cleared his throat, fussed with some

papers, then continued, "A last concern is the lack of security. There are no fences to prevent patients from leaving the facility's grounds and walking into town."

"They're not inmates," Justin snarled, eyes glinting hard enough to throw sparks. He practically crackled with unleashed energy. With his black cowboy hat jammed low on his forehead, a worn biker jacket clinging to his wide shoulders and chest, his long, muscular legs filling out his jeans, he looked as dangerous and magnificent as a diamondback, coiled and ready to strike.

"They should be!" shouted one of the locals filling the folding chairs.

"Druggies!" someone else muttered.

Brielle cringed at the ignorance, mistrust and fear.

"As such, I vote to revoke Fresh Start's charter," Brent concluded to resounding applause before resuming his seat.

Panic fluttered in Brielle's stomach. One vote against Fresh Start, and the assembly was starting to resemble a mob. What next? A call to storm the facility with pitchforks and torches? Her clients were *not* monsters. Her back teeth ground together.

"I'd like to remind the public that Fresh Start's mission is to provide treatment for mental health as well as addiction issues," Brielle said into her microphone. "Our clients are searching for help, not trouble."

A low muttering rose from the crowd. Mayor Cantwell tapped on his microphone until the group quieted. "Thank you for your thorough report, Mr. Jarvis."

A hand clamped on Brielle's knee, squeezed, then withdrew. "Don't let them see you sweat," Miss Grover-Woodhouse murmured from the side of her mouth.

Brielle stopped fidgeting and straightened her slight slouch. A toddler whined about a cookie, and Brielle wanted to cry along with him.

"Better." A faint smile ticked up the corners of Miss Grover-Woodhouse's mouth as she stood to speak. "Using my twenty-five years of experience as an administrator, I deem Fresh Start to be a well-run organization beneficial to its clients and the community. It provides treatment, education and the needed motivation for its patients to make lifelong changes. Client engagement is high, which speaks to its effectiveness. My vote is to maintain the current operational charter for Fresh Start."

Hope glimmered to life. One for, one against. How would the others vote?

Dana Stoughton slouched over the table, one

hand propping up her head as though it might roll off her shoulders. "The patients seemed out of control to me," she carped in a nasal voice. "Some were openly crying while others were noncompliant in following directions."

"They were learning to tie a lasso," protested Justin, fists thrust into the front pockets of his jeans. "No one gets that on the first try."

"But some…were…*crying*," Dana repeated slowly, drawing out each word as though she spoke to the hearing impaired.

"Our activities challenge patients to learn to work through stressful situations. In those scenarios, an emotional response may be part of the process," Brielle countered.

"It wasn't normal," Dana stated flatly, her thin lips folding into her pinched expression. "I vote to revoke the charter."

Miss Grover-Woodhouse's quelling stare snuffed out the smattering of applause. Even the fussing toddler hushed.

Goose bumps prickled Brielle's spine. Two to one in favor of shutting down Fresh Start. Her gaze fled to Justin, who chomped hard on a toothpick. His eyes looked up into hers. In them, she caught a hint of frustration, a hint of loss, a hint of worry.

One more revoke vote and they'd never see each other again. She knew their separation would inevitably happen, one way or the other. He'd leave once his mandatory sentence ended.

But after only a couple of weeks of having someone challenging her, comforting her, calling her out and pulling her in, the thought of being on her own again felt...lonely.

She gripped her microphone stand so hard she was surprised it didn't crumble.

"Like Miss Grover-Woodhouse, I was impressed with the patients' participation in the observed activities," Judge James said, her hands pressed flat on the table, fingers spread starfish wide. "Their commitment to improving their lives is admirable, and I believe they deserve to have the second chance Fresh Start affords. I vote to continue the facility's charter, as it not only helps its patients, but our community as well. In fact, it's my understanding that Cole Loveland recently spoke at an Al-Anon meeting attended by several local Carbondale residents."

The crowd craned their necks, looking at one another, mouthing "You?" as they attempted to figure out who'd crossed sides.

"I was honored to be invited." Cole Loveland's husky bass reverberated through the room. His slow, lazy smile at Brielle only widened at Justin's fierce scowl. "Some of the attendees mentioned previously driving to Lancing, forty minutes away, to find an Al-Anon group. Providing those services locally, neighbors helping neighbors, that's Carbondale's way. Or it used to be."

Several nodded in agreement with Cole's assessment, while others whispered to each other or stared off into space, arms folded against their chests.

"I'm abstaining," Doug Rowdy declared into his microscope.

"Why's that?" demanded the woman who'd worn the pug sweatshirt at the last meeting. Tonight, she'd donned a sweater with a repeating dog bone and bow pattern.

"Just am." Doug's chair scraped against the linoleum-tile floor as he shoved back from the table. Justin smirked at him and Brielle blew out a breath. If not for Justin's roping, Doug would've been the third vote against Fresh Start.

So, tied at two, leaving Mayor Cantwell the swing vote.

"Any final words before I make my decision, Ms. Thompson?" Mr. Cantwell asked, standing.

"You're a woman of God." The sweater-wearing woman wagged a finger at Brielle. "Is it un-Christian to want to protect your own from harm?"

Brielle swallowed, shoving her heart from her throat back down into her chest and drew in a calming breath. Justin jerked his chin at her, a you've-got-this gesture that settled her.

She leaned into her mic. "Wanting to protect loved ones from a perceived threat is a common wish regardless of your faith. However, I would like to leave everyone with one thought—the importance of taking people from the fringes of society and placing them at the center of our life's narrative. When I think about the people on the edges of society, they don't cross our paths often, right? In most cases, we must search for these people. Fresh Start is an opportunity for us to extend a hand to those in need, to honor them. Please, make Fresh Start the center of your community."

Several people cheered, and Brielle sagged back in her chair. *Phew.*

Mr. Cantwell sat, tucking the hem of his gray suit beneath him so it stopped bunching around his shoulders. "Thank you. You've given me much to consider...so much so that I believe it best if I abstain in voting as well."

Utter relief washed over Brielle, relaxing muscles she hadn't realized were tense.

Her eyes flipped to the ceiling. *Thank you.*

"That leaves us tied!" exclaimed Doug Rowdy, red blooming in his cheeks.

"What do we do now?" Dana Stoughton tapped her pen on the table, punctuating each word.

Judge James raised a hand, quieting the cacophony. "If I may?" She raised an eyebrow at Mayor Cantwell, who answered with a nod. "The bylaws state that in the case of a town council tie, the mayor may cast the deciding vote. If he abstains, then the vote is turned over to the community."

Brielle's mouth dropped open and fear prickled the back of her neck. A town-wide vote? She eyed the animated, chatting assembly. Who knew how that'd turn out? She feared the worst.

Mr. Cantwell banged a gavel when Judge James sat again. "We'll set the vote for two weeks from today."

"But them nutjobs could escape!" exclaimed the portly man with the short tie predilection. "You heard Brent. No security over there."

"They've got me," Justin boomed.

"And me," Cole thundered, his voice hitting the group like a shotgun blast. "Though I think *they* might be the ones in need of protecting from you townsfolk."

"Two weeks," Mayor Cantwell repeated. "And you'll have your chance to make your voices heard. Any other questions?"

"Do we vote here?" asked the pregnant woman who'd admitted to being a recovering alcoholic at the previous meeting.

"Yes, we'll have ballots here, as well as monitors to oversee the process and guarantee the authenticity of the results. The town hall will be open from 8:00 a.m. to 9:00 p.m. Meeting adjourned."

Brielle watched as the room emptied, her stomach roiling. A warm arm circled her and helped her stand.

"Come on," Justin said. "Let's go."

Her shoulder muscles relaxed, the tension seeping out at the sight of him. He looked down at her, his jewel-toned eyes more brilliant than ever in the soft light.

They walked outside to a chorus of crickets, slamming car doors and vanishing taillights. Dry pine needles crunched under their feet as they strolled to the rear parking lot. Yellow birch leaves drifted down from above, tumbling along with her thoughts.

She leaned into Justin's strength until she realized what she was doing, then pulled back abruptly. She didn't have the luxury of leaning on anyone, least of all a man who occupied her every thought, who laid her bare with one touch, one look, one kiss…

The wind cut through her sweaterdress and

teased a strand of hair loose from her bun. Her body felt cold and vulnerable once his warmth was gone. She bit the inside of her cheek to give herself something more demanding to feel.

"Hey," Justin said. "It's going to be okay."

"No, it's not." She didn't even realize she'd said it aloud until she heard her voice choked with tears.

His callused palms cupped her cheeks and he peered down at her, his pupils enormous, his lips parted as he momentarily forgot to marshal his expression. She'd swear he stopped breathing for several heartbeats.

So did she.

Was he going to kiss her again?

Would she let him?

"We're not going down without a fight," he said quietly. His words came out husky and velvety, as if he was saying something personal.

She bit her lip to focus on the fact that he was just giving her reassurance. He couldn't help it if his voice was mesmerizingly sexy.

His thumb stroked her jaw. "I've got a plan."

She drew back, and his arms dropped to his sides. "Bribery?"

One side of his mouth lifted. "Now, why

didn't I think of that? You're supposed to be the good one."

"There's a lot you don't know about me," she said, meaning it, longing to reveal more of herself to Justin. The good, the bad and the monstrous. Would he still look at her the same way if she did? "What's the plan?"

"It's right up your alley." A teasing light entered Justin's eyes. "Lots of mingling with strangers. Sharing…"

She moaned. "Why do I think this is going to hurt?"

He pressed his forehead against hers, and her breath caught. "Just for a day."

"What is it?"

"A community open house."

"I had one the week before we opened. No one came."

"That's because I wasn't involved."

"And how will that make a difference?"

"This time, we're putting on a rodeo."

Her breath caught as she juxtaposed the image of downed riders with downed soldiers. "No. Too dangerous." Especially for her, since it might trigger her PTSD and send her back down the rabbit hole. "I don't want anyone getting hurt."

"No one will. Promise. Cross my fingers and hope to—"

"Don't say it!" she cried.

"Trust me." His eyes held hers until she nodded. Then he led her to the car and held open the door for her. Once she slipped behind the wheel, she watched him scoot over the hood, daredevil as ever.

Did she trust Justin?

She wanted to…very, very badly.

With her heart most of all…if she dared.

CHAPTER ELEVEN

"Isn't she just the cutest little baby you've ever seen?" Justin's mother tapped on the maternity ward window. "Hi, baby! It's your grandma!"

"Ma, she can't hear you," Justin said without tearing his eyes off the red-faced infant wearing a miniature pink cap. She had Jesse's nose. His winged eyebrows. And her eyes were the same golden-green hazel he avoided in the mirror.

"Oh, yes, she can," cooed his ma. "She's very alert. See—she's not sleeping like the rest. She's pointing at us. She's very smart."

"Wait here while I call Harvard admissions."

"Nonsense. Did I tell you her Apgar score was a ten?"

"A couple times." More like twenty…

"She's perfect…" His ma sighed.

"How's Sofia?"

"She was finishing a shower a half hour ago, so this is a good time to visit her and James."

"I just came to see the baby. Don't want to

keep Brielle waiting." Or drag down the happy family with his long face.

"I'm in no hurry," Brielle remarked, joining them. She plucked a cup of coffee from a cardboard container and passed it to Joy. "You said cream and sugar?"

"Thank you, honey." Ma lifted the lid, letting out the strong scent of burned roast. Her eyes closed in appreciation. "I needed this. We've been here since Sofia's water broke. Sixteen hours of labor, bless her."

"Black for you?" Sofia's fingers brushed Justin's as she passed over his drink.

He relished the electric feel of her skin against his. Since last week's incredible kiss, he could no sooner stop reliving the moment than he could stop breathing.

"Thanks." The bitter brew scalded his tongue and throat as he gulped it back.

"Thank you for bringing Justin," Ma gushed, twinkling at Brielle. "We're grateful for all you're doing."

He felt Brielle's eyes on him. "Fresh Start's thankful for him, too. We couldn't do without him."

Did she include herself in that statement?

It was clear *he* was getting attached...and he wasn't sure if he could do without her. Not that he'd burden Brielle's already troubled life with his issues. If he committed, full on, to Fresh Start's treatment, though, might he become worthy of her? Be someone she could lean on and open up to fully, at last?

Plain and simple, Brielle made him want to be a better man.

Incentive enough to try.

He'd made his first counseling appointment with Dr. Sheldon for tomorrow and then another, with psychiatrist Dr. Fulton, the following day. Along with his volunteer work, his visits with the doctors would satisfy the court's ruling. The Al-Anon session and Brielle's insistence that he face his supposed anger about Jesse also factored into his decisions.

Since his twin's death, Justin's emotions had settled deep within, where they couldn't touch him. Now, they swirled around him, shaken loose by recent events, leaving him disoriented. He needed to clear his head and his heart.

Most importantly, he had to save Fresh Start with a kick-butt open house that'd keep the facility's charter and Brielle in Carbondale while he figured out his growing feelings for the chaplain.

"She's the spitting image of Jesse and Justin," he tuned back in and heard his mother exclaim. "You know, my husband and I weren't expecting twins when they were born." Justin's ears perked up. "Justin came first, screaming and red, mad as a hornet."

"Justin?" Brielle's eyebrows rose. "But he's so mild-mannered." She hid a teasing smile, but Justin could see her amusement in her eyes. It warmed him through.

Joy chuckled. "Oh, yes, very out of character. Then along came Jesse, catching us all by surprise. I hadn't had an ultrasound, and when we'd listened to the heartbeat at the doctor's office, we'd only heard the one."

"You heard both," Justin asserted.

"Justin and Jesse were close," his ma sighed. "They say mothers are supposed to be able to tell their twins apart, but I sure couldn't."

"Then why'd you dress us identical for so long?" he grumbled.

He glimpsed Brielle taking in his mother's color-coordinated outfit: rose-colored earrings that matched her blouse, necklace, a braided wool belt and heels.

"I like things that match." Ma shrugged. "Besides, I made you wear those colored wool string bracelets. It was the only way I could keep track of who was who before Justin got stitches on his fifth birthday."

"We switched those strings all the time," Justin confessed with a grin.

Brielle mouthed "terrible" at him behind his mother's back.

"You little devils!" huffed Ma. "I knotted them myself!"

"We'd just grab more wool from your basket and Jared would tie them."

His mother turned to Brielle and placed her hands on her hips. "Do you see what I had to deal with?"

"Nothing but trouble and heartache, right, Ma?" A pinching throb began on the right side of Justin's head, directly behind his eye.

"And love," Ma added with a long sigh. "Despite everything, I feel like the luckiest mother in the world. And grandmother."

Justin thought of Cole's mother, of the note where she'd confessed to never feeling like a mother, and caught his ma in a fast, tight hug.

"Oof!" she said when Justin released her. "It's been a long time since you've given me one of those. Thank you, honey."

"There you are!" huffed his sister, Jewel, as she turned into the corridor and spotted them. "James sent me to fetch you all."

"We're heading out." Justin pointed to his watch. "Dinner starts in ten minutes."

"We can grab something from the kitchen later," Brielle insisted, completely misreading him…or was she just sticking her oar in again, imposing her aid when he didn't need it? Not from her, especially since he didn't want to be treated like one of her patients, even if she wasn't counseling him.

How did he want her to view him?

As a beau? A boyfriend? More?

Jewel linked her arm in Justin's and nearly yanked him off his feet as she dragged him down the hall. "That settles it. Come on!" Then— "Sorry!" when she nearly ran over a volunteer pushing a flower-filled cart. Coffee spouted from Justin's cup and burned his wrist.

"Careful!" his mother yelled behind them.

At a closed door marked with the name Cade, Jewel stopped and turned to face him. "Smile."

He wrenched his mouth slightly.

Jewel poked her fingers on either side of his lips and shoved them up. Her eyes narrowed as she considered him. "Better. Show some teeth."

He bared them, and she rolled her eyes. "Now you look like a rabid rottweiler. Just be happy for them, okay?"

An arm slipped in his, slender and strong. Brielle. He breathed in her light, fruity scent, and his headache backed off.

"I *am* happy for them." Deep down…where he couldn't fully feel it.

Justin followed Jewel inside, Brielle sticking to his side like a burr. One he didn't want to shake.

"Uncle Justin!"

He instinctively crouched to catch Javi midleap. "How're you doing, bud?"

"I'm a big brother." Javi's small chest puffed. "Which means I'm the boss."

"You sound like your father more every day." Justin eyed James, who'd officially adopted Javi after marrying Sofia. An exasperated nurse watched as James modeled proper swaddling cloth–folding techniques.

"Sofia, you look beautiful!" his ma raved, moving to the hospital bed.

Brielle nudged Justin, and he stepped forward to pause at the headboard.

Sofia's damp hair clung to her flushed face. Dark circles pouched beneath her eyes, and her exhausted smile waxed and waned, but Justin agreed with his mother. Sofia gave off a light all her own. Was this what perfect happiness looked like?

"I feel like I've been run over by a tractor trailer. Twice." Sofia laughed. "Did you see the baby?"

"She's adorable," Brielle said.

"Beautiful," Ma gushed. "A dainty little lady."

"Dainty?" Jewel scoffed. "Did you see her arms and legs? She's built like a sumo wrestler."

Justin's laugh cut off at Brielle's light kick.

"Jewel! That's insulting," Ma chastised.

"She meant it as a compliment," James said, joining them.

"Exactly." Jewel rolled up her plaid shirt's sleeve and flexed her ranch-honed bicep. "A real cowgirl. She's going to be a barrel racer and roper, just like her aunts."

"I'll teach her," Amberley offered as she and Jared entered the crowded room with her service dog, Petey.

The place was practically wall-to-wall smiles and good cheer. Justin tried to back up and was stopped by a wall—that wall being Brielle. Darn that stubborn woman.

She'd said everyone needed someone to challenge them…and she did that to him in spades. Aces, even.

"Do girls wrestle?" Javi hugged Jared and Amberley then threw his arms around a tail-thumping Petey.

"Heck yeah," Jewel insisted. "Just ask your father how many times I've pinned him."

James rubbed his chin, rueful, as he smiled at his sister. "My ego pleads the Fifth."

A knock on the door quieted his family's

laughter. A nurse wheeled in a clear plastic bassinet holding James and Sofia's baby. "The doctor's finished with her, so I thought I'd bring her down if that's okay?"

James lifted the pink-swaddled bundle carefully, the expression on his face one Justin had never seen before. His know-it-all brother looked awed and slightly terrified. It tugged at Justin to witness his tough sibling vulnerable. James, who'd devoted his life to the ranch and their family, now had one of his own.

The other night Justin had wanted to kiss Brielle more than he'd wanted anything before. Now another need flickered to life inside him, a simmering, more intense burn.

He wanted to make someone as happy as James made Sofia. He wanted someone to love and protect. He wanted to know that he could create something so perfect…so pure. A second chance… He wanted someone to look at him with such adoration, such unadulterated faith and love. If he committed to therapy, put in the hard work, could he find this life with Brielle?

He had to find out.

"She's twenty inches and eleven pounds," the nurse proclaimed.

"See," Jewel said. "A sumo wrestler."

"I hope the newborn-size dresses fit her," James worried out loud.

"Good thing you've alrcady bought a hundred more in the next size up," Justin drawled, earning him a smile from Brielle that lit him up inside.

"Justin, would you like to hold the baby?" James asked once the nurse left.

Justin froze.

"Of course he would," Brielle replied for him.

Without further ado, James thrust the warm pink bundle into Justin's arms. Instinctively, he cradled the baby close, and his chest lifted as he inhaled her fresh talcum powder scent. She opened one hazel eye and squinted up at him, a spit bubble forming on her pink lips, and in a heartbeat, Justin fell head over heels in love with the munchkin.

"What's her name?" he asked gruffly without looking away from her rosebud of a face. If she was a future sumo wrestler, there'd never be one prettier.

"Well. We've thought long and hard about it and—uh—we think we've come up with something real special," James nattered, sounding uncertain.

Justin slipped his index finger into the baby's hand, and her sudden, fierce grip squeezed his heart, too. He'd never seen such a beautiful baby. Perfect in every way.

"I'm your uncle Justin," he whispered. "I'm going to make you proud to call me kin," he vowed, discovering another reason to work on himself…another person to be worthy of.

"What's her name already? Sheesh!" huffed Jewel.

"Do you need a drumroll?" quipped Jared.

"Sofia?" James prompted.

"Jesse. Her name's Jesse," Sofia said slowly, and the family gasped.

A shudder tore through Justin. *Jesse.* He was holding Jesse. His hands trembled, and he handed the baby to James lest he drop her.

Brielle's fingers laced in his, halting his bolt from the room, from the name, from the reminder of everything he'd lost and would never get back. How could they?

"We want to honor Jesse," James said, his voice hoarse. "So we'll never forget him."

"I'll never forget Jesse." Justin fought to keep his voice from cracking while his heart splintered. "Don't need a reminder."

"Is it too late to change your minds?" Jewel asked, biting her nail and shooting Justin a worried look.

"We already filled out the birth certificate,"

James said heavily, his eyes on Justin. "We'd hoped you'd be happy."

"It's a lovely name." Ma blew her nose with a loud honk. "And a beautiful tribute. We'll have another Jesse in the family again."

"No, we won't." Justin shoved the words from between clenched teeth. "You can't replace Jesse. Give the baby her own identity."

"She'll have it. Her name won't change that," James argued. "If it wasn't for Jesse, she wouldn't be here."

"You mean if Jesse hadn't died, you and Sofia wouldn't have gotten together?"

"Justin!" Ma's face transformed in shock and horror. "Apologize."

"No, Joy," Sofia said, accepting the infant from her husband and cradling her close. "Justin's right. We owe Jesse a lot, and this is our way of paying tribute. We both have a special connection to Jesse, one that no one else in the family shares."

"And you're the closest to my first daddy." Javi slid his small hand into Justin's. "Baby Jesse will love you special like I do."

Justin nodded, anger draining from him, anguish and regret rushing in to take its place. "I'm sorry, Sofia. James."

"Perhaps we should be heading back," Brielle said. "Congratulations. God be with you and your beautiful, blessed baby."

"Wait!"

Justin halted in the open doorway at James's shout.

"We wanted to ask you a favor."

"What?"

James dropped a hand on Justin's shoulder. "It'd mean a great deal to me and Sofia if you'd be Jesse's godfather."

Justin's mouth dropped open, and his heart stuttered to a stop.

"Please, please, please, Uncle Justin!" Javi bounced before him. "Will you?"

"I—I—" The word *no* built in the back of Justin's throat, constricting it.

"He'll think on it." Brielle tugged him backward before he could refuse.

"Why'd you do that?" he asked as she hurried him down the hall then outside, where the setting sun cast the world in rosy hues of gold. "I was about to say no."

She angled her head, and her strong chin jutted. "You just answered your own question. Think seriously before you blurt out an emotional answer you might regret."

He shook his head and whistled. "You do beat all, woman."

"I aim to please." Her cheeky grin almost made him feel better.

Almost.

What were his brother and sister-in-law thinking? He wasn't anyone's idea of a good role model. Besides, he'd already failed one Jesse. He wouldn't repeat his mistakes.

Unless this could be a second chance, a voice whispered inside.

"Justin Cade. Just the fellow I'm looking for!"

Justin tore his eyes from Brielle's determined face and braced at the sight of a rapidly approaching Boyd Loveland.

The last person he wanted to see.

Boyd swept off his hat to reveal a thick head of clipped silver hair. His tanned, weathered face creased into a smile when he turned to Brielle and stuck out a hand.

"Boyd Loveland," he said, shaking her hand. "Haven't had a chance to visit your place yet, but it's on my list. Sure do appreciate all you're doing for the community."

The old cowboy hadn't lost his country-boy charm, Justin noted, given Brielle's pink flush and quick smile. She appeared to have lost her tongue as she stared into the Loveland blue eyes the local ladies nattered on about.

"Come on, Brielle." He cupped her elbow, but she dug in her heels.

"Cole's been a real help to us," she said, still smiling, while sliding Justin a narrowed side-eye stare.

Boyd rubbed the back of his neck, and his expression turned pensive. "It does him good. His mother's death hit him hard, and I'm glad he's getting out. He's not much for socializing."

No kidding.

Not that Justin could talk.

Boyd's sober expression deepened when his gaze shifted to Justin. "I've been hoping to catch you. As you know, your mother and I've been courting."

"Is that what you call a con these days?" Justin challenged, staring hard at Boyd.

"Justin!" Brielle hit him with her death-by-glare expression, and he felt a pang of guilt. She always caught him at his worst. Would she ever see his good side?

Did he have a good side?

Boyd held up a hand. "There's a lot of history between our families, Ms. Thompson. No apologies needed. Still. I love Joy and, for some reason, she's decided to take pity on this old cowboy and love me back. I'm hoping to ask for her hand, but I won't do it unless I have the support of all her children, since I know how important that'd be to her. It's important to me, too. I promise to make her the happiest woman, to cherish her as she deserves and to always take care of her."

"With what money?" Justin spit with bubbling frustration. "Hers?"

Brielle's mouth dropped open, and her disappointed expression cut him deep.

Boyd lifted his chin, staring down from his imposing height. "I won't deny we've had our challenges at Loveland Hills, but I've always provided for my family—and I'd never touch a dime of Joy's money. Her heart's all I want. And her hand."

"Right." Justin schooled his tense face back to neutral and forced his shoulders to relax. "Then sign one of those things, uh, a prenup, and prove it."

Boyd crushed his hat between his hands. "You think I haven't offered? When I was feeling her out about the general topic, she vowed marriages were not business transactions."

Yep. That sounded like his sentimental, softhearted ma.

Justin watched the last of the sun slip over the horizon and wished he could chase after it. He wanted to escape this tangled moment, extinguish this anguished day.

Boyd stepped closer and cocked his head. "Would you consider thinking on it some?"

A muscle in Justin's jaw pulsed as he ground his teeth. "No."

Boyd's face fell, softening Justin a touch.

"Besides," Justin added, "I'm not the only holdout."

Boyd donned his hat and cupped the brim into a C shape. Despite his polite smile, his expression was one of pain, the kind you couldn't stop with aspirin. "That's true. Though I'm grateful for Jack, James and Jared's support. Hoping, in time, I can convince you and your sister to change your minds, too." A fleeting smile twisted his lips. "Everyone deserves happiness, especially your ma. Y'all have a good night, now." He tipped his hat then climbed the hospital stairs with a slight hitch in his step.

Justin gaped after Boyd's broad back, mind in overdrive. Jared caved?

Now only he and Jewel stood between his mother and the biggest mistake of her life.

Brielle cleared her throat. "He's right. Everyone deserves happiness."

He stared into her beautiful green eyes, and his heart constricted. "But they don't always get it."

A rushing family jostled them on their way

into the hospital while a driver honked at a waving woman in a wheelchair.

"Let's go over there." Brielle pointed to a large duck pond farther down the hospital's front lawn. "I'm not ready to head back yet."

A couple of minutes later they stood on the grassy embankment, their hands brushing, the slight contact seizing him with a hard, hungry need to hold her, kiss her and forget everything but the incredible feelings only she aroused.

"What are you afraid will happen if your mother marries Boyd?" Her voice startled a pair of geese who took to the sparkling water with indignant squawks.

Justin watched the V-shaped wake trailing behind the paddling birds. "She'll get her heart broken. It took her years to smile again after Jesse's passing. It wasn't until Javi and Sofia showed up that she became herself. I don't want to lose her again."

"Ah." Sofia tucked her skirt and knelt on the grass.

"What's that mean?" he asked, joining her on the soft, cushioned ground. Above, squirrels scurried and chittered on an oak's branches, sending missiles of acorns thudding to earth.

"You don't want to lose her to the Love-lands."

"I—" He snapped his mouth shut as the

truth hit him square on the jaw. He didn't want to lose anyone he cared about ever again…his mother or…

He studied Brielle's strong profile.

Or Brielle.

He was falling for her, hard, and if he wasn't careful, his mother's heart wouldn't be the only one broken. "I've already lost someone I love."

Her fingertip traced his rough knuckles, quickening his pulse. "You won't lose her."

"She'll move away."

"Next door."

Another acorn pinged on a rock and jetted into the water. "Cades live on the Cade ranch."

"Doesn't your brother Jack live across state?"

"Yes," he admitted, stealing a glance at her.

"You and Jesse planned on traveling, climbing mountains, seeing the world," she insisted, earnest. "You were okay leaving the Cade ranch then."

He let the thought roll around in his head. Anything he felt during that time of his life had gotten shoved into a vault, its ten-foot-thick door slamming as soon as it went in, just in case something in there had any intention of crawling out. "That was with Jesse."

"Nothing's stopping you from going now."

Nothing except his growing feelings for Brielle...and his loyalty to his brother.

He picked up an acorn and rolled it between his thumb and index finger. Then he took a deep breath and let it out slowly, making sure all residual feelings were under control.

"I won't leave Jesse." With a snap of his wrist, he flung the acorn far out into the middle of the pond. Concentric rings spread from where it dropped.

"Jesse's gone, Justin," Brielle said gently.

"He's still here. Six feet under, but he's right there beside Pa in our family plot."

"I see."

Did she? Silence expanded between them, a quiet understanding that loosened the pressure in his chest. Her willingness not to press, to back off and let him breathe and feel, shoved the truth from his heart. "I won't abandon my brother like I once did."

"But you're abandoning the dream you two shared. Would he approve of that?"

He shook his head, thoughts swirling. "It's not up to him," he croaked.

"It's up to you. How you live your life. How you honor your brother. How you find happiness again."

"What about you?" he asked, turning the

tables, needing to switch the spotlight, fast. "Are you happy?"

Brielle plucked a brilliant orange leaf beside her feet and twirled it by its stem. "I'm working on that," she answered obliquely, no mention of the dog tags belonging to William Pelton. Would she ever trust him with her painful past?

"I hoped I'd find happiness when I moved out here. With the community against us, though, I suppose I'll be leaving once they vote." She shooed away a hovering fly.

"Carbondale's a small town, and they don't take easily to outsiders." Justin shrugged. "If you spent time with the community, socially, they'd get to know you. They'd grow to trust you…listen to you."

Her brows scrunched together. "We're doing the open house."

"How about meeting locals on their turf? There's a Halloween parade on Friday. I could take you to it. Introduce you around."

Her sudden, teasing smile made her eyes glow and his breath catch. "Because you're the perfect person to help me socialize." She smacked her forehead with her palm. "Now why didn't I think of that?"

"Hey," he protested, enjoying her tweaking,

his dark mood lifting. "I can be a charmer when I want to be."

"Oh, yeah?" she challenged, leaning in.

"Yeah."

Her face was so close their breath mingled. "Then it's a date, cowboy."

CHAPTER TWELVE

"You look nice."

Brielle turned from Fresh Start's reception desk and smiled uncertainly at Craig Sheldon's compliment. "Too much?" She yanked down the fluttering above-the-knee hem of her white angel costume while simultaneously holding up its neckline. The feat required intense focus, Olympic coordination skills and a blessed miracle. Was she a celestial being or a pole dancer in a halo, for goodness' sake?

"She's one hot angel." Doreen blew a plate-size bubble then sucked it back in, the red of her gum blending with her bright lipstick. "Wish it'd looked that good on me."

"Maybe there's still time for me to change…"

Doreen traipsed to the bottom of the stairs wearing a white handkerchief masquerading as a nurse costume. Leaning on the banister, she barred Brielle's flight. "You've got nice legs. Show 'em off for once. Besides, the only other costume I could loan you is my *Playboy* librarian outfit."

"A playboy librarian?" Craig's voice rose, skeptical.

"Yeah. See, it's mostly just pages from books that are glued in, ah, strategic places. Real classy, though. Oh, and a bookmark." Doreen twisted and pointed over her shoulder. "Goes right down there. You know. For modesty."

"*Right,*" Craig drawled, chuckling.

Brielle shuddered and stared down at her bare knees, toying with one of the elaborate curls Doreen had arranged around her face earlier. Since Brielle had spent most of her life in sensible skirts, uniforms or fatigues, she'd nearly forgotten what her legs looked like. Smooth and not too knobby…was she being horribly vain in thinking they passed muster?

Would Justin think she looked pretty?

She squelched the question.

She'd spent too much time obsessing over it today as she'd prepared for their Halloween parade date. A shiver of anticipation danced up her spine whenever her dark rider came to mind, leaving her hot and cold and full of jitters.

At the stable, bad boy Justin had behaved like a gentleman, giving her space to make up her mind about kissing him again. Since then, whenever their eyes met, she heard the unspoken question between them. Did she want to kiss him again?

Yes.

Badly.

But what a person wanted and what they needed were often two different things, as her training had taught her.

Seeing tough Justin cradle his niece the other night had melted her through and through. His rough facade crumbled as he'd cooed to the newborn, his big heart out on his sleeve. Then, when he'd confessed his fear of losing people he loved, she'd understood it'd be wrong to toy with his heart, especially when she didn't understand her own. She had a history of abandoning those who relied on her...to tragic ends. And Justin's careless disregard for life already made him susceptible to rash decisions.

If anything happened to another person on her watch, especially someone she was developing strong feelings for, she'd fall, too...and this time her bootstraps wouldn't be enough to pull herself up again.

William Pelton's letter flashed in her mind's eye.

Without you, I had no one else to turn to...

She shuddered. Too much blood stained her hands already.

Plus, if the community voted to revoke Fresh

Start's charter, she'd leave Carbondale and Justin for good. Disappointment whirled inside, a dark funnel. Better to keep her distance emotionally. Now she just needed to convince her yearning heart of that.

She jerked her gaze off her limbs, folded her arms across her chest then yanked them down again when they pushed her cleavage higher in the scoop neckline. Argh. She really needed to change. She turned back to Craig. "Do you have everything in hand for the night? Any last questions?"

"Where do you keep the vodka?" Craig deadpanned.

"Right next to the Jack Daniel's, sheesh." Brielle rolled her eyes, and Doreen giggled. "Seriously. Are you all set?"

"I've only read a third of your list—" Craig shook her ink-covered sticky note "—but I hope to finish before you return."

"Okay. I get it. I'm being a mother hen. It's just…we can't afford even the slightest mess up, or we'll lose whatever chance we have of winning the town vote."

Craig saluted her. "Yes, ma'am. We'll hold down the fort."

She stiffened at the familiar gesture she no longer deserved.

"Nice hippie costume, Dr. Sheldon," Doreen observed, chomping on her gum.

Craig smoothed a hand over his fringed suede vest. Wearing a tie-dyed scarf, a Have a Nice Day T-shirt, bell-bottom jeans and flip-flops, he exuded a laid-back chill Brielle envied. "Oh, I didn't dress up."

Brielle bit back a grin when Doreen momentarily choked on her gum.

And where was Justin? He should've been here fifteen minutes ago.

A loud gasp sounded, and Brielle's gaze flew from a bug-eyed Doreen to a tall, masked bandit stalking across the entrance hall. His boot spurs clanked with each menacing stride. Wearing a black cowboy hat with a matching kerchief tied around his face and a pair of gleaming, holstered pistols in a cartridge belt, he resembled a Wanted: Armed and Extremely Dangerous poster.

A shiver danced up her spine until brilliant hazel eyes gleamed at her.

"Justin?"

He bowed, pulled down his kerchief, lifted her hand to his lips and seared her flesh with a light, heart-stopping kiss. "M'lady."

"Holy Wyatt Earp!" breathed Doreen.

Justin's eyes dropped to Brielle's toes and dragged slowly up the length of her body, his gaze a scorching caress, making her skin flush red-hot. *Oh. My.* He was gorgeous, all edgy, dangerous swagger, confidence oozing from every pore of his muscled flesh. He wasn't just playing an ominous outlaw, he was one—a desperado who made women swoon and lesser men flee. Except beneath his hard exterior beat the heart of a tender, caring, sensitive man... layers upon layers that made her care more for him every day.

Was she falling in love with Justin?

"What's your costume?" Doreen asked, avidly staring, chewing openmouthed.

"A Teletubby."

Brielle chuckled. "You nailed it."

"And *you* look beautiful." His low baritone vibrated in the short space between them, bending the blood streaming in her veins.

"Thank you," she answered breathlessly.

"Don't do anything I wouldn't do," Craig called as they strolled to the door.

"That's a pretty short list," Doreen teased, and then the door shut behind them and silence descended.

"Will you be cold in that?" Justin asked when they stepped off the front porch, his eyes sticking to Brielle, wide and unblinking.

Her heart beat loud in her ear. "No. The weatherman said we're breaking a record today. Warmest temperature ever measured in October."

"It sure is plenty hot." Justin mock leered at her, and she swatted him away, her hand lingering on his firm chest before she dropped it.

"We'd better get going," she blurted, her words halting as she struggled to catch her breath. "The parade starts in a half hour."

When Justin looped his arm in hers, she pulled away. "We're not a couple in front of them." She pointed to the lit Main Street down the hill.

Justin stopped and traced a finger down the side of her cheek. "What about in private?"

"Justin." She sighed. "Things are complicated."

He hung his head a moment then nodded. "Whatever m'lady wishes," he teased lightly, yet she heard the bruise behind his words.

"It's not that I don't like you…"

"You like me?"

"Too much," she admitted.

His eyes sparkled, and a smile lifted the edges of his kerchief.

"But you also scare me."

"Why?"

"Because I don't want to lose anyone else I care about again."

"Oh."

She tore her gaze from his and resumed her trek. "How about we just have fun tonight and forget everything else?"

"Your wish is my command, m'lady."

"And what's with the 'm'lady' thing?"

"I promised to be charming. Men say that in romance books, right?"

"When did you start reading romance books?" Justin Cade, renegade cowboy, sensitive rebel, wounded bad boy and now a romance reader?

"Ma has a stack of them by her knitting basket. Jewel, Jesse and I used to act them out on rainy days."

He fell silent and the houses they passed began to crowd one another, side yards disappearing as they turned into duplexes, then eventually businesses.

"That sounds like fun."

Out of the corner of her eye, she caught his quick nod. Given the dark night, his large hat and kerchief, she couldn't discern his expression.

"I always played the Viking or the pirate."

"Sounds like typecasting to me."

A deep chuckle rumbled out of Justin. "Suppose. Jewel always wanted to play the cowboys, which meant Jesse got stuck acting out the women mostly. Not that he minded. He'd pinch his nose with a clothespin, wear one of Ma's aprons and swish around the room until we had to stop reading for laughing."

"You were so close."

"Always thought we were the luckiest family."

"Good times are ahead, Justin. Now you've got baby Jesse…"

A truck festooned with orange and black crepe paper rumbled past on its way to join the parade. White fog belched from a smoke machine placed amid the elaborate graveyard constructed on its bed. Justin didn't return the driver's wave. "Uh-uh…we agreed to only talk about fun things."

"I wish you'd reconsider being her godfather."

"They've got better role models than me to pick from."

"Not true," Brielle countered. "You've started going to therapy and you're working with the patients, who adore you. You're making a positive difference in their lives and yours."

And hers…

He made a noncommittal sound then stopped when someone called his name.

"Justin Cade?"

A woman led by a waddling, one-eyed pug

approached. Brielle remembered her from the first town meeting, but instead of the pug sweatshirt she'd worn then, she now wore a doggy onesie. A hood with ears covered her broad face and hair, and a felt tail dragged on the leaf-covered pavement behind her.

"Howdy, Mrs. Leonard." Justin doffed his hat.

"Ruff!" The pug jumped on Brielle's legs, drooling slightly as he panted up at her, one bulging eye shining expectantly. The other socket was shriveled and empty.

"Otis! Down!" ordered Mrs. Leonard.

"Oh. He's okay." Brielle crouched and let Otis lavish her face in frantic, rough licks. "Just," she sputtered as she dodged Otis's determined tongue, "fine."

"There's no stopping him when he takes a shine to someone," Mrs. Leonard declared as Brielle did her best to avoid getting frenched by the pug.

"You're just so cute," Brielle cooed, planting a final—she hoped—kiss on Otis's soft head. "How old is he?"

"I found him ten years ago by the town dump. The vet thought he might be two or three back then. Can you imagine tossing out this little sweetie? Some people have no heart." Mrs. Leonard scooped up Otis and cradled him.

"Must have dumped him because he only had one eye," Justin observed.

When Otis's short legs kicked, Mrs. Leonard set him back down. "That only makes him more perfect."

"You made him the center of your life story," Brielle noted, referencing the lesson she'd shared at the last town hall meeting. Justin released a low whistle.

Mrs. Leonard's smile fell, and she peered hard at Brielle. "I see what you're doing. You're trying to compare Otis to your patients at Fresh Start."

"All they need's a second chance," she insisted and straightened her slipping halo, "people to care about them, flaws and all…"

Mrs. Leonard sucked in her lips and her extra chin appeared as she retracted her face, considering.

A couple of kids dressed as Power Rangers sauntered by, pointing at Otis. One of them called out, "Cyclops." At Mrs. Leonard's glare, they raced off, screaming and laughing.

Mrs. Leonard's eyes rose to Justin's then swerved to Brielle. "I've been thinking hard about what you said…how we should go looking for people to help."

Brielle held her breath as Mrs. Leonard reached into a belted pouch, retrieved a treat then fed it to a leaping Otis. "I might be wrong about Fresh Start."

Justin lowered his bandanna, and his even teeth flashed white against his dark beard. "Will you vote against revoking Fresh Start's charter?"

Mrs. Leonard passed another biscuit to her wriggling dog then nodded. "I suppose."

"Maybe you could bring Otis over to meet the patients sometime," Brielle said, inspiration striking. "We could include him as part of their therapy."

Mrs. Leonard pressed a hand over her heart. "Otis? A therapy dog? Oh, I believe I'm going to like Fresh Start after all." Someone waved to her across the street. "Elaine! Wait until you hear my news about Otis!" And without another word she hurried across the street. Instantly, a bevy of nodding and smiling women surrounded her, aiming speculative stares at Brielle.

How many more locals could Mrs. Leonard sway? Enough to help Fresh Start keep its charter?

"And that's how it's done." Justin pulled his bandanna over his smirk as they resumed strolling down the now crowded thoroughfare. Costumed children darted in and out of stores carrying plastic pumpkins full of candy. In the distance, a marching band's snare drum rat-tat-tatted while a cotton candy machine whirled, offering orange and black cones to customers.

"You *were* pretty charming," Brielle admitted. Especially to her, she added silently, falling even more under Justin's spell.

"*Pretty* charming?"

"Okay. Very charming."

"And you were very clever. Mrs. Leonard will chain herself to Fresh Start before she lets them close it down now."

Brielle laughed at the visual. "Let's hope it doesn't come to that. Oh! Look!" She stopped and pointed to risers filled with hundreds of carved, lit pumpkins.

"Our annual jack-o'-lantern contest. Want to check it out?"

"Yes!"

She dashed to the elaborate display. While Christmas was her favorite holiday, Halloween was a close second…a sacrilege, really, considering her profession. But everything about it fascinated her: creepy music, outrageous costumes, jack-o'-lanterns, trick-or-treating… Growing up on international army bases, it'd been a piece of America, a sense of normalcy.

She stopped at the risers and scanned the entries. Painted, carved, bedazzled and even automated, spinning pumpkins occupied every inch of space. Some had flickering votive candles while others used electronic strobe lights or colored illuminators.

"Who could pick one over the other?" she wondered out loud.

"We were hoping you might help us, Ms. Thompson. Howdy, Justin." Mayor Cantwell, dressed in a Harry Potter robe and a red-and-gold-striped Gryffindor tie and scarf hurried closer. "One of the judges got sick bingeing on apple fritters and dropped out. Could you step in?"

"Sure she can," Justin answered for her, nudging her forward just as she'd done to him at the hospital.

"I'd love to," she said. Justin vowed that socializing with the locals would increase Fresh Start's chances of winning the vote, and she trusted him…more and more every day.

Was she starting to depend on him, too?

Twenty minutes later, she bestowed a blue ribbon on the man who'd called her patients "a bunch of crazies" at the last town meeting.

"I'm sorry about what I called your patients, ma'am," the man said, clutching his ribbon.

"I appreciate that, though you're entitled to your opinion."

He shook his head. "You're a kind lady. Can I make a confession, Reverend?"

She hid her surprise and glanced down Main Street to a tall, white church. "Would you like to stop by and see me at Fresh Start, or I could meet you at the church…?"

All around them, the sidewalk teemed with parents ushering costumed children, shoving teens dressed as horror film villains and strolling elderly couples seeking curbside seats for the imminent parade.

"Nah. No one's paying attention." The man grabbed a cloth from his back pocket, blew into it, then stuffed it away. "Just wanted to say my dad was an abusive alcoholic. One time my little sister Theresa ended up in the hospital for a month. We thought she was lucky since she'd escaped for a while."

"I'm so sorry. Did your father seek help?"

"Nope. He killed two people and himself in a drunk-driving accident my senior year of high school. Never touched a drop of liquor myself. Grew up too scared of him, and it, to be tempted."

"Then you're lucky, too."

He pulled off a Broncos ball cap then resettled it on his bald head. "You suppose a program like Fresh Start could have helped him?"

"We assist lots of parents. Many have children hoping we'll get them well."

His Adam's apple bobbed. "Well. Then. I'm man enough to admit when I'm wrong."

"Meaning?" Her stomach rumbled when a sizzle rose from a nearby apple fritter stand. The butter-and-cinnamon scent of fried dough wafted in the unseasonably balmy air.

"I won't vote against your charter. Kids should have parents better than mine."

"Thanks, Mister…?"

"Kolchek. Sam Kolchek." He tipped his hat and ambled away, instantly swallowed by the seething crowd.

"Won over another one, I see." Justin offered her a caramel apple and pulled his bandanna down to his neck, revealing an approving smile.

"I can be charming when I want to be," she mumbled around a sticky, tart-sweet apple bite then passed it back.

"And…?" He chomped on the treat, and a smear of caramel clung to his upper lip. It took every bit of willpower not to lean forward and lick it off.

"And I'm glad you suggested meeting the community. Thank you."

For a moment, their eyes clung and neither seemed to breathe. Then a cymbal crashed, nearly on top of them, making her jump.

"Parade's starting," Justin murmured in her

ear, the savory caramel-cinnamon smell of his breath rushing over her skin. He led her to a spot by a lamppost and stood directly behind her, sheltering her from the pressing crowd. This close, she could feel the heat of his rising and falling chest against her back, and she gripped her hands to keep from leaning back against his muscled firmness.

A *Wizard of Oz*–themed hay wagon trundled by, distracting her wayward thoughts. Across the back, a banner read Carbondale Medical Center. Its scrubs-wearing driver winged Tootsie Rolls into the crowd, and children darted out to snatch up the candy rolling on the pavement.

Next, the local high school band marched by playing "When the Saints Go Marching In," the infectious tune animating the swaying and cheering crowd. A young girl, seated on her father's shoulders, clapped her hands in time to the beat. Brielle caught Justin staring at the father-child pair, the naked longing on his face twisting her heart.

Did he want a family?

He'd held baby Jesse so tenderly the other night. Could a reformed bad boy make a great father? A loving partner? Someone she could depend on, who might not threaten her stability after all?

Mayor Cantwell cruised by in a vintage yellow convertible tossing miniature candy bars to the crowd. When a pack of kids nearly shoved her off her feet to grab some, Justin's arms encircled her, warm and steady. Her body trembled against his lean, muscular frame. With the crowd's rapt attention on the parade, she let herself indulge in the delicious feel of him for a couple more minutes before reluctantly shifting away.

Twenty minutes later, the parade ended with a whistling bang. A starburst of steaming red lights bloomed against the black sky then faded, followed by another burst of yellow, then two purple circles.

Boom!

Brielle instinctively ducked and covered her head, blinking back the sting in her eyes as she recalled similar, less innocent explosive sounds in Kandahar. Justin crouched beside her.

"You okay?" He peeled back her arms and peered into her eyes.

She rose quickly, unwilling to make a fool of herself and jeopardize the goodwill she'd built with the townspeople tonight. "I'll be fine."

Oohs and ahs followed a spray of sparkling white that screamed to earth. A streak of white smoke sailed upward then exploded in a sizzling green pulse.

Justin's hands clamped over her violently shaking shoulders. "Let's go," he murmured in her ear, and this time when he slid a firm arm around her waist, she didn't protest. It was all she could do not to drop to her knees and cover her head the way she had when lobbed IEDs struck inside the base.

They wove through the crowd then jolted to a halt at someone's scream.

"He's going to jump!"

The crowd turned as one, following a woman's finger pointing to the town church. What Brielle saw sent a jolt through her.

Paul, her former artilleryman patient suffering from PTSD, stood on the edge of the steeple's bell tower.

CHAPTER THIRTEEN

BRIELLE SHOOK FREE of Justin and shot down the street like a bullet. Her lungs screamed for air, but she ignored them.

"Who's that?" she heard someone ask.

"One of them mental patients," another spat.

A young child wailed. Another cried, "Is he going to die?"

"I'm scared, Mama!" a third pleaded. "I wanna go home."

She pulled up before the church and stood panting on the street, watching Paul pace in the minuscule square of space surrounding the belfry. The wind whipped his T-shirt and a flock of pigeons took flight, squawking. Her heart practically stopped at the thought of him dropping from that height.

"Paul!" she yelled up to him, but he only paused, gripped the railing encircling the area, then threw one leg, followed by the other, over it. A needle of fear punctured her lungs, and all the air seemed to leak out of her. But her determination to save Paul swamped it, a tsunami overwhelming every cell in her body.

"He's going to jump!" someone screamed.

"Please, quiet!" Brielle ordered the pressing crowd. In the distance, the fireworks built to a crescendo, a barrage of firepower that had Paul cringing. As an artilleryman, the sounds of explosions must have sent him spiraling back to his darkest times and triggered his PTSD.

How had he gotten out of Fresh Start? Had the exit's security keypad malfunctioned again?

Travis Loveland arrived wearing his brown sheriff's uniform and a commanding air. "Is he one of your patients?"

"Yes," she said, relaying Paul's information through clamped teeth. "Tell whoever's running the fireworks to stop," she ordered briskly in her captain's voice.

Travis nodded and conferred rapid-fire directions into a walkie-talkie. Several officers arrived and began pushing back the avaricious crowd.

"I'd like to talk to him," Brielle said when a sheriff's deputy handed Travis a bullhorn.

"We have a crisis negotiator coming, but it'll be at least fifteen minutes before he arrives." Travis passed her the bullhorn. "Can you keep him up there and talking?"

"I plan on getting him down. Safely."

Justin's eyes warmed just enough to let her know he approved of her intervention. "Paul, it's Brielle Thompson," she yelled, her amplified voice echoing in the night air.

When Paul turned to face her, a gust snatched his hat from his head. The locals squealed when it fell to the ground.

Such a long way...

Her heart constricted like an iron hand was squeezing it as punishment. Once again, she'd abandoned her post and another soldier in her charge might pay with his life.

No.

She could not let that happen.

"We blew a fuse and the electricity went out, deactivating the security system," panted Craig Sheldon, joining her. "We counted heads, discovered Paul missing and headed straight out."

Doreen bent over, grabbing her waist. "We were about to call you when we heard the commotion."

"Leave me alone!" Paul screamed, his body bowed out from the railing like a sail, his knuckled grip and toehold all that kept him from tumbling to his death.

Brielle's muscles stiffened in sheer terror. "You don't have to do this," she said into the bullhorn, striving to keep her voice level and calm, to defuse the intense moment.

"You don't know the bad things I've done." He dipped a toe over the edge, and the crowd shrieked.

"You don't know the bad things I've done, either, but I'll tell you if you'll listen. And I've never told them to anyone else before."

She caught Justin's sharp look out of the corner of her eye.

Oh, Lord. Could she do this?

If she opened the door to her darkest moments, would the shadows consume her, break her once again? Her fingers turned cold at the thought.

Justin's large, warm hand enfolded hers. He looked grim, his muscles taut, his face pale as though all the blood had drained from him. She knew she didn't look any better, but they were in this together, his handhold communicated, the kind of grip that said *never let go*.

Paul pulled his toe back and glanced at her again. "You're a chaplain. Reverends don't do bad things," he shouted, though, at this distance, she had to strain to hear his words.

"I have. The very worst. A soldier died because of me." The wind whipped her hair around her face, and Justin gently tucked the wayward curls behind her ears. "If you go back over the railing, I'll come up and tell you about it."

A loud murmur broke out and dozens of eyes pummeled her like arrows, finding their mark. Justin's firm touch, however, steadied her, as did Paul's plight. Carbondale could judge her all they wanted; her reputation was moot compared to saving this deserving soldier's life.

Paul stared at her then slowly slung one leg, followed by the other, back over the railing.

She blew out a long breath once he was behind the short iron railing. It wasn't much of a deterrent from jumping, and the decorative piece wasn't designed to stop a human from falling, but it was better than having him completely exposed. All he had to do was lean over it to tumble to his death. She shut down the thought and compartmentalized, forcing her mind back to her task—bringing a fellow soldier back to safety.

"Thank you, Paul. Hold on. I'll be right up.

"Sheriff," Brielle said, "no one comes up there unless I say so, okay?"

"You've got it," Travis Loveland vowed.

She handed him the bullhorn, charged inside the church then turned when she felt Justin right behind her.

"Paul only agreed to me."

"Tough. You're not going up there alone."

His eyes lasered into hers in the shadowed church interior.

"You might not like what you hear."

"Trust me, Brielle. Let me in."

After a moment, she nodded then hurried up the curving stairs to the belfry. She paused at the door and breathed a sigh of relief to see Paul still safely inside the narrow space.

"Don't come any closer," he warned.

"I won't. I'm going to sit right here and won't budge."

"Promise?"

"Promise. Is it okay if Justin's here, too?"

"Yeah," Paul called a moment later, and she drew in a long, cold breath.

"After attacks, sometimes marines wanted to talk to me. They were incensed, mourning, numb, confused, frightened, though they wouldn't always admit it, exactly… Yet I'd never seen a marine like the man who stopped by one day after his company's tenth KIA."

"That's killed in action, right?" Justin whispered in her ear."

"Right."

"What was his name?" Paul asked.

"I'll just call him Bill, out of respect for his privacy. You understand, right?" Despite the relative shelter of the doorway, the late-October wind, colder at this height, seeped through her angel costume and raised goose bumps on her skin.

Paul nodded, a small motion difficult to discern in the dark.

"He came to me outside medical, where the surgeons had just called time of death for one of his platoon members. A buddy he'd grown up with back home. Blood smeared across Bill's face and stained his hands and uniform. He was so angry he was snarling, his face contorting like an angry dog's. I wasn't sure if I wanted to be alone with him, not when his anger had the better of him. I told him to meet me after supper, but he didn't show up. I should have sought him out, but I had the memorial service to plan and figured I'd take him aside later, after he'd had time to calm down."

Paul moved closer, away from the flimsy rail. "Did you?"

"At the service, I read from Second Timothy—'I have fought the good fight. I have finished the race. I have kept the faith.' Do you know that one, Paul?" she asked, desperate to hold his attention, to keep his mind off his plan to jump.

Two cruisers rumbled to a stop down below, and an ambulance siren wailed in the distance.

"No police up here!" Paul shouted, angling over the banister.

"No police, I promise. I told the sheriff

no one else comes up here without my say-so." She dragged in a shaky breath when he straightened. Justin's hand now rubbed a slow, steady circle on her back, a soothing motion, a caring one, too.

Did he care for her?

If he did, those emotions would disappear after he learned the truth about her horrible, selfish choices.

"The company commander spoke next," she continued. "He vowed revenge, but I noticed Bill hardly seemed to listen. He stood apart, his expression closed off. Surly. After the commander spoke, Bill talked about how his friend was a good guy, the only decent one in the squad because he didn't think the country would be better off if they razed it to the ground. Then he glared at his fellow soldiers and accused them of teasing his friend for being sympathetic. For caring."

"I had a friend like that." Paul swiped at his face, and his wet cheeks gleamed in the starlight. "His squad leader said he left his position to help a little girl caught in the cross fire. Then she blew up and killed them both. Insurgents strapped an IED on a three-year-old. What kind of world is that?" Paul screamed, a primal, guttural sound of raw pain.

"I'm sorry for your friend."

"We signed up for it," Paul sobbed. "We were doing our duty. Just never knew our duty would mean watching kids die, dogs die, old people, everyone...die. What happened to Bill?"

"He kept ranting at the squad. I was about to step in when he stopped talking. At the end of the service, the company approached the battle cross, knelt together, arms over one another's shoulders, leaning close until they were one silent, weeping block—all except Bill."

"They cried?" Paul said.

"Like children." Marines were terrifying warriors on the battlefield, but they hurt, they bled, they cried like anyone else—maybe harder. To survive, they bottled up their feelings, becoming powder kegs of emotion. One spark, one loss and some exploded, the shrapnel of their pain striking everything in its path, including loved ones. Others imploded, the wound a black hole inside, draining their life away, their souls crushed in its vacuum...like her.

For so long she'd thought herself the lucky one to have survived, but now she understood she was a casualty, too. But she shoved the realization deep into a dark corner where she could examine it another time, when Paul was safe and out of danger.

"Then one by one they stood up, touched the helmet, and walked back to their commander. All but Bill. He tried to get my attention, but the commander waved me over. He wanted to talk about low morale, about ideas he had for the upcoming Easter service. By the time I finished talking to him, Bill had disappeared."

Paul cupped his hands around his mouth when the wind picked up and raised his voice to ask, "Was he in his tent?"

An officious-looking man in a blue windbreaker appeared below, bullhorn in hand. The crisis negotiator. Should she stop?

Justin thundered downstairs, and his fierce scowl and animated gesture backed the officer off a couple of paces, leaving her room to continue this life-and-death task. Paul knew her. Trusted her. What's more, Justin had faith she could do the job, and so did she.

She had to talk Paul down; they stood on the precipice together, their fates irrevocably entwined.

"Is Justin coming back?" Paul paced in the narrow, slanted space.

"Right here, bud," Justin affirmed, rejoining them.

"Did you find Bill?" Paul asked again.

"I didn't look for him. I wanted to write down the commander's ideas while I still had them fresh in my mind. I made myself the priority, thinking I still had time with Bill. Then another squad went out on patrol, one I'd gotten to know well. They were only days away from going home, but they got hit. Bad. Twelve casualties. When I gave the Easter service the next day, I lost my words. My thoughts. My faith. I broke down."

Justin's arm slid tight around her waist, clamping her against his side. Down below, the impatient crowd's chattering rose in volume, static-filled judgment she forced herself to tune out.

"I walked out of the service and found Bill waiting for me by my tent. He begged to talk to me, but I refused. I didn't have anything to say to anyone. No comfort to give. He came back later that night, but I told him to leave. When he returned in the morning, I called the MPs, had him ordered away. I couldn't handle any more grief. A few days later, I was put on leave then given an honorable discharge, though there was nothing honorable about it. I was weak. I forsook my flock."

Paul slid down the bell tower wall and drew his knees to his chest. "What happened to Bill?"

Her stomach filled with ice. "When I got

home, an envelope waited for me. Inside it was a note from Bill and his dog tags."

"Only next of kin get those…" Justin murmured beneath his breath.

"He didn't have any family, he told me in the letter, and his friend who'd died had been like a brother. He said when I left he had no one to talk to, no other choice but to kill himself, because he couldn't take the pain of being alone anymore. If I hadn't broken down, if I'd done my duty, Bill would still be alive. So, you see." She lifted her arms and pressed her palms to the sky, her heart splintering. Her eyes stung so hard she could barely see.

"These aren't clean. I can never remove Bill's blood from them. It's why I'm at Fresh Start, why I'm here now, asking you to come down from the ledge. Don't add your blood to these hands. They can't hold any more. If you fall, I fall. Please, Paul. Come down and take another day to think about it," she pleaded, ignoring the storm of conversation flowing through the crowd behind her like an electric current. What they must think of her…what Justin must think of her… But none of that mattered, not right now, when Paul's life was on the line.

Paul rose and stepped to the rail again. "All of my buddies died when our launcher backfired. I was the last one to sign off, to check it, before we set it off… I thought it was a go, gave the signal, then it blew up in our faces."

Understanding fired through her, compassion swift on its heels. "You made a mistake, too. I understand. I do."

Paul nodded, his shirt dappled with the tears streaming down his face. "They'd be alive if it wasn't for me. If you kill somebody, that means you're going to hell."

"God always offers forgiveness," she said, keeping her tone soft. "To those who are truly sorry. But sorry isn't a feeling. It's an action. A determination to make things right. You have that chance now."

"I can't make anything right." He beat his fists on the banister, and the rubberneckers erupted in screams and shouts.

"Yes, you can. Come down the stairs with me, come back to Fresh Start, and I'll listen to you. I'll listen to you talk about the friends whose names are inked on your arm. Tell me about your dreams to ride in the rodeo, your favorite pizza toppings—what were they? Pineapple and ham?"

A bit of white flashed—possibly a smile?

"Pineapple and jalapeño peppers," he called, his tone lightening.

Justin whispered, "Good work," in her ear.

"Right," she forged on, her voice gaining in conviction. "You can't make Maya try a pineapple-jalapeño pizza from up there. Please, come down and I'll help you find a path to forgiveness, one which already runs through you. Will you take it, Paul?"

"How do I know you won't ship me to a hospital in a straitjacket?"

"You'll go to the hospital for a little bit."

Lying might increase her chances of talking Paul down, but she wouldn't betray his trust. Justin had told her to connect with her patients and the community. She'd done both today and would never go back to her days of hiding, of isolation. Despite opening the Pandora's box of her past, here she stood, straighter than ever. "Just for a few days, and not in a straitjacket. And then you'll come back to Fresh Start."

If the facility was still here, she qualified silently. This dramatic display fed into the locals' fears about disruptions to their idyllic small-town life. The vote to revoke the charter loomed darker and more ominous than ever.

"Promise?"

"I give you my word. Now give me yours to come down these stairs with us."

Paul leaned over the railing, his body far out into the air. When he nodded, the crowd erupted in a gasp. As soon as he backed away from the railing, Justin wrapped an arm around Paul's shoulders and hustled him down the stairs and outside. A moment later, EMTs helped Paul inside an ambulance and drove away.

The crowd erupted in cheers, while others sobbed. As they dispersed, many stared at Brielle as she stood on the church steps, their faces full of accusation, confusion and shock. She sagged against Justin and finally managed to suck in a decent breath. It burned as it went into her lungs, but her muscles unclenched as they got oxygen again. She reveled in relief. She twisted to watch the ambulance lights disappear around a corner.

"Private William Pelton," Justin said quietly, leading her back inside the dark church. They held hands as they sat in a pew.

"Yes," she admitted after a long moment, staring at a shadowed cross. The haunting silence threatened to suffocate her.

He tipped her head down to rest on the strong curve of his shoulder and cradled her close. "I'm proud of you."

"Don't be." Her heart was racing so hard she thought she'd have to swallow it to keep it from galloping out of her mouth.

"Admitting your past took guts."

So, he didn't despise her...a lightness seized

her limbs, making her buoyant until reality crashed her down to earth again.

"Carbondale will never let Fresh Start stay now, or if they do, they won't allow it to be run by a director with a history of breakdowns."

"First off, they have no say in that," Justin vowed, firm. "Second, breakdowns are like bone breaks—you heal stronger than before." His fingers combed through her curls slowly, making her scalp tingle and her shoulders lower.

"Not the heart," she said, thinking of Justin.

"Especially the heart." His fingers now grazed along the length of her neck.

"Not me. It took me a long time to get out of bed after my discharge, a long time to stop seeing the casualties. So many good men died. It's like mortality is a game, and God maneuvers us like chess pieces." The words, whispered in His house, sounded like blasphemy but tasted like truth. Her truth.

Justin traced her jaw with the callused pad of his index finger. "Do you still believe in God?"

The moon disappeared behind clouds, and the light coming through the stained-glass windows dimmed.

"I do, but I don't hear Him anymore. He stopped answering me after my breakdown, stopped talking through me—like He blames me, too. Bill wasn't the only suicide. Another member of his squad killed himself on leave, with his personal handgun. A couple months later, a third member of his company over-dosed. A year later, Stan Dobbins, one of the only survivors of the group ambushed before Easter, redeployed for the third time and shot himself in the head." She leveraged herself up to face Justin. "That's why I'm not stronger."

"You haven't healed yet. Didn't you tell me therapy's hard work?"

"Maybe I'll never get better. When you drove into my truck, when you showed how little you cared about life, I couldn't handle it. Still can't."

"But I don't feel that way. Not like I did. Not as much."

Justin's face was so close to hers their breath mingled. She had a strong compulsion to try to pull them both out of this melancholy mood, to distract them. She placed her hand on his bearded cheek. It was soft and warm. When he didn't move, she lifted her face and tenta-tively touched her lips to his.

At first, she got no response, and she consid-ered backing off. Then his kiss turned hungry. It was not the gentle kiss of a couple on their first date, nor was it the kiss of a man driven by simple lust. He kissed her with the desperation of a dying man who believed the magic of eternal life was in this kiss.

The ferocity of his grip around her waist and shoulders, the grinding pressure of his lips, had her off balance so her thoughts whirled out of control. It was a knee-melting, gut-twisting, vein-tingling, nuclear meltdown kiss. And then the pressure eased, and the kiss turned achingly tender. A tingling warmth shot from the silken touch of his lips and tongue straight to her core. Her body melted into his, and she was hyperaware of the hard muscles of his chest, the possessive feel of his fingers denting her waist, the wet slide of his mouth on hers. Then he pulled back, taking a gulp of air as if surfacing from choppy waters.

She took a deep, deep breath. Held it. Let it out slowly.

His lids lifted, and his eyes were deep pools of swirling emotion. "You should know," he murmured, low and husky, "you make me want to live. You lost Bill, but honey, you're saving me."

"But you should save yourself," she murmured just before his lips found hers again, melting into the delicious, stolen moment.

Later, she stared at the cross. *Thank you*, she thought, and a warm, joyous answer expanded in her heart. She'd been listening so hard she'd forgotten to simply feel, or had been too afraid to feel until now, until Justin encouraged her to face her emotions instead of locking them away.

Did she dare give her heart to the reckless daredevil?

Could she convince him love was all the reason anyone needed to live?

CHAPTER FOURTEEN

JUSTIN DROPPED THE last rib eye on the grill and inhaled the juicy sizzle hissing from the grates. With a flick of his wrist, he dabbed liquid smoke on each thick steak, followed by Worcestershire sauce. An extra dash of salt, pepper and garlic powder followed. After a quick glance to determine no one watched him, he shook smoked paprika, his secret ingredient, over the marbled meat, then slipped the bottle back in his pocket.

"Smoked paprika, huh?"

Justin's back snapped straight at the instantly recognizable voice. Cole Loveland. How did he miss the goliath? He must have crawled out from under a rock.

He *was* a Loveland…

"What are *you* doing here?"

Cole hoisted a tray of foil-wrapped baked potatoes. "Helping. Now move over."

"There's no room for those." Justin pointed his spatula at the steak-filled grate.

"We'll make room." And then, like every

other arrogant, stubborn, condescending Loveland, Cole muscled in, smooshed Justin's pristine steaks to one side, and dropped the potatoes next to them. "See? Plenty of room."

"They won't cook evenly packed that tight," grumbled Justin, tamping down his irritation the way Dr. Sheldon taught him in anger management. He nudged the potatoes with the spatula to give his steaks room and to keep himself from decking Cole smack in his smug Loveland face.

"Potatoes are mostly cooked already." Cole inched the potatoes closer to the steak, rolling them with a mitt.

Justin slammed down the grill cover, trapping the heat inside against the cool November air. "Then why grill them?"

"To enhance the flavor. *My* secret ingredient needs to soak in."

"What is it?" Using a grill fork, Justin poked at the ears of corn steaming in a tall kettle on a side burner.

Cole smirked. "Wouldn't be a secret if I told you."

Justin brandished the fork at his longtime enemy. "You saw my smoked paprika…"

"Herbes de Provence," Cole admitted beneath his breath, eyes flitting to the oblivious residents enjoying the good weather before winter took hold. Some milled around cloth-covered picnic tables while others competed in a game of horseshoes.

Justin whistled, grudgingly admiring Cole's culinary style. "Parsley, sage, rosemary and thyme mixture, right?"

"How'd you know?"

"I rub it on chicken then brush the pieces with olive oil before grilling."

Cole nodded slowly. "Good to know."

"What are you two talking about?" Brielle asked as she joined them. Her blond ponytail gleamed beneath the cloudless sky, emphasizing her square jaw and high cheekbones. Her face was strong. Beautiful. Magnetic. It stirred Justin's heart. A week had passed since their kiss in the church, seven days since they'd agreed to delay a relationship until his discharge, one hundred and sixty-eight hours of longing for the woman who'd captured his heart. "Boring manly stuff like sports, I bet."

Cole cleared his throat, and Justin muttered, "Yeah. Go Broncos."

"Great game last night," Cole added, scuffing the brown grass with his boots.

Brielle cocked her head, swinging her ponytail. "Thought they were playing tonight."

Justin and Cole swapped conspiratorial

looks. "Right," Justin blurted. "That's what he meant."

She eyed them suspiciously then wandered off with a plate of deviled eggs.

Cole guffawed. "That was pathetic."

"Think she bought it?"

"Nah. Speaking of sports, are you riding in the motor cross race day after tomorrow? Saw your name listed but didn't know if you'd chicken out."

"Why would I do that? Should be an easy win."

Cole flashed Justin an irritable look. "I'm riding in that race."

Justin grinned. "Exactly."

He shoved down his unease about telling Brielle he intended to race his bike, something he'd been postponing since his brother called last night to remind him about the annual benefit event for the local VFW. He didn't want to worry her or, worse, trigger her PTSD. She had a thing for protecting her patients, saw it as her obligation to keep them safe and free of harm. Him riding his bike at ninety miles an hour across a rutted dirt track was far from what she'd consider safe. On the other hand, he couldn't tiptoe through life like she did.

"Guess we'll see, then." Cole shrugged. "And I heard from Maverick. He agreed to compete against you at the open house rodeo next weekend. Called it a grudge match since you bested him at the junior championships before you quit the circuit. Now he can even the score."

"Maverick Loveland's coming here?" Paul exclaimed, sidling close. "Watched him win the PBR world championship last January. What a rider."

"He's the best," Cole affirmed in ringing tones of pride.

Would any of Justin's siblings ever speak of him this way? Not with pity or anger or regret, but with straight up admiration? In this morning's session with Dr. Sheldon, they'd discussed how Justin's anger at Jesse turned inward. He couldn't hate his deceased brother, so he'd hated himself instead. Now he needed to love himself, Dr. Sheldon insisted—a concept Justin struggled to accept. Was he lovable?

His eyes flitted to Brielle as she poured cups of coffee and chatted with her patients. Since publicly opening up about her struggles, she'd seemed more at ease with them and herself. Could a strong, principled woman like Brielle love him?

One thing was certain. He was head over heels for her.

Thankfully Paul hadn't fallen during the

Halloween parade, but Justin had tumbled hard. When he'd heard Brielle's courageous story, witnessed her strength in confessing her mistakes as she worked to save Paul, Justin's heart had ripped loose and cleaved to her.

If Fresh Start's open house failed to convince the locals to keep its charter, she'd leave, taking his heart with him. He didn't have much experience with women, not like reformed lady-killer Jared. Yet Justin always knew if he ever fell in love, it'd only be once. And it'd be forever.

"You two used to be rivals?" Paul asked, looking healthier and steadier after his release, yesterday, from his week-long hospital stay.

"Bitter rivals," Cole clarified.

"Never saw Maverick as competition." Justin raised the grill lid and speared each steak, turning them. Brown juice ran off the seared tops. With an exasperated sigh, he prodded Cole's potatoes, rolling them to ensure they cooked evenly, too.

"Are the steaks almost done?" Maya stuck her hands above the heated air wafting off the grill. She'd replaced her usual black nail polish with blue, Justin noted, and her complexion looked brighter, too, her cheeks rosy and filled out slightly. She'd put on a few pounds. Last night, Paul had challenged her to take a bite of his pineapple and jalapeño pizza, and she'd gone one better and polished off an entire slice.

"Five minutes," Cole said.

"Six," countered Justin. No one called time on grilled steaks except him. "There's sweet and spicy pickles on the table if you're hungry. My ma brought them over. It's a family specialty."

"I'll try them." She jogged back to the picnic table and snatched a pickle from one of the bowls. Satisfaction filled Justin to see the strides she'd made…the progress they'd all been achieving, even him, who'd thought he needed it least of all.

Fresh Start could not close. The work here was too important. Brielle's smile caught his eye as she accepted a pickle from Maya. Brielle was too important…to him… If she left town, would he follow? It'd mean abandoning his brother, but Dr. Sheldon insisted Justin needed to let go of Jesse to find his own happiness.

Crazy psychobabble.

But darn if it wasn't working on him.

"You think I'm ready to rope at the open house rodeo?" Paul fidgeted with his ball cap, shaping the brim, lifting, lowering and turning it.

"I wouldn't let you ride if you weren't." The grill lid thudded shut again.

"Thanks, Justin." Paul stared up at the bright sky for a long moment. "You taught me a lot. And not just about ranching. About myself and what I can do."

"Go on, now," Justin protested, never comfortable with praise, especially when he didn't feel like he deserved it.

"Paul!" Maya yelled from the tables. "Try these pickles. Some of them are hot!"

"It's true, dude. I owe you and Ms. Thompson everything." Paul strode off, leaving Justin to stare after him, openmouthed.

"Hey, appreciated you talking about Jesse at Al-Anon last night," Cole said quietly.

Justin shrugged and stared at a group of wild turkeys pecking in a distant field. Behind them, scarlet maples glowed, brilliant beside golden-leafed birches and orange-shaded oaks. Piles of leaves heaped beneath their trunks. "Helped me more than them."

"Not true." Cole lifted the grill lid and transferred the potatoes back onto his plate. Puffs of fragrant stream rose from their charred foil wrappers. "You're a role model—people look up to you," he added, then strode away.

"What about you?" Justin called after Cole. "Do you look up to me?"

"I've got you by five inches. It'd be impossible."

"Jerk." Justin laughed under his breath, his respect for Cole rising.

Was he starting to like a Loveland?

"He's right, you know." Brielle arrived bearing a large platter for the steaks.

"About?" Justin poked the thickest steak, noting the color of its juice with an expert eye. Another minute...

"You've inspired the patients. Like it or not, you're a role model." Her lips tipped up sadly. "I wish you'd reconsider being baby Jesse's godfather. Your brother would want you to do it, for his namesake."

"Don't do that, Brielle," Justin said, his voice low and urgent.

"Don't do what?"

"Guilt-trip me."

"I'm trying to talk sense into you!" Her eyes sparked with a won't-back-down challenge.

"Don't hold back on my account," he said drily.

"Hold back? I'd hit you over the head with a blunt object if I could," she huffed.

He choked on a laugh. "You beat all, darlin'. Shouldn't you be praying for me instead of threatening violence?"

"I'm doing both, and you're the only one I'd

like to beat some sense into—you and Brent Jarvis," she amended, then laughed along with him. "Cole mentioned his brother Maverick participating in our rodeo."

Justin poked the steaks one last time, then transferred them to the platter. "We're lucky he has a break in his schedule. His star power will draw a big crowd, exactly what we need after Halloween."

Brielle's eyes swerved to Paul. Worry etched faint lines around her mouth. "There've been a lot of letters to the editor about it."

"I know." He stabbed a rib eye clear through and had to shake the fork twice to release it. "It spooked them, but they'll come around once they meet the patients…see them in a different way."

Brielle blew out a long shaky breath. If she weren't holding the laden tray, he'd pull her in his arms and reassure her properly.

Although his thoughts, when it came to Brielle, were seldom entirely proper…

A reformed bad boy was never going to be completely good. At least, not all the time. His thoughts veered to the upcoming motor cross race, and guilt pinched him hard for keeping his participation in it from her. He'd wait a little while longer to fill her in rather than risk ruining the festive afternoon.

"It's tough staying positive. What if Fresh Start shuts down?"

Their eyes met and the unspoken question—what would happen to them—wavered between them.

"It won't. Maverick's competing and so's Amberley, both big names in rodeo."

"Barrel racing's fine, but you and Maverick bull riding? Too dangerous. What if someone gets hurt?" The thread of desperate worry in her voice confirmed his decision to hold off on mentioning the motor cross race.

"It's a possibility." He snapped off the burners, tucked a bottle of steak sauce under his arm and relieved her of the tray.

"We can't risk that," she said, but her lips barely moved as they strolled to the picnic tables.

"We or you?"

"What do you mean?"

"People risking their lives, getting injured, are triggers for your PTSD."

"I don't know what'll happen to me if I see someone hurt." She said it so quietly he barely heard the words. "Especially someone I care about."

Touched by her admission, he moved closer, wishing for privacy. "I'll be there. I'll make sure you're okay."

"What if *you* get hurt?"

"Could happen." He wanted to put her mind at ease, but he wouldn't lie to her. Though, technically, postponing the news about the motor cross race was a lie of omission…one he'd rectify soon. "But I used to be the best bull rider in the state and never got more than a busted rib. Why do you think a PBR world champion's willing to come home to compete against me?"

"A good cause?"

"That, too," Justin agreed, one side of his mouth hitching up. Brielle never tiptoed around his ego. "We're doing everything we can to keep Fresh Start open. Don't block our best chance of drawing a crowd to support us."

Brielle stopped and turned to stare at him, lips pursed, green eyes considering. "How about this. I'll agree to the bull riding if you'll agree to be Jesse's godfather."

He shook his head, stunned. She never stopped surprising, challenging or pushing him, and he supposed he did the same for her. At least, he hoped he did.

"Well?" she prompted, hands on her trim hips, her lips stretched into a gotcha smile.

Oh, she had him all right…

He had to grin back. Brielle's smile was infectious. "It's a deal *if* you'll go to the christening with me."

"Deal." And without another word, she walked away, swishing her legs under her dress and dissolving into the sunlight streaming in from the west.

He settled the steaks in the center of the picnic table and backed away from the descending, ravenous pack.

Now that he wanted a life, he wanted a person to live it with, and only one would do: Brielle.

He'd never believed in himself much, but he believed in them.

The open house rodeo had to go off without a hitch.

His life—his heart—depended on it.

Justin splashed stinging aftershave on his clean-shaven jaw then faced himself in the bathroom mirror. In a black suit and a deep blue tie against a crisp white shirt, borrowed for today's christening, he hardly recognized this spiffed-up version of himself. His first shave since he'd learned his twin had died.

"Hello, Jesse," he said, and his brother's wide-open, easy smile twinkled back at him, his hazel eyes swirling with anticipation and hope. It'd been a long time since he'd seen his brother content…since *he'd* felt at peace…

So, this is what happiness feels like.

Hope I do you proud today, brother.

And just like that, his anger at Jesse, his war on life, evaporated, the weight in his heart gone. He still hadn't told Brielle about the motor cross race, but he found that worry dissipating, too.

A knock rattled the bathroom door.

"Chop-chop, sweet cheeks," Doreen called. "Ms. Thompson's waiting on you."

He yanked open the door, and Doreen stumbled back, her hands rising to her face. Her lids snapped up, revealing the whites of her bulging eyes.

"How do I look?"

Doreen swallowed hard. "Like a god."

His lips twisted sardonically at her exaggeration. "Not a devil, then?" he asked, half seriously. It'd been a long time since he'd looked and felt human. He no longer wanted to scare anyone off, not baby Jesse, not his family and especially not Brielle. Although he had to give it to his scrappy sparring partner—she didn't back down, and she didn't take any of his guff.

And he liked—no, *loved*—that about Brielle.

Loved her.

"Is he ready, Doreen?" Footsteps clattered up the stairs then stopped on the landing. "We'll be late."

A thrill jumped through him at the sight of Brielle. A tangible, head-to-toe current singeing his nerves, searing across his skin and snaking along the seams of his fitted shirt. Wearing a gray sweaterdress that darkened her eyes and brightened her upswept golden hair, her beauty, her presence, walloped his chest and stopped his heart. Everything receded around her like a camera trick.

"Can I help you?"

He quarter turned to face Brielle fully. "You already have."

Brielle's pretty mouth dropped open, and Doreen rushed to her side, steering her faltering boss from the stair's edge.

"Breathe, Ms. Thompson, and don't look at him directly, not for too long. It'll stun your brain. My retinas are still burning."

"Justin?"

He closed the space between them in two strides. "Hey." His greeting seemed inadequate given all he'd been thinking and feeling about her in the last few days, but one look at her had scattered his thoughts.

Rendered him breathless.

"Should I leave?" Doreen asked while he

held Brielle's wondering gaze, hoping she liked what she saw…this new man she'd created.

Brielle touched his face, as if not trusting her eyes.

"Yeah," Doreen murmured to herself. "I'll just be going now."

"You look so different," Brielle marveled as Doreen's steps receded.

He raked a hand through his newly shorn hair. Pam—a salon stylist, it turned out—had clipped it after breakfast. It'd take him a while to get used to the cool rush of air around his neck and ears. "Different good?"

"I just didn't know…" Brielle hesitated.

He raised an eyebrow. "Know?"

"You were this handsome."

Shameful heat stung his cheeks. He wasn't a pretty boy like his brother Jared, and he'd never paid his looks any mind before. Now he was absurdly pleased at the compliment. How much had changed.

"Should I start humming the *Beauty and the Beast* song?" he joked, relishing his proximity to her body while he ate up her presence with his eyes.

Her fuzzy gaze sharpened. Then her mouth twitched into a smile. She biffed him on the shoulder and he knew, in that instant, everything was going to be all right today—and maybe, if he was lucky, forever, too.

"You look beautiful." His husky voice rasped in his tight throat.

She glided closer and her intoxicating berry scent made him want to bury his nose in her shoulder, taste and explore every inch of her mouth. Her forehead brushed his chin as she angled her face up to his. "So do you."

Electric emotion crackled between them and heated the very air around them. His hands reached for her, skimming her slim waist through the knit of her dress. "We're going to make people talk."

She rose on the balls of her feet and brought them nose to nose. "Let them," she teased, knowing, as he did, everyone except Doreen was in the kitchen completing a cooking lesson. Then she pressed her soft mouth to his and the gentle caress ignited his wild, hungry need for her.

He hauled her close and captured her lips fully, savoring their minty flavor, their silken texture. His pulse sprinted to every corner of his body, and his breath grew ragged. "I didn't know how hungry I was until I tasted you," he whispered into her mouth.

From their first kiss at Miracle Point, she'd stirred a longing in him that hadn't come close to being quenched. He suspected he'd never get enough of Brielle. His tongue stroked a path along the curve of her full lower lip, his blood simmering in his veins, every nerve ending jumping to life.

He smoothed his palms down her spine, pressing her closer one vertebra at a time, her body molding to his. His heart pounded so hard he could feel the pulse leap at the bottom of his throat. Her soft, feminine sigh filled him with satisfaction, sharp and sweet.

"Ah-hem!"

They broke apart. At the stair's base, Doreen waved frantically then pointed at the kitchen doorway. Chatting residents began filing out. Luckily, none peered upward.

Justin's hands itched to hold Brielle, but he forced them in his pockets instead and followed her down the stairs, past a grinning Doreen and out into the crisp fall day.

A couple of hours later, he stood by the two-story hearth in his family's ranch house, Brielle by his side, feeling at home for the first time since Jesse's passing. He wasn't on the outside looking in anymore, a squeaky, busted-up third wheel.

He'd been broken, and Brielle was the only one who could have fixed him.

"Come on, Justin, let someone else hold

her," Jewel pleaded. In a concession to the formal occasion, his tomboy sister had worn a denim skirt and polished her battered cowgirl boots. Behind her, red-orange flames engulfed a large log pile in the fireplace, their cedar scent wafting through the crowded, festive room.

"You'll have to put her down sometime, at least to eat. Want me to fix you a plate?" Brielle offered.

Justin shook his head and cradled the baby closer. Now that he'd embraced sweet Jesse, he never wanted to let her go.

"You planning on keeping Jesse all night?" demanded James.

Justin peered down at the sleeping infant, and warm tenderness filled his heart. "Probably. She didn't cry once in the church."

"Oh, she's the most well-behaved baby that ever was," gushed his ma. She'd gussied up in a cream suit, and her rose-and-lavender corsage matched her shoes and a beaded necklace. "Quite the little lady."

Jewel lifted one of Jesse's limp, pudgy arms. "Sumo wrestler, Ma."

"Then she's a lady sumo wrestler, yes, she is," Joy cooed before deftly scooping Jesse out of Justin's arms and wandering away.

"Hey," Justin protested, earning him a chuckle from his older brother and Brielle.

"Looks like someone's getting attached," Jewel teased before she threw her arms around him and squeezed hard. "You look good, Justin. And you've never brought a girl home before. Brielle must be special…"

Out of the corner of his eye, he glimpsed Brielle's face flame with color. A log popped in the sudden, uncomfortable hush.

"Justin couldn't drive himself here," his practical brother proclaimed, easing them past the awkward moment. "Not with his license still suspended. Lucky you don't need one to compete in the motor cross race tomorrow."

"What motor cross race?" Brielle's voice rose half an octave.

Justin swore beneath his breath.

"You didn't tell her, Justin?" Jewel's nose curled like she smelled something rotten.

"I was planning on telling you after the christening," he hurried to explain, unsettled by Brielle's dilated pupils and the rapid rise and fall of her chest. "It's a fund-raiser I participate in every year. Nothing ever happens."

"Except that year you broke your arm," Jewel supplied, not helping one bit. Whatever happened to family loyalty?

"If you don't want me to participate, I

won't," he offered then held his breath, hoping she wouldn't try to clip his wings. He already felt like a fallen angel.

Brielle's eyes darted from one Cade to the other, then she nodded slowly. "I think Sofia needs help with the cake." She hurried off.

Justin started after her then jerked to a stop when the kitchen door opened and a tall man ducked inside. "What's he doing here?"

James turned and Jewel eased away as Boyd Loveland doffed his hat and strode across the room to Joy. "We invited him."

"No one told me."

"We didn't even know you were coming until yesterday," Jared said as he wandered over. He adjusted Justin's tie and smoothed down one side of his collar.

Justin shoved his fussing brother's hand away. He was no peacock. Besides, there were more pressing matters than his appearance. An archenemy had just crossed their threshold. A Loveland on Cade turf. Dad would be turning over in his grave...especially at the way Ma was smiling up at Boyd, wide-eyed and twinkly, in a way Justin had never seen her smile at their stern, sober father.

"Better get used to it." James accepted a slice of cake from Sofia with a thank-you then cut into it with the side of his fork. "He's close to being our stepfather."

Justin's body went hot then cold then numb. "He promised he wouldn't propose without all of our support."

Jared shrugged. "Boyd's nearly got everyone on board."

"Jewel won't ever say yes," Justin insisted, eyeing his sister as she sat cross-legged on the floor with Javi beside a large train set, his brother Jack's eight-month-old son on her lap.

"She already has," Amberley surprised him by saying as she approached, Petey leading the way.

The black-and-white rescue dog butted his wet nose against Justin's clenched hand.

"What? How?" Justin scratched behind Petey's ears, a hard heaviness roiling his gut.

Amberley leaned in and lowered her voice. "No one knows for sure since she's not saying…but it happened after Heath talked to her between sets during his performance last weekend."

"Heath?" Justin and his brothers chorused.

"She likes him the least of all the Lovelands," Justin added.

James nodded. "Remember how she used to tease him in school?"

"And she always gets upset whenever we

joke about her liking him. Unless..." Jared tapped his chin. "Unless we're too close to the truth."

"Have all the women in our family lost their minds?" Justin exploded, and Petey woofed at his frustrated tone.

"Hey," protested Amberley. "I take exception to that, considering I'll be a Cade woman this summer."

Jared nuzzled her neck. "The wedding can't come soon enough."

"Looks like you're alone, Justin," James mumbled around a mouthful of cake, his lips purple from the frosting roses.

Justin's shoulders hunched and the old, familiar isolation of the past returned. "What else is new?"

"You could change your mind," Jared said, nonchalant, like people did that every day. Like it was easy.

"Never."

"You'd stand in the way of Ma's happiness?" James demanded, his features tight, the ends of his cropped hair practically crackling with electricity. "You've done some wrong things, made some bad choices, brother, but this might be the most low-down, meanest thing you've ever—"

James cut off and stared at someone behind Justin's back.

"Your brother has a right to his own mind," Boyd Loveland said, coming to Justin's defense.

Justin spared the older man a brief, grudgingly appreciative look then strode out onto the back porch. He leaned against the railing and stared up at white-capped Mount Sopris. In a flash, he was eleven years old again, standing with his dying father in this very spot.

"You see the top of that mountain?" his pa said through a long, rattling cough. "Any time you want to talk to me, I'll be up there, watching over you."

"That's not heaven," Justin had protested, fighting with his parent even then, frustrated and disbelieving his larger-than-life, tougher-than-boot-leather father couldn't lick his illness.

"It's heaven to me," his pa countered. "Every blade of grass, every tree, hill, stream and mountain, they're all God's creations, just like us. I believe when we pass, we become a part of that miracle. I'm not afraid to die."

"I'm not, either," Justin had vowed, though he was frightened, scared to death, to lose his father. Not that he'd show it.

"Good," his pa had said, clapping him on the

back. "Because I want your promise to look out for Jesse."

"Why?"

"Because you're the stronger twin. I'll rest easier knowing you'll watch over your brother when I'm gone."

A burst of laughter erupted inside the house, dragging Justin back to the present.

"Sorry, Pa." White clouds punctuated his words as he spoke to the mountain. "But that was too big of a promise for an eleven-year-old to make. I did my best, and I hope, somehow, you might still be proud of me…proud of what I'm doing now to turn things around, to do right."

"If you were my son, I'd be proud," Boyd said, joining him at the railing. He handed Justin his leather jacket.

Justin stared at the coat, grabbed it then shoved his cold arms through its sleeves before zipping it up. "I'm not your son. And you're not my father."

"I'd never want to take your dad's place."

"But you want to marry Ma."

"That's different."

"You'd be replacing my father as her husband."

"I don't see it that way. Joy and I had our

own relationship before your pa came into the picture."

"I already heard about how a mix-up separated the two of you, then Pa stepped in." Justin flicked his hand impatiently, wishing he could shove Boyd off the porch and out of their lives. He sucked in a deep breath to calm down before he said anything else. His temper cooled, just like Dr. Sheldon promised.

"Have you heard about how your ma and I first got together?"

"No."

"Wanted nothing to do with her at first." Boyd's voice lowered and grew fainter, as if he'd jumped back in time and spoke from the past. "She was a tiny thing. Scrawny. A couple years younger than me. Big eyes and a nervous smile. My friends called her my shadow because she trailed me around everywhere I went, especially after she kissed me when we got stuck in a closet playing seven minutes in heaven."

"Ma chased you?" Justin scoffed.

"She was terribly persistent." Boyd let out a long, suffering sigh, a hint of amusement running through the white plume of air.

"I don't believe you."

"Have you ever known your ma to take no for an answer?"

Justin turned and studied the merry group through the porch window. Ma still held baby Jesse while she cut slices of cake with her free hand. "No," he admitted.

"I knew, straight off, to keep my distance. She wasn't a casual dating kind of gal, and I was too young to get tied down. Some people called me wild back in the day." Boyd leaned against a pole and stared at the lowering sun riding through swells of clouds.

"What happened?" Justin asked when the silence stretched too long, curious now, despite himself.

"Homecoming dance my senior year. I'd been crowned homecoming king and scored the winning touchdown against our rivals. I felt invincible. Untouchable. Then your ma asked me to dance."

"You turned her down," Justin guessed, bristling on his mother's behalf.

"First time." Boyd rubbed his hands together then blew on his fingers. "Second and third time, too."

"You made a fool of her!"

"When I saw some gals laughing at her, I got angry, so I asked her."

"You took pity on her?"

"It was more complicated than that." A smile curled Boyd's mouth, and his eyes took on a faraway look. "She was real pretty that night. I still remember her dress. Yellow with beaded straps. It kind of floated around her like a cloud. She'd done her hair different, too. Usually she wore it long and straight, but that night, she'd pulled it up on the sides and curled it. I remembered thinking how pretty her ears were." Boyd laughed to himself. "Funny the things you remember."

Justin nodded, thinking about the first time he'd seen Brielle, how'd he'd thought her an angel ready to usher him into the afterlife.

"When we hit the floor, the band swung into a slow tune. She put her arms around my neck and smiled up at me, her eyes big and dreamy, and I said to her, 'I'm not falling in love with you.' She just kept smiling."

Boyd scrubbed a hand over his eyes, and a short laugh escaped him. "But I did. As soon as I held her, I knew she was the one."

"You knew that quick?"

"It was more a feeling than a knowing."

Justin stopped breathing, his love for Brielle pounding through him.

Boyd was right. Love had no rhyme or reason. It didn't care about timing or convenience. And once created, it could never be destroyed. Events might pull them apart, but his feelings for Brielle would remain, just as Boyd and Joy had never stopped loving each other all these years.

He would not be another obstacle to their happiness. His chest inflated as he gulped the fortifying cold air. "I support you proposing to Ma." Justin stuck out his hand.

Boyd stared at him, hardly seeming to breathe, then he gripped Justin's hand and pumped it, a firm handshake, communicating strength, steadiness, commitment. "Thank you. It means more than I can say. I won't ever try to replace your pa, but I hope you don't mind me saying I'm proud of you, son."

Boyd pivoted and disappeared into the house, his broad smile nearly splitting his face in two. Justin peered through the window and spotted Brielle surrounded by his ma, Amberley, Sofia and Jack's wife, Dani. She'd somehow wrangled the baby from his mother, and the sight of her holding a child, his kin, turned his heart to pulp.

Then the mountain drew his eye again, and he pictured Jesse's globe, the pins marking the spots they'd planned to see.

Healing untethered him from Carbondale, and the distant horizon beckoned. His old, dark need to challenge life was replaced with the desire to explore it, to enjoy it and live it to its fullest.

Yet he wanted a life, a family with Brielle, too.

Could cautious Brielle love a man with an adventurous side? He recalled her unsettled reaction to tomorrow's motor cross race. She feared risks, injury, the unknown, and wanted a more secure, predictable life. Did that extend to a partner, too?

Pain brought them together; would his healing now drive them apart?

CHAPTER FIFTEEN

BRIELLE PULLED THE staple gun's trigger, embedding an open-house flyer on the bulletin board beside the motor cross's covered ticket booth. She stepped back and swiped at the icy rain pelting her face as a steady drizzle fell from a dark gray sky. In the distance, engines whined as racers completed practice runs, the noise more chilling than the freezing water dripping down her collar.

Shouldn't they cancel the race? Cold dread shivered through her as she imagined Justin among the pack. What if he got hurt or worse? Justin's brother had offered to drive him, but she'd wanted to come and support him, despite her fears. Somewhere along the way, she'd fallen head over heels for him and needed to demonstrate those feelings, even if she didn't dare voice them yet.

Accepting his mother's impending engagement last night showed his progress in therapy, healing old wounds and breaking negative habits. She wanted to meet him halfway and prove she'd changed, too. If she couldn't handle his risky, adventurous lifestyle, the future she envisioned for them might disappear. She shoved down the terrifying thought. She loved Justin and had to make this work.

A whistle shrilled behind her.

"Maverick Loveland's competing? In Carbondale?" asked a teenage boy, eyeing the flyer advertising the matchup between the PBR world champion and Justin.

At her nod, the boy whipped around to face his frowning father. "Can we go?"

His parent yanked money from his pocket and slid it across the ticket booth counter. "Too expensive."

"No, it's not, it's free. See!" The teenager pointed to the flyer and shook his dripping bangs back from his eyes. "Says right here. Free. Plus, there's food. Roping, barrel racing. Please, Pa!"

Brielle scanned the parking lot, watching the streaming race goers splash through puddles as they hurried to the first heat. Was Justin finished with his practice run? He'd promised to meet her here, but waiting for him while this family argued was making her all kinds of uncomfortable.

"There's other stuff there I don't want you around." The man pocketed his change and tickets, avoiding Brielle's eye. Fine by her. She didn't want intolerant people at her open house…but what if no one came? What if the town shunned the event and voted against keeping Fresh Start's charter?

"There's kids in school that do drugs," challenged the boy, his red-marked chin jutting. "Lots get counseling. You don't stop me from going to school."

"He's got a point, Jeb." A woman arrived holding a ladybug-print umbrella, her young daughter planted on her hip. "We can't protect him from everything."

"Who's doing drugs?" Jeb demanded, but his son clamped his mouth and shook his head, mutinous.

"Fine," Jeb relented then whirled to face Brielle and jabbed a finger in her face. "But if any of them weirdos pull a stunt like on Halloween, I'll ride you out of town personally."

"The heck you will," growled Justin, shoving between them. His aggressive advance backed the other man up fast, his face blanching. "You ever threaten Ms. Thompson, or any of the fine people at Fresh Start, I won't be riding you out of town, I'll be throwing you out on your—"

"Justin," Brielle interrupted, pulling down his raised fist. "Everyone's entitled to their opinion. I hope we can change yours at the open house tomorrow," she said to the man and his family, mustering a half smile. It was the best she could do with her nerves scraped and raw, a painful sensation intensifying as Justin's race time neared.

"Well, now." The man spat a brown stream at the ground. "At least someone knows how to be civil."

"Any time you want a lesson in manners, I'd be glad to teach you," snarled Justin as the family beat a hasty retreat.

"You've certainly won their vote, Mr. Congeniality," she teased, her smile wavering then fading as she took in Justin's bright padded racing suit and the helmet tucked under his arm. How much protection did they provide?

"He can take his vote and—"

"You ready to ride?" asked Cole, joining them. Streams of light rain snaked down the clear plastic goggles he'd pulled over his open-faced helmet.

"You ready to get beat?" Justin rejoined, his handsome mouth, perfectly shaped like the rest of his flawless features, lifted in a taunting smile. Brielle caught herself staring at Justin's gorgeous, chiseled face and almost wished back his beard. Like Doreen said, looking at him was like peering directly at the sun; it scrambled her brain.

"Should be asking you that question." Cole led them past the entrance through a muddy back field toward the course.

The sopping ground stained her jeans' hem brown, the moisture-filled air frizzing the ends of her hair. It was a light rain, but enough to seep through everything. The wet chill froze her hands, and she shoved them deep in her pockets.

How would Justin hang on to his bike in this slippery mess? An image of him lifting his fingers from his motorcycle bars, moments before he'd slammed into her moving van, stabbed her between the eyes.

No.

That was a long time ago.

He'd been a different person then—someone who didn't care if he lived or died. Now he had a reason to live…didn't he?

Although you haven't told him you love him yet, a voice inside said.

True. An omission she'd rectify after the race and the open house, when her panic had subsided, allowing her to think more clearly.

"See you at the riders' meeting, stepbrother!" Cole boomed then jogged off toward a huddle of riders gathered at the start of the course.

"They're not married yet!" Justin shouted after him, shaking his head.

"Did Boyd propose?" Brielle drew the strings of her hood tighter around her wet face.

"You look cute like that." Justin pulled on his helmet and goggles. "And not that I've heard."

"Cute?" She glanced down at her drenched, stained jeans and her shapeless rain parka, flattered by the outrageous compliment. "Never known you to be a liar."

He pressed the tip of her nose with a gloved finger. "Cute. Like a bundled baby."

"I think you've got baby fever."

"Can't deny starting a family's been on my mind lately." His hazel eyes gleamed down at her through his plastic googles, steady and certain.

Her mouth dried up, and her heart beat double time. "Why?"

He stepped closer and sank his gloved hands into her pockets, gathering her chilled hands in his. "You make me want to live, to have a life...with you."

"Justin," she sighed, breathless, her knees dipping slightly as she melted at his proclamation. "Please don't race."

He stiffened and slowly withdrew his hands. Someone with a bullhorn announced the first heat's start time in ten minutes. "We'll talk later," he promised. "Nothing's going to happen. Look." He turned and showed her a large patch with Fresh Start's name and logo sewn on the back of his suit. "I'm wearing your colors, m'lady. So, wish me good luck. I need your blessing."

His eyes twinkled down at her, mirroring the brilliant smile lighting up his face. He was in his element here, amid the scents of diesel, burning rubber and adrenaline-fueled testosterone. But she was in misery. His blessing request reminded her of soldiers who'd asked the same thing before heading out to battle... and then never returned—at least, not alive.

"Good luck," she choked out. "And be careful!" she called as he jogged away after a last reassuring hand squeeze.

Please, please, please, she thought, her eyes raised to the dripping sky, wanting to cry along with it.

Moments later, she huddled with the sodden group crowding the muddy track. Flags, buffeted by the chill wind, flapped along its sack-lined course. Engines sputtered and revved as the drivers sat astride their bikes at the gated starting line. Across the way, Justin's family waved at her and she returned the gesture, jerking her lips into a smile, wishing she could feel as excited as they looked, cheering and holding a sign spelling out Justin's name.

Her heart felt full of ice when she spotted Justin in the middle of the pack. He stared straight ahead, his lean body taut as a wire and angled forward. Even from this distance, she sensed his intense concentration, his fierce drive to win.

Just make it through in one piece...

Come back to me...

She pushed back against the images of men who hadn't returned to her base, the door to her dark past cracking open.

Somewhere far away, thunder rumbled. The wind raced off the mountaintops, snatching off hats and flapping women's skirts. She spotted a couple of officials conferring while some of the riders swapped concerned looks. Would they cancel?

No.

An official shook his head and strode back to the starting line. The wind picked up, pelting the assembly with stinging cold rain. She realized she was cradling her elbows like she was hugging herself. She relaxed her arms and stood tall. Body language said a lot about you, and the last thing she wanted to do was look vulnerable in front of potential voters, especially after the Halloween debacle.

"Hey, Ms. Thompson." A dark-haired woman a couple of feet away waved. "Heard Maverick Loveland's coming to the open house."

Brielle strove to force words off her sluggish tongue. "That's right."

Another man smiled, revealing a crooked row of teeth. "I'll be there with my grandkids. Maverick's a hero around our place."

"Justin Cade used to give him a run for his money," someone volunteered. "Can't wait to see those old rivals throw down."

The crowd's answering, bloodthirsty roar deepened her trepidation. She struggled to watch Justin in a motor cross race today. How would she handle seeing him astride a raging thousand-pound bull?

She willed back the sting rising in her eyes.

"If Maverick supports Fresh Start, so should we," a middle-aged man mumbled, chewing his way through a bag of sunflower seeds.

"Vote's in a couple of days," the brunette reminded the group. "Everyone needs to come out and vote."

Brielle nodded, appreciating the support. Hopefully a large attendance at the open house would equal a big—and favorable—turnout for the charter vote.

"What's the holdup?" asked the snacking

man, nodding to the riders revving their engines on the start line.

"An official's walking the track to make sure it's safe," someone supplied.

"I've seen worse," another attendee grumbled then shouted, "Let's go already!"

Cowbells clanged along with the man's shout while others whistled and hooted. Why couldn't Brielle be as excited?

Because you've seen too much...

Plumes of white exhaust billowed from the waiting riders' bikes. Justin hadn't shifted an inch, his eyes still aimed dead ahead, despite the bustle of race officials. At last, one of them waved and, without any fanfare, the half gates lowered and the competitors blazed off the line, engines gunning.

Her ears filled with the mechanical roar, and her heart leaped to the back of her throat. It clung there, beating frantically. She tracked Justin's blue-and-white suit as he zoomed to the head of the pack, Cole hot on his wheels. They zipped along a hairpin turn then ripped up a steep hill.

"Face of that's rutted," someone exclaimed.

"Tracked right up," came swift agreement.

At the crest, Justin launched his bike, whizzing through the air lightning fast, before his front wheel, then the rest of the bike, touched ground without losing his breakneck speed.

"That boy will kill himself," someone swore, and Brielle pressed her shaking lips.

"And break his mother's heart," another answered.

Brielle tuned them out, her eyes peeled on Justin as he whipped around another sharp turn, narrowly avoiding a mud patch that dragged down a rider behind him. Cole, however, now drew even with Justin, the pair increasing their lead as they sped into a higher incline.

"Can't they go around that?" she gasped, not realizing she spoke out loud until someone answered.

"Not if they plan on winning."

Her lungs stilled as Justin gunned straight over the top, standing in his seat as he went airborne, before bouncing back down to the course. How did he keep his seat at such a crazy speed?

"Nice block pass!" the sunflower eater shouted when Justin passed Cole in a corner, forcing his rival to slow down and fall slightly behind.

"Way to go, Cade!" shouted the teenage boy Brielle met earlier. *"Brraap..."*

A series of three shorter jumps loomed

in the final turn of the first lap. Justin led, trailed by Cole and an advancing group who'd made up time on the last jump. The crowd screamed as the pack raced through the triple then gasped when one of the riders came up short and landed on the back side of the obstacle.

"He cased it!"

"Here comes medical."

"Looks like he busted his nose."

Brielle fixed her eyes on Justin, trying not to focus on the injured, bleeding rider.

Please, please, please...one more lap to go...

The diminished group barreled around another ninety-degree turn, and Cole edged out Justin just before the next jump. His rear wheel kicked up mud, spraying Justin full force, obscuring his vision. A sinking sensation dragged her stomach to the boggy ground. Justin wouldn't take second to a Loveland, even if he had called a temporary truce last night.

Justin let out his throttle, his bike leaping forward, wheels barely touching ground. When he launched over the next hill crest, his body and head bent low over his handlebars to pick up speed. He and Cole banged to the ground at the same moment.

"Go, Cole!"

"Get him, Justin!"

The crowd had clearly picked their favorites, and it was anyone's guess who'd win given how evenly the pair was matched. Another insane turn appeared, and this time Justin zipped slightly ahead then tapped his brakes, slowing Cole's momentum so that he faltered, wobbled and nearly lost his balance. The rest of the racers streaked by Cole, hot after Justin, who now commanded the lead.

Despite everything, excitement mounted inside Brielle. Watching Justin expertly navigate the treacherous field was exhilarating, his skill, confidence and daring on full display. Maybe she should have more faith in him and trust his promise nothing would happen to him. He looked invincible.

On the next jump, Justin twisted his bike in midair, a showy feat earning him wild cheers from his growing fans.

"Goon ridin'," a voice roared from the back of the crowd.

At last, Justin approached the final obstacle, the triple jump, and her tight chest eased as the finish line loomed. He flashed over the first two bumps effortlessly and pumped his fist, catching the cheering crowd's mood.

Then his bike splashed down into a mud puddle, his wheel sinking instantly before he could steer it away. He flew over the handlebars and slammed into the ground. A scream ripped from her throat and she rushed to the track, halting when Cole skidded to a stop. He blocked Justin, protecting him, as the rest of the racers careened around them while warning flags waved.

Cole helped Justin up, and the pair dashed off the field. Dizzy and disoriented, she wobbled one step, two, then her knees gave out.

She sank to the ground and the world turned black on the edges, tunneling down, down, down until only a tiny prick of light remained, then—nothing.

"BRIELLE!" JUSTIN GENTLY tapped her ashen cheek as she lay motionless on a sofa inside a nearby RV. Minutes ago, he'd snatched her limp body from the ground and carried her to the makeshift medical spot, feeling every one of his trembling muscles, every staggering step, every struggling breath. Had his accident caused her to faint? To relive her time in Afghanistan and trigger her PTSD?

Pain radiated from his right wrist, but he ignored it, his eyes fixed on Brielle's motionless face. "Wake up, sweetheart."

"Should I call an ambulance?" asked Cole, poking his head through the door.

Justin opened his mouth to say yes then noticed Brielle's lashes flutter. Slowly her lids lifted, and she stared at Justin blankly, as if he were a stranger.

"Brielle? It's me, Justin."

Her eyes welled, pain shading them a dark forest green. "Justin's dead."

Her anguish stung his heart to a stop. He never wanted to cause her suffering. She'd already endured so much. "No, I'm not darlin'. I'm right here."

"Ambulance?" Cole prompted from the door.

"No. She's awake now."

"I'll be outside if you need me." The door slammed shut behind Cole.

Justin gathered Brielle's small, cold hands in his. "Do you know where you are?"

She looked up at the ceiling. A tear sparkled on her lashes. "No."

"We're in a medical RV at the racecourse. You fainted."

"I—I don't remember."

"What's the last thing you recall?"

When she pushed herself up on the cushions, he slipped his arm around her shoulders and supported her, careful not to jostle his aching wrist. A moment later, she nestled against him and he breathed in the subtle raspberry scent of her shampoo.

"You were thrown off your bike." Her entire body shook, and he pulled her onto his lap gently, cradling her close, pressing her head to his chest.

"But I'm all right."

She shook her head slowly, looking down. A tear dropped onto her jeans. "You could have been killed."

"There was little chance of that."

"But the possibility existed."

"It always does, no matter what we do in life. Last year Carl Letty fell off a ladder cleaning his drainpipe and broke his neck. Year before that, Martha Clearmont slipped on icy pavement crossing the street and got run over by a car. Then there was a silo incident with—"

"Stop." Her lips moved against his shirt fabric. "I don't want to hear any more about death."

"It's a fact of life."

"You think I don't know that?" she rasped. "I lived with it day in and day out in Kandahar."

"That was an extreme situation. Not reality."

"It was *my* reality."

"Not anymore."

"Yes, it is," she insisted, her voice low and tight, as though forced through a tiny straw. "I can't handle it, Justin. Today proved it."

"Handle what?" he asked, already suspecting the answer, dread settling hard and heavy in his gut.

"Danger. Thrills. Whatever you want to call them. It's not exciting for me. It's torture."

"What are you saying?"

"If that's a part of your life, I can't be in it." The sadness in her voice was the sound of heartbreak, splintering him in two.

"You want to keep me in a box? Clip my wings?"

"You make living a quiet, safe life sound terrible."

"It wouldn't be terrible, but I wouldn't be happy. I want to live, not hide."

"You said you wanted a family, marriage…"

"I do, but…"

"It's not enough." Brielle scooted away. Her face looked tired and drawn. From the circles under her eyes, Justin was pretty sure she was near her breaking point—a condition he'd created.

His body turned numb with remorse. "I want both."

"Both isn't possible. Not with me."

"What if someone had prevented you from enlisting? Said you weren't allowed to—"

"I risked my life for something bigger than myself," she interrupted, fury giving her voice authority. "To serve and protect my country.

I held up my hand and said, 'I'm willing to die for America.' But you. You're doing it for thrills."

"Once, yes. I wanted to feel something, anything after Jesse passed. But before I lost him, I was always chasing an adventure. I once told you Jesse wanted to climb those mountains more than me, but I wasn't honest with myself. I wanted to scale all of them, just as bad. Even Mount Everest."

She slid farther across the seat. Now there was an energy around her. The air all but hummed. "That's one of the world's deadliest mountains."

"Yes."

"You're still trying to cheat death." She trembled and her hands clenched into fists.

"No. I want to live life to the fullest, and I can't do that hiding out in Carbondale, unable to leave it like when I felt tied to Jesse."

"You'd choose Mount Everest over me?"

"You said you wanted me to live, and it can't be just for you—I see that now—or for Jesse, but for myself. I choose freedom over suffocation."

Her harsh intake of air cracked in the cramped space. "That's how you see me, someone who'd smother you?"

"Not on purpose." He tried to lace his fingers in hers. When she snatched them away, he winced.

"Are you hurt?"

"Just my wrist." He waved his good hand. "I'll have it checked later."

"Then you're not bull riding tomorrow."

Something inside him fluttered like captive wings. "Why wouldn't I?"

"Because you won't be able to hang on."

"I'll use my other hand."

"No. As head of the facility, I forbid it."

"And disappoint all the people coming to see me and Maverick square off? We need their goodwill and their votes." This time when he reached for her with his uninjured hand, she didn't pull away.

"I need you alive. I need you safe with me."

He looked down at their entwined hands. He found himself staring at them, as if he had to memorize how hers felt against his. "I need you, too, but I wouldn't feel alive if I always played it safe. That's not me."

"I'm not enough, then." Brielle's gaze met his and slid away.

Grief, longing and regret swelled in the silence. A strange panic rose inside him, and he thought she must have felt it, because she squeezed his fingers.

"I'm not enough," she repeated, her voice waterlogged, her lashes spiked.

"No." The admission kicked its way out of him, bruising his heart, cracking his ribs, scratching his throat out so every part of him hurt. For most of his life, he'd been part of a pair. Therapy had taught him how to live without Jesse.

Strange how he'd finally learned to live without Jesse, discovered his own identity, and now must figure out a path forward without Brielle. But he couldn't just be part of another duo. He had to discover himself, regain his identity, if he was ever to be whole.

Brielle began to pull away, but he tightened his grip. He didn't want to let her go. He felt like a magnet gone awry, being pulled between two poles.

He leaned forward and kissed her, like people kiss at train stations and airports, full of love and desperate longing, kisses meant to last the weeks, the months, the years, the lonely forever ahead. With that kiss, he tried to tell her how much she meant to him. He tried to show her that she was the answer to a question he hadn't even known he'd been asking.

"Stop." She pressed her palms against his chest and eased away. "I don't know what you want."

"I'm hoping you'll want me to be me," he said, trying to ignore his pounding, aching heart. "More than you want to stash me in some bubble. I wouldn't be able to breathe in it."

"And I can't breathe outside that bubble…" Her voice dropped. "Or while worrying about you out of it. Today proved that, though I tried, Justin. I tried."

He pushed a lock of hair back from her eyes, and her face crumpled. "You did, sweetheart, and that means a lot."

"So neither of us gets what we want." Brielle's voice cracked, and her eyes filled with tears.

"Not each other," he said hoarsely.

She placed her damp cheek against his, and he clenched his jaw and breathed in the scent of her, trying to embed some of that solidity into himself, to carry a bit of her with him, wherever he roamed.

As for his heart, it'd remain with Brielle. He'd given it to her, and there it'd stay.

She stood, let out a strangled "'bye" that might have been a sob or a cough or a gasp, and dashed outside.

He stared at the shut door, his feet stuck to the linoleum floor, processing that a part of him had been ripped loose and left him half a man. In a flash, he bolted to the door, shoved it open and clambered down the short stairs.

Cole stepped in front of him. "Let her go, buddy."

"Out of my way!" Cole matched Justin's sidestep, blocking him. "This isn't your business."

"Any woman in distress is my business," Cole said stoutly. "She said goodbye."

"How did you…" Justin looked over his shoulder and stared up at the RV's open windows. "You heard everything."

"Yes."

"Then you know why I can't let her go."

Cole folded his thick arms across his chest. "Are you going to ride tomorrow?"

Justin nodded.

"Still planning on climbing Mount Everest?" Cole's eyebrow rose.

Justin's back teeth ground together as he craned his neck, searching out Brielle. "What's your point?"

"If you love her, then let her go."

The simple, powerful statement hung in the space between them then exploded in Justin's chest, ripping him wide-open.

His head bowed, weighed by the truth of Cole's words.

He loved Brielle, and because he loved her, he had to let her go.

Dr. Sheldon told him no one moves on without a backward look. You moved on always carrying with you those you'd lost. Justin had learned how to carry Jesse, not as a burden, a weight keeping him stuck in the same place. Jesse's presence now felt like a gift.

Would he ever come to think of Brielle that way?

The resounding answer, *no*, crashed through him. With Jesse, he'd had no choice but to let go. Brielle's loss was a self-inflicted wound, one that'd never heal if he stayed away. On the other hand, he'd hurt her if he remained, his unhappiness at being hemmed in turning to arguments and resentment.

Better to leave it this way so she'd have a chance to move on, to be happy, to have the life she deserved, a life he longed to give her but knew he couldn't.

As for him, no matter how far he traveled, he'd never move on, not with his heart with Brielle, in Carbondale.

Tomorrow, he'd do everything in his power to deliver an unforgettable open house and rodeo show which would give her everything she wanted.

Everything but him.

CHAPTER SIXTEEN

"QUITE A TURNOUT," Craig Sheldon observed, handing Brielle the paper plates she'd requested after running through her third stack. He squinted at her in the bright sunshine while he pulled up his striped poncho's hood against the cool afternoon air. "Maverick Loveland's appearance did the trick."

"I can hardly believe it." She cut a wedge from one of the apple pies dotting the foldout table and slid it onto a plate. Doreen squirted a dollop of sweet cream. Next, Craig carved out a square of cheddar cheese, emitting a creamy, mouthwatering aroma, then placed it atop the pie before passing it the next person in line.

"Can I have pumpkin?" a middle school–aged boy asked, stepping forward. "And apple."

"Don't be greedy," chided his pregnant mother.

Brielle smiled at the woman who'd identified herself as a recovering alcoholic and pledged her support for Fresh Start at the first town hall meeting. "We've got plenty."

"Well, in that case, I'll have both as well, since I am eating for two. No cheese on mine, though. And extra cream, thanks." She rubbed her rounded stomach, and the small, serene smile playing on her lips filled Brielle with longing.

Would she ever have a child, a family, a partner to love?

Her eyes searched out Justin. Wearing fringed black leather chaps over faded jeans and a denim shirt stretched across his lean, muscular torso, his white cowboy hat contrasting with his dark hair and hazel eyes, he looked incredibly handsome. Soon, he'd ride against Maverick, yet he appeared completely unconcerned, despite his bandaged wrist, as he conversed animatedly with a group of stern-faced men. She recognized the rude father from the motor cross race among the group. Was Justin persuading them to vote for Fresh Start? Given their grudging nods, he was making headway.

Were others being convinced?

Today's high turnout boded well for the upcoming vote. Locals crowded the property, eating barbecue, playing horseshoes and sticking their heads through cutouts of cartoon characters painted on particle board for photo ops. Children lined up for face painting while women and men examined the arts and crafts tables, some purchasing the tooled leather belts, turquoise bolero ties and beaded jewelry the residents had created for the open house. A group of adolescents crowded Maya, who modeled studded black leather wristbands while Paul, wearing his combat fatigues, enthralled an older group as he assembled an unloaded AR-15 blindfolded. Everyone seemed to be having a good time.

Everyone but her.

Brielle should be over the moon, but instead she felt stomped flat, her heart still battered from yesterday's devastating conversation with Justin. Since the moment they'd met, she'd wanted to help him, heal him, and in so doing she had, ironically, given him the wings he needed to fly away from Carbondale.

From her.

She could travel with him, on her vacations, but not on the kinds of trips he'd want to take.

Mount Everest?

Hundreds of people died trying to scale it. And weren't there frozen casualties along the trail? She'd seen enough for one lifetime...

What was the saying?

Whither thou goest, I will follow... But she couldn't pledge this to Justin, and he wouldn't be happy trapped in Carbondale.

She'd been worried about abandoning him

the way she had her other charges once. But now he was leaving her, moving on, no longer needing her help, no longer a wounded man.

Did that mean she was the one still wounded?

"How about a break?" asked Cole, sliding behind the table with a young woman Brielle remembered seeing with the Lovelands at the town hall meeting.

"I'm fine." Idle hands were the devil's workshop. She'd have a devil of a time not imagining Justin trampled or worse in his imminent bull ride if she didn't stay busy. X-rays showed he'd sprained his wrist yesterday, yet he insisted on riding.

Stubborn, obstinate daredevil of a man.

"This is my sister, Sierra." Cole picked up a pie cutter and helped the next person in line.

"Howdy." A petite blonde with piercing blue eyes stuck out a hand. "We're excited to support Fresh Start. Cole's been raving about it."

"We've been lucky to have his help," Brielle said after a brief handshake, returning Sierra's warm, friendly smile.

"Dr. Loveland! Yoo-hoo!" shrilled a woman's voice.

"Oh, Lord, save me," muttered Sierra before she beamed a smile at the one-eyed pug's owner. "How do, Mrs. Leonard? I see Otis is doing fine."

"His hip is bothering him terrible. He needs me to carry him everywhere I go."

Otis wriggled against his owner's tight grip, half of his body smooshed into the folds of her torso.

"Would you like some pie?" Brielle pointed her cutter at the apple then the pumpkin.

"No, dear. I have to watch this figure or no one else will." She winked at Cole, who erupted in a red-faced coughing fit, then asked Sierra, "Would you mind giving Otis a checkup?"

"Right now?" Sierra passed a slice of pie to another visitor.

"Well…" Mrs. Leonard's tongue darted between her lips as her eyes lingered on the pies. "Maybe I will have just a sliver of apple first."

"Everything on it?" Brielle asked before sliding the wedge to a hovering Doreen.

"Yes. And pumpkin, too. But not too big. Just a sliver, now."

"Got it."

"But put some extra on for Otis, so I can share."

"Yes, ma'am."

Doreen rolled her eyes and Craig chuckled beneath his breath as they heaped the plate.

"Thank you, dears," trilled Mrs. Leonard.

"This really is quite the event. Now where were the patients you said Otis could help?"

"How about you and Otis lend a hand at the craft table?" Brielle pointed out the spot. "I bet that cute face of his will sell us out, and you can meet some of the residents."

"Wonderful! Dr. Loveland, I'll stop by your practice tomorrow. Otis has an important job to do today."

"Indeed, he does." Sierra smiled. "I'll see you then."

"Thought you specialized in wildlife." Cole doled out a huge cut of apple to a pint-size girl holding a stuffed pig.

"Otis is pretty wild." Sierra laughed.

"Cole, Sierra and Doreen have everything in hand," Craig said, catching Brielle's eye. "How about a stroll?"

Before she could refuse, he cupped her elbow and guided her through the throng to a stack of hay bales beside the horse stable. He removed his poncho, laid it over the rough straw and gestured for her to sit.

"Why do I feel like I've just been called to the principal's office?" Brielle perched on the stiff square. All around rose the pungent smell of horse manure mixed with fresh hay and sweet corn feed.

"Nothing that formal." Deep lines radiated

from the corners of Craig's eyes as he smiled. "Just wanted to check in with you."

"I'm fine." Her gaze flitted to Justin, who now spoke to a mountain-size man she recognized from the flyer photos. Maverick Loveland. A cluster of admirers hovered nearby, some holding paper and pens for an autograph.

"I heard you fainted at the motor cross race." Her head snapped around. "Who...?"

"Justin and I had a session this morning." Craig sat cross-legged on a hay bale, his eyes closed and his face lifted to the cloudless sky. With his open palms facing up, he looked ready to meditate, not chat.

"What else did he say about me?" As she watched, Maverick clapped Justin on the back and the two strode toward a corral encircled by filled risers. Seated attendees cheered wildly. In a few moments, they'd ride the bulls...

Her mouth vacuumed itself dry.

One eye cracked open. "You know I can't divulge that."

"Patient confidentiality," she affirmed, for the first time in her life hating rules.

"You care about him," Craig said without inflection. Or judgment. Like developing a personal attachment to a patient wasn't any big deal at all. As if it didn't break the biggest rule of all.

Her heart quivered, panic-stricken, as Justin and Maverick climbed up to the chute holding the bulls. "I care about all the facility's residents."

Craig popped both eyes open and studied her until she squirmed. "Fine." She tossed her hands in the air. "Yes. I have feelings for him."

"He returns them."

Mounted speakers interrupted her next question, announcing the start of the barrel-race competition. A moment later, Amberley appeared in the corral astride her horse and thundered around the course at breakneck speed. Her daring, flawless ride was jaw-dropping considering the genetic condition that left her legally blind. Justin had mentioned his brother Jared, a former NFL star, guided her using a walkie-talkie system.

It must take an incredible amount of trust to follow a partner, blind, into an extremely dangerous situation, yet Amberley made it look easy.

"Did Justin say he cared about me?"

Craig shook his head, his lids lowered again like a Zen Buddha…one she wanted to throttle for being so cagey. A horse nickered on the other side of the stable wall.

"Then how do you know?"

"It's my job to study people and emotions."

She waited for the cheers to die down as Amberley finished her race then asked, "How about everyone else? Do they know?"

"Yeah. I'd say they do."

She dropped her head in her cupped hands and groaned.

Craig tsked. "Anyone who looks at the two of you can tell you're in love."

"I might be," she gasped, "but…"

"Justin loves you."

Hope ballooned inside her, inflating until it butted against reality and burst. "It doesn't matter." Another barrel racer streaked onto the course to rip-roaring applause.

"Why?"

She scooched back on the hay bale to rest her back against the stable wall. "Because I have to let him go."

Craig plucked sticks of hay loose and began plaiting them. "What makes you feel that way?"

"He wants a life I can't handle." An invisible steel wire strung itself around her chest then tightened. The barrel racer thundered out of the corral as a pair of ropers entered. Her eyes widened when she recognized Paul and Justin.

"He's come a long way," affirmed Craig, professional pride ringing in his voice.

"Yes—maybe too far. He's left me behind,"

she admitted, eyeing Justin as he expertly tossed a lasso around a bolting heifer's head, checking its wild rush. An instant later, Paul unleashed his rope, snagging the kicking calf's ankles. Justin leaped off his horse and bound the thrashing animal in a movement so fast, it blurred.

Craig dropped to the ground and leaned forward, his fingers twisting one strand of hay over another and another in a repeating pattern. "You can catch up."

"How?"

"You shared your experiences to help others." His hands paused in their task. "How about talking about your past to help yourself?"

A moment passed, then two, before his meaning sank in. "You think I need therapy?"

"What would you tell yourself if you were one of your clients?"

She opened her mouth, then closed it, unable to formulate her tumbling thoughts into a coherent sentence. All the while, Craig continued braiding his straw plait as if he had all the time in the world. The cheering crowd snagged her attention again. Another pair of ropers, this time Jewel and Jared, expertly trapped and trussed a bellowing calf.

She knew how the poor, panic-stricken

creature felt. While in Kandahar, she'd been mostly trapped on its base, waiting for disaster to strike, never knowing how or when or where. The constant state of anticipation, of dread, had never left her. Sometimes she'd simply wished for a strike so she could stop worrying about it…crazy as it sounded.

Did she need therapy?

Unlike her fellow vets, she hadn't seen true combat… "I don't want to keep reliving the past—it needs to stay there," she said at last as James galloped into the arena and circled it atop a massive stallion, performing tricks in the saddle.

"What's behind that belief?"

"Because I can't find peace if I don't put it behind me." As she watched, James deftly switched sides in the saddle, touching the ground with his feet before popping up and over his horse. How many more acts before Justin's bull ride? She couldn't stick around to watch.

"Is it ever truly behind you if you don't deal with it?"

She thought of the advice she gave her patients and had only one answer. "No."

"And how do you feel when you consider a life without Justin?" Craig twisted his braid, forming a circle.

Miserable, her heart said before she could answer.

Craig continued looping and tucking his straw plait. "You can't go forward when obstacles from the past block the way."

"You're saying I need therapy." A couple of brightly dressed clowns appeared in the corral, catching her eye. One she recognized as Cole, while the other bore him enough of a resemblance to be another Loveland sibling. Her pulse sped. They had to be there for the bull riding.

"What do you think?"

She'd been so worried about falling apart and abandoning others if she relived the tragedies that triggered her breakdown, she'd abandoned herself in the process. Justin said he had to live his life for himself as well as for her. Devotion to another didn't mean giving up everything—it meant compromise, it meant work, it meant being true to yourself and each other.

Yesterday she'd panicked when he'd fallen off his dirt bike. She'd thought it meant she couldn't handle his life, but it'd really proved she hadn't learned how to cope with her own, despite all her experience counseling others how to do so.

She'd faced her past when she'd confessed

it to Paul and a listening Justin at the Halloween parade, but she hadn't dealt with it. She'd considered herself lucky for surviving the war unscathed, but she was wounded, too. Surviving and living weren't the same thing.

If she'd addressed her issues, worked through them, she might have coped better. She'd warned Justin she might never get better when they'd spoken in the church, but what steps had she taken to heal?

Physician, heal thyself...

"I want Justin. I want happiness."

A bell shrilled and metal clanged as a gate opened. Maverick shot out atop a wildly bucking bull, spinning in a blur of circles. Justin would be next. And she needed to be there for him. She wouldn't abandon him like she'd abandoned others. She wouldn't let her weakness get the better of her. Not when it came to Justin or anyone else. Including herself. Not ever again.

"How do you achieve happiness?"

"I need to deal with my past. Thank you, Craig." She kissed his cheek and sprinted across the field as Maverick flew off the gray beast. Clowns rushed in, waving their hands frantically to distract the enraged, twirling bull as the professional rider effortlessly leaped over the fence and out of harm's way.

"Justin!" she shouted when she reached the corral.

He stopped adjusting the rope attached to the black bull he straddled in the chute and looked up sharply. When his eyes met hers, they rounded in surprise.

"Good luck!"

The bell shrilled and the animal bolted, carrying Justin with him.

She forced her eyes to stay on Justin as he grappled to keep his seat atop the incensed animal. His bandaged hand swayed overhead, the other firmly gripping the rope. His body bent and leaned, forward then back, side to side, as the bull kicked, drove, stopped, spun then full-out sunfished, all four legs in the air, to dislodge Justin.

The moment they touched ground, the animal whirled in a head-snapping 360-degree turn, then jerked at whiplash speed in the opposite direction. Justin sailed through the air and crashed, headfirst, at the bull's stamping hooves.

The crowd screamed, and a sob flew from Brielle's mouth. She grabbed hold of the fence to keep herself upright, refusing to be weak.

"Justin!"

A flurry of hooves pounded over Justin's body before the clowns distracted the furi-

ous beast, driving it away from the motionless rider.

She ducked through the arena's fence and
rushed to an unconscious Justin's side. Blood
gushed from a deep thigh gash, and she yanked
off her scarf and tied it around his leg, her
breath rasping harsh in her throat. She'd seen
men bleed out in seconds without a tourniquet.

Please, please, please, she pleaded, *Lord,
save him.*

"Don't move him," cautioned Sierra, joining
her. "He might have a spinal injury."

Tears blurred Brielle's vision as she dog-
gedly maintained pressure on his wound. "I'm
here, sweetheart," she whispered in his ear. "I
love you."

Would he wake to hear her say it again?

Would he wake at all?

"You SHOULD GO home and get some sleep,
dear."

Brielle shook her head at Joy's advice and
raised stinging eyes to a heavily bandaged Justin. He lay beneath a white sheet, his hand,
strapped up to various monitors, lying motionless alongside his body. A foot-to-hip cast en-
cased his raised left leg, his head was swathed
in white gauze and a metal splint protected his
broken nose. After an emergency surgery to

repair his femoral artery last night, he'd briefly woken, then slipped back into unconsciousness, his brain recovering from trauma.

"You must need to eat. Can I get you anything?"

Brielle shook her head.

Joy's warm hand covered hers and squeezed. "Justin's tough as old boots, honey. He's going to pull through this."

"How do you know?"

"I have faith," she said simply, her expression grave, her eyes red rimmed and exhausted. "Call me as soon as he wakes. I hate to leave, but I've got to pick up a prescription for the baby and run it to the ranch. He and Sofia are still down with the flu. James texted and said Jewel's tire blew, but they'll be here shortly once they change it. Jared's at Amberley's race, but they're coming back, too, once she's finished. Will you be okay on your own for a bit?"

Brielle nodded, glum and guilt ridden since she'd thrown off Justin's concentration just before he went out on the bull, probably causing his accident.

Joy swooped down and hugged her briefly. "See you soon then, honey."

The door clicked shut behind Joy, snuffing

out the rattle of a wheeled medical cart and a nurse's greeting to Mrs. Cade.

When Brielle closed her eyes, she heard the crowd's screams again, the bellowing of the rampaging bull, the splintering of bones that cracked loud enough to be heard over the din, then the siren's wail.

She kept seeing Justin's wound—a messy, deep gash like she'd seen in the war…a living, pulsing thing, pumping out blood as if trying to rid him of it. Her jeans were still dark with it.

And she saw Justin's face, the moment after his fall when he briefly opened his eyes and looked at her. There had been concern, not for himself, despite being on the ground unable to move, but for her. He'd whispered, "Don't worry," before passing out again, his last conscious thought about her.

He wasn't her dark rider, but a white knight. She'd thought herself his rescuer when he'd been the one on the fatal day they'd crashed, heaven-sent to save her. To bring her out of the dark and into the light.

She sat motionless on the plastic chair because she didn't know how to do anything else. She'd stay by Justin's side, praying for a miracle, a second chance to make things right between them. She sank her head into her hands and listened to her breathing, in and out.

In and out. Her body smelled unfamiliar, of blood and antiseptic and something acrid left over from primal fear. She noticed her hands shook, but she wasn't sure if it was low blood sugar or exhaustion, and somehow the thought of trying to find food was way beyond her.

Movement was beyond her.

She closed her eyes and tried to remember what it felt like, a couple weeks ago, to lie in the hay beside Justin, how he'd held her tight, the reassuring scent of his warm shirt, the low rumble of his voice, sweet kisses he'd showered on her face.

This was what catastrophe did: it stripped away the white noise and the fluff, the *what if I,* and the *should I really?* She loved Justin. She knew it with a stinging clarity. She wanted to feel his arms around her, hear him talking as they sat atop Miracle Point and howled at the harvest moon. She wanted to lasso him right there in bed and pull him to her. She never wanted to be apart again. Whatever storms the world held, they'd face them together. Whatever mountains loomed, they'd scale them side by side.

Why hadn't she been able to tell him her feelings? Why had she wasted so much time worrying about what she couldn't control instead of what was important?

And then she let out an involuntary sob.

"Don't," a voice croaked.

Hope shoved her from the chair and over to Justin's bedside.

"Justin?"

His dark eyelashes fluttered then slowly lifted. Golden-green hazel eyes gleamed. "Am I dead?"

Tears welled in her eyes as she lifted his hand to her mouth and pressed a kiss on the back of his knuckles. "No."

"Good."

A small smile tugged up the corner of her trembling mouth. "Very good."

"How long?" he rasped.

"Since the accident?"

He nodded.

"Over twenty-four hours."

"The vote?"

A gasp burst from her. She'd forgotten the town was determining Fresh Start's fate today, her thoughts focused only on Justin. It figured her tough guy's first thought would be for someone, or something, other than himself.

"I haven't heard. I'm just relieved you're awake. I was so worried you might not…" She stopped, unable to finish the thought.

"I'm tough." His fingers skimmed over the bandages covering his head as his eyes flitted down to his cast leg. "How do I look?" Despite everything, a glimmer of amusement lightened his eyes, only making her cry harder.

"Invincible."

"No, that's you."

Was that how he saw her, despite her fears, her hiding, her avoidances? Crazy. "Want some water?"

He nodded, wincing at the small motion, then gently but firmly took the cup she held and brought it to his mouth. After a long sip through the straw, he passed it back.

"We have to stop meeting like this," he said, his voice stronger, clearer. He slid farther up the pillow to peer at her more directly.

She recalled the first time she'd seen him, inert on the highway, semiconscious and injured, and she smiled, despite everything.

"I thought you were dead," she whispered.

"Heard the nurses talking this morning. Seems some amazing woman who shouldn't have been in the arena slowed my blood loss."

Her face contorted as she strove to stop the steady drip of tears. "Some amazing woman, huh?"

"Yes, she is." He extended his free arm out

to the side and crooked his fingers. "Come here."

It was all the invitation she needed. Gingerly, she stretched out on the bed beside him. She closed her eyes, feeling the warmth of his skin against her cheek. Underneath the chemical disinfectant smell emanating from his body, she breathed in Justin, the warm spicy scent assuring her he was alive. That he was here with her.

She didn't think about anything. She just let herself exist in the moment, the deep, deep pleasure of being there next to him, of feeling the weight of him beside her, the space he took up in her world.

She shifted her head and kissed the firm skin on the inside of his arm and felt his fingers trace their way gently through her hair.

"You wished me good luck."

"Yes." She let out a long, shaky breath. "I wanted to see you ride, but I never should have distracted you. You got hurt because of me."

"My pride and ego are to blame, not you. I shouldn't have done it with a bum wrist. It was reckless and stupid. I could have died. Triggered your PTSD."

"You did it for Fresh Start, for Jesse and yourself. Besides, I was too worried about you to fear anything else." Her voice was so calm, she almost laughed.

Then she did.

Justin stiffened, taken aback at her reaction. It might have been leftover shock. But she wanted to think it was because she suddenly understood she wasn't afraid of anything anymore.

"You saved my life...twice," he murmured, his warm breath rushing over her temple.

She shook her head. "No. You saved me. It took me a while to see it, but I understand now."

"Understand what?"

"That you were heaven-sent the night we crashed, to rescue me."

"No. You were *my* angel."

She slid her arms around his neck, careful not to jostle him, reveling in the feel of his body close to hers. "And you were mine."

"I recall you said something else in the arena."

Her heartbeat thudded so hard it practically shook her entire body. "I did. I love you, Justin," she breathed and laid her head against his muscular chest, unafraid of what it meant, how he'd react, what he'd say.

Oh. Please say you love me, too...

By living in the dark, hiding from pain,

she'd closed herself off from joy. From now on, she'd only live in the light. In the truth.

He looked at her then, as if he were drinking her in, and something inside her weakened with relief. "I love you, too, darlin'. With everything I am, which might not seem like much right now," he admitted with a rueful twist of his lips.

"You're everything," she said, crying and laughing, almost unable to take in what he was saying, her heart pounded so hard. "Everything to me."

"I'm not perfect, even at a hundred percent, but you saw past that and loved me anyway. Any time I needed you, you've been there."

"I fainted at the motor cross," she reminded him…and herself.

"But you were there, my love," he insisted, fervent.

"Well, let's not go overboard. I ended up on the ground like a lump," she joked, though her heart was just as soft and mushy as all her other parts were becoming.

He chuckled and then grimaced, as if laughing were painful. "Hey. You're talking about the woman I love."

She let those words sink in.

"I'm starting therapy to deal with my PTSD," she said, snuggling into the crook of his arm. "Reliving my past is less painful than a future without you. I can't make any promises about being able to do risky things, but I want to try."

"Just your trying is enough. Getting kicked in the head by a thousand-pound bull has a way of making you see sense. Puts things into perspective." One side of his mouth quirked. "Makes danger a tad less exciting."

"You asked me to want you for you, and I do. I never want you to change."

"Too late, darlin', because you've changed me," he told her huskily, his hand weaving through her long strands, pressing her to him. "You woke me and made me whole. I didn't know what I was missing until you showed me. I thought Jesse was my better half, but it was meant to be you, all along."

Their eyes locked, and in that moment, everything shifted. She saw she could be his center, his reason for living. And he was hers. She knew now she could be enough.

She took Justin's face in her hands and kissed him carefully, softly, as he pulled her into his arms, his hold strong and sure, as he kissed her back. Then she pressed her cheek against his, half laughing, half weeping, unmindful of the nurses chattering outside—

unmindful of anything except the incredible man beside her.

Her cell phone buzzed in her pocket. She yanked it out and gasped when she read the text.

"What is it?"

"Carbondale voted to keep Fresh Start's charter," she whispered. Her gaze found his.

He expelled a rush of air, and his eyes exploded with light. "Knew they had too much sense to let a good thing go." His arm tightened around her. "Like me."

"Whither thou goest..." she began.

"I will go," he finished for her, his voice deep and full of promise. Somehow Brielle had never heard anything more beautiful.

"I want to climb those mountains with you."

"Are you gonna start singing that nun song from *The Sound of Music*?" His breath stirred the hair at the crown of her head.

A chuckle escaped her. Oh, how she loved her sarcastic cowboy. "Lord, no."

"Good. I have better plans for that beautiful mouth." His eyes twinkled down at her devilishly. "We'll hike the peaks on our vacations."

"You're going to keep working the Cade ranch?"

"And at Fresh Start. Carbondale's my home.

Especially now that you're in it. You'll marry me." It wasn't a question but a statement of fact.

"Yes," she breathed happily.

"Children?"

"As many as we can handle."

The bandage above his eyes rose as he lifted an eyebrow. "I can handle a lot," he teased with a smile of intense satisfaction.

"I'm counting on it," she said shakily and raised her head to meet his descending mouth. Her lips parted under his, and blood rushed through her veins as he kissed her tenderly, passionately. No longer did she question whether she'd break down again. She'd found her center of strength, and it was rooted in love, in Justin. Love made her strong, for Justin and for herself, for those she'd lost and those she'd gained.

Her arms encircled his broad chest, returning his kiss until she lost track of everything except Justin, the heat and softness of his lips and the incredible joy bursting inside her like fireworks. Red. Yellow. Green. Gold. She melted against him, heart utterly light.

Possessively, his hand slid down the curve of her back and gripped her waist. He shuddered and buried his head in her neck. "I'll make you the happiest woman on this planet," he vowed. "I promise you that *and* the world."

"I promise you forever."

He drew back, and his warm eyes studied her intently. "It'll do," he whispered, lowering his mouth again until it hovered a breath away from hers. "For starters…"

* * * * *

*Be sure to check out the next book
in Karen Rock's*
ROCKY MOUNTAIN COWBOYS *miniseries
coming out later this year.*

*And if you missed the previous titles,
now's the perfect time to catch up!*

*CHRISTMAS AT CADE RANCH
FALLING FOR A COWBOY*

Also, don't miss these other great reads!

*A COWBOY TO KEEP
UNDER AN ADIRONDACK SKY
HIS KIND OF COWGIRL*

*All available now from
Harlequin Heartwarming.*

Get 2 Free Books,
Plus 2 Free Gifts—
just for trying the Reader Service!

Love Inspired®

Get 2 Free Books,

Plus 2 Free Gifts—

just for trying the Reader Service!

LIS17R3

HOME on the RANCH

YES! Please send me the **Home on the Ranch Collection** in Larger Print. This collection begins with 3 FREE books and 2 FREE gifts in the first shipment. Along with my 3 free books, I'll also get the next 4 books from the Home on the Ranch Collection, in LARGER PRINT, which I may either return and owe nothing, or keep for the low price of $5.24 U.S./ $5.89 CDN each plus $2.99 for shipping and handling per shipment*. If I decide to continue, about once a month for 8 months I will get 6 or 7 more books, but will only need to pay for 4. That means 2 or 3 books in every shipment will be FREE! If I decide to keep the entire collection, I'll have paid for only 32 books because 19 books are FREE! I understand that accepting the 3 free books and gifts places me under no obligation to buy anything. I can always return a shipment and cancel at any time. My free books and gifts are mine to keep no matter what I decide.

268 HCN 3760 468 HCN 3760

Name _____ (PLEASE PRINT)

Address _____ Apt. #

City _____ State/Prov. _____ Zip/Postal Code

Signature (if under 18, a parent or guardian must sign)

Mail to the **Reader Service:**

IN U.S.A.: P.O. Box 1867, Buffalo, NY. 14240-1867
IN CANADA: P.O. Box 609, Fort Erie, Ontario L2A 5X3

* Terms and prices subject to change without notice. Prices do not include applicable taxes. Sales tax applicable in NY. Canadian residents will be charged applicable taxes. This offer is limited to one order per household. All orders subject to approval. Credit or debit balances in a customer's account(s) may be offset by any other outstanding balance owed by or to the customer. Please allow 3 to 4 weeks for delivery. Offer available while quantities last. Offer not available to Quebec residents.

Your Privacy—The Reader Service is committed to protecting your privacy. Our Privacy Policy is available online at www.ReaderService.com or upon request from the Reader Service.

We make a portion of our mailing list available to reputable third parties that offer products we believe may interest you. If you prefer that we not exchange your name with third parties, or if you wish to clarify or modify your communication preferences, please visit us at www.ReaderService.com/consumerschoice or write to us at Reader Service Preference Service, P.O. Box 9062, Buffalo, NY. 14240-9062. Include your complete name and address.

HRCBPA18

READERSERVICE.COM

Manage your account online!

- Review your order history
- Manage your payments
- Update your address

We've designed the Reader Service website just for you.

Enjoy all the features!

- Discover new series available to you, and read excerpts from any series.
- Respond to mailings and special monthly offers.
- Browse the Bonus Bucks catalog and online-only exculsives.
- Share your feedback.

Visit us at:
ReaderService.com